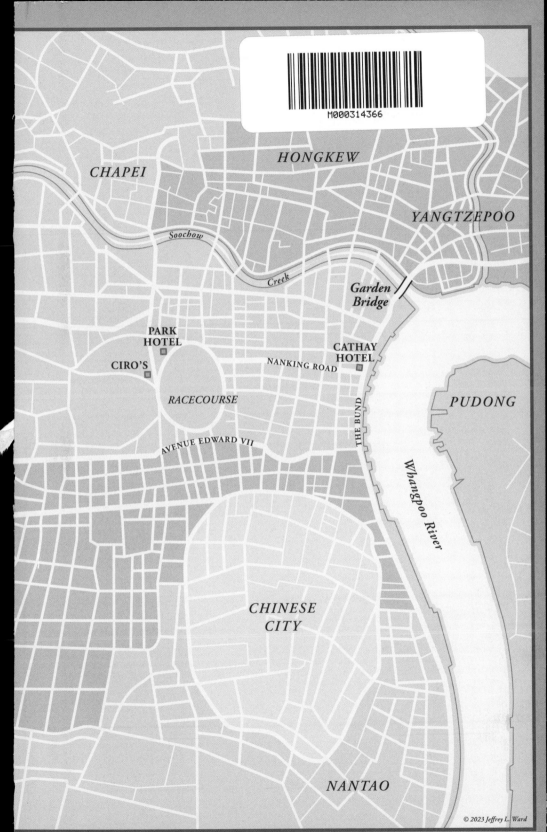

SHANGHAI

A NOVEL

JOSEPH KANON

SCRIBNER

NEW YORK   LONDON   TORONTO   SYDNEY   NEW DELHI

Scribner
An Imprint of Simon & Schuster, LLC
1230 Avenue of the Americas
New York, NY 10020

First Scribner hardcover edition June 2024

SCRIBNER and design are trademarks of Simon & Schuster, LLC.

Simon & Schuster: Celebrating 100 Years of Publishing in 2024

For information about special discounts for bulk purchases, please contact Simon & Schuster Special Sales at 1-866-506-1949 or business@simonandschuster.com.

The Simon & Schuster Speakers Bureau can bring authors to your live event. For more information or to book an event, contact the Simon & Schuster Speakers Bureau at 1-866-248-3049 or visit our website at www.simonspeakers.com.

Manufactured in the United States of America

1 3 5 7 9 10 8 6 4 2

Library of Congress Cataloging-in-Publication Data

Names: Kanon, Joseph, author.
Title: Shanghai : a novel / Joseph Kanon.
Description: First Scribner hardcover edition. | New York : Scribner, 2024.
Identifiers: LCCN 2023031812 (print) | LCCN 2023031813 (ebook) |
ISBN 9781668006429 (hardcover) | ISBN 9781668006443 (ebook)
Subjects: LCGFT: Novels.
Classification: LCC PS3561.A476 S53 2024 (print) | LCC PS3561.A476 (ebook) |
DDC 813/.54—dc23/eng/20230717
LC record available at https://lccn.loc.gov/2023031812
LC ebook record available at https://lccn.loc.gov/2023031813

ISBN 978-1-6680-0642-9
ISBN 978-1-6680-0644-3 (ebook)

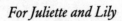

For Juliette and Lily

SHANGHAI

CHAPTER 1

Trieste 1939

He was only a few blocks from the hotel when he realized he was being followed. The sudden rain had emptied the big square, so there were only a few scattered umbrellas, no crowd to melt into. Footsteps you could hear, keeping a steady pace with his. When he stopped by one of the streetlamps, haloed in the misty drizzle, the footsteps stopped too. Not professional, then. In Berlin they'd be almost on top of you before you knew, your skin tingling with it, the fear. But maybe the Italians weren't as well trained. Or maybe he was imagining it, so close now, escape just hours away, alert to any sound, ears turned up like a dog's.

Still, he'd be better off in the lighted street across the square. In the empty piazza he'd be easier to grab, hustled off before a solitary walker could lift his umbrella to see what was going on. Unless it was all nerves. His last night, the boat already at the pier, waiting for morning and the desperate passengers. A new life, any life. The piazza was like a stage set of Europe, everything he was leaving behind, the old shipping offices and insurance companies as weighty

as imperial ministries. At the far end, open to the Adriatic, cafés
once filled with passengers having the last *mocha* before boarding,
official cargo boxes stamped K u K, Kaiser und Koenig, the port of
an empire that would last forever, already gone.

The steps again, keeping up. An amateur. But hadn't he been
too? All of them, everybody in the group? Wanting to do something, to stop what was coming. Enemies of the Reich. Remember two things, Franz had said. You have to survive, or the rest of
it won't matter. So don't take chances. Two, someone will betray
you. So don't give him anything to betray. Your real name. Who
you are. You're just someone in the group. Party discipline. It had
worked for Franz, still alive, so they listened, became careful, because just being in the group now was a death warrant. And when
Willy was caught, the training held. There was nobody to betray,
not even when they tortured him. False names, nothing more to
give, until he was dead and they were safe.

The only weak link, ironically, was Franz himself. He had recruited the group, knew who they really were. So when they arrested
Franz—Who had given him away? Someone in the Party?—Daniel
felt the air go out of his chest, a vise squeezing his ribs. One night,
then two, imagining the basement in Prinz-Albrecht-Strasse, the
screams, the blood on the floor. Then they came for Josef. Because
Franz had been broken, given them someone? Another night sweating, staring at the ceiling. He'd be next. But they didn't come. And
then Franz was dead, his body pulp, and Daniel knew he'd been
saved. For what? To finally join the Party—did he owe Franz that?
In the end, he did nothing, ignored the faint signals Joachim sent,
fell out of the group. First you had to survive. And by that time
Kristallnacht had happened, fires leaping out of the smashed windows, and his father beaten and thrown into a truck collecting Jews
for Sachsenhausen, and he knew he had to get out of Germany.

Now everyone knew it. The lines at the consular offices, the waiting lists that stretched years into the future. No Jews, not even for money. You could buy a visa to the Dominican Republic and then you couldn't. Uncle Nathan finally arranged it, the impossible tickets, the exit visas. Blood was blood. Was it Nathan's fault his brother, Eli, was the way he was? Save your skin. China's still open. You don't have to stay in Germany. All this through emissaries from the real underground in Berlin, not the Communists, the criminal world Nathan knew and Daniel's father, Eli, despised. But then it didn't matter what his father thought, his body just ashes somewhere in the camp. Sudden illness, the official notice said. So Daniel would make the trip alone. If he got out. What had happened to Eli's ticket? Resold probably, pocketed by Uncle Nathan's fixer. Worth a fortune now. He glanced toward the pier where the SS *Raffaello* was being loaded. The vise pressed his ribs in again, the moist air caught in his throat. Only a few more hours. And someone following.

He passed the big fountain and left the square by the old stock exchange, another imperial flourish, drawn by the lights of the cafés that lined the canal farther along. A thief would prefer shadows. But what was there to steal? If the Germans let you go now, they took everything, bank accounts, property, passport. Ten Reichsmarks and a suitcase, the clothes on your back. And your life, a fair trade. No papers. A meaningless Nansen passport for an ID. A citizen of the Lloyd Triestino line until you reached Shanghai, where you wouldn't even be that. So what was there to steal? But a thief wouldn't know that. Daniel started walking faster, toward the safety of the lights. Another Canal Grande, but not like the real one, broad and dazzling. Here it was a narrow inlet of nearly stagnant water, just enough movement to rock the boats that tied up along its edges. Melancholy, like the rest of the city, even the lights reflecting on the water slightly dim. At the door he looked over his shoulder. Which one? Nondescript wool jackets and cloth hats, nobody meeting his eye. Maybe gone, already looking for another victim.

The café was a postcard of old Vienna—bentwood chairs and newspaper rods and the hiss of steam from the coffee maker. Daniel took a seat, watching the door. No one. A waiter in a long apron took his order. Why not a last seed cake? Who knew what the ship food would be like? Probably rich and heavy. First class, the only tickets left. Another debt to Nathan. Daniel sat back, his eye still on the door, feeling calmer. How could it be the Gestapo? There was no one left to give him away. Just footsteps in the dark. Imagining things. And then there he was, coming through the door, shaking the rain off his hat, a quick glance around the room, then looking straight at Daniel, almost a smile. He made a *you don't mind?* gesture at the other chair and sat down.

"Herr Lohr," he said, not waiting for an answer. "You like to walk in the rain? I thought, maybe he's meeting somebody." Another glance around the room. "But no, just a walk. So it's better here. I didn't want to talk at the hotel. Maybe somebody sees."

"Somebody who?"

"The police."

Daniel looked up. "Who are you? What do you want?"

The man patted the air with his hand, calming it. "Nothing, nothing. It's just a job. Make sure everything's all right. If you need anything."

"What would I need?"

The man shrugged. "People need things. Somebody wants to make sure—"

"Who?" But who else could it be? Another emissary.

4

"I don't know. It's better. A man who works with me says do me a favor. Make sure he gets on the boat. That's all."

Daniel tried to place the accent, as mongrel as Trieste—German and Italian and something flinty, like the karst that overlooked the city.

"I can get on the boat myself."

"So get on yourself. But meanwhile, a little advice? You're a Jew, I assume?"

"Half," Daniel said, a reflex. What did it matter? There were no *mischling*s to the Nazis, one drop of blood enough. His father had been a veteran, with medals, and still ended up in Sachsenhausen, his eyes already dead the one time Daniel had been allowed to see him. Get out, he'd said. Don't wait for me. There's no time. They're going to kill you. Even with a gentile mother, just a memory now. What did it matter?

"Half, then. You want to be careful tomorrow. Going through customs. One suitcase. Just clothes. Nothing in the lining. No valuables sewn in the hem. They know all the tricks. You get on the boat, you're picked clean, understand?"

Daniel nodded. "They already went through everything, leaving Germany."

"And now here, just in case. People think they're in the clear, they get careless."

"All right," Daniel said.

"You want to get out. You don't want anything to go wrong." He stopped as the waiter brought Daniel's coffee, shaking his head no to another cup. "So no funny business."

"He asked you to say that?"

"It's not like that. I'm saying it. I'm just supposed to get you on the boat. Clean."

"What else?"

"Get there early. You have a single cabin but sometimes they double up. What it's like now, everybody trying to get out. You know, a bribe maybe, and they find a berth. So you get there first."

Daniel looked at him, waiting.

"First class, they have these silent butlers. You know, a compartment, the other side opens in the hall so they can take your laundry, shine your shoes while you're sleeping. Like royalty, first class. So you get there early, there's a package in there. Put it somewhere safe. Nobody's looking hard—you just got through customs so you're clean. Just somewhere safe. They'll be waiting for it at the other end, whoever you're meeting."

"What's in it?" Daniel said quietly, dismayed. Not even on the boat and already compromised, involved in something. Stay away from Nathan, his father would say. He's a crook. Everything he touches—I know, you think it's all smiles. But it's rotten underneath. You touch something rotten, the stink gets on your hands. And it'll suck you in. One day, you're in it. Stay away from him.

"I don't know. Neither do you. And don't look. You just keep it safe and hand it over."

"How'd you get it through customs, if you don't mind my asking?"

"*I* didn't get it through anything. I'm just a messenger here." He paused. "But you know the service crew, people come on board before the passengers, bring the food, clean out the ashtrays, they don't go through customs, they're not going anywhere. Maybe somebody like that puts it in the silent butler. Maybe. Look," he said, glancing away. "It's nothing illegal. I don't get involved in anything illegal. I'm an expediter, you know what that means?"

"You move things along," Daniel said, leading him.

"That's right, I move things along. I don't have to know what they are. That way, nobody gets hurt. So get on the ship all right.

6

And I'm done." He looked up at the waiter, who'd been hovering nearby, still hoping for an order. "Maybe a brandy. You?"

Daniel shook his head.

"Your last night. On me."

"I can pay," Daniel said.

The man raised his head. "You have cash? Besides the ten marks? You can't take it, so you might as well spend it. Enjoy yourself. I can get you a nice girl if you're interested. Slovene. Young."

Daniel looked over at him. Nobody gets hurt. "I don't have that much."

"Suit yourself," the man said, hearing the edge in Daniel's voice. "*Salud.*" He tossed back the brandy. "Where are you going anyway? He never said. Lloyd's goes everywhere. I figured—you know, Jews—maybe South America—"

"China."

"China. Christ." He finished off his glass. "Why China?"

Daniel looked around the room, everything familiar, what he knew.

"It's not here."

———

When Daniel got there, hours early, the pier was already swarming with people pushing against the closed doors of the customs shed as if they were afraid there wouldn't be enough time later. When the Vienna train pulled into the station just down the *riva*, walking distance, a noise went through the crowd, an anxious moan. There were so many now, hundreds more. How could they all get on? The train passengers, seeing people already on the pier, surged forward, calling for porters, hurrying. In the hotel there had been pictures of the Franz Josef days, women in day gowns and big hats, parasols, followed by maids. Husbands in bowlers looking at vest pocket watches. People with all the time in the world, lucky to be on the big white liners with their welcoming stewards and champagne at dinner. Not this, the crush at the gates.

"Taxi!"

A young woman a few heads away, waving a hand toward the street. Young, but not a girl, someone used to hailing cabs. A long black coat, too heavy for the spring weather, bulky, an extra layer of clothes underneath. Whatever they could carry. Lugging two suitcases, barely off the ground, an older woman behind her, clutching a purse, looking bewildered. "Taxi!" Exasperated now, turning to check on the older woman and catching Daniel's eye instead, a flicker, just a second, but aware, returning his look. "Mother, keep up. Don't get separated."

"How can we just leave?" the woman said.

"Don't start," the younger woman said, still struggling with the bags.

Daniel pushed past two people. "Can I help? There aren't any taxis. It's not far."

"We can manage," the young woman said, a whiplash answer, her voice stretched taut, about to snap.

"It's no trouble," Daniel said, reaching for the suitcases.

"A gentleman," the mother said, coming to life.

The woman shot her a glance. "I can manage," she said again, stopping him, then hearing herself, dropped her hand. "I'm sorry. It's just the train was late and–" The words rushed out, then faded, tripping over themselves. Curly brown hair jammed under a cloche hat, off her face, which seemed to be without makeup, the cheeks flushed just from the morning damp. A tiny dimple in her chin, as if a fairy had put a finger there, the story she was probably told as a child.

8

"Leah thinks she can do anything," the mother said. "She was always like that."

"There's plenty of time," he said, bending over the suitcase, then let out an involuntary "unhh" as he tried to lift it.

Leah looked over at him, surprised, covering a smile with her hand.

"There's a strap," she said. "I should have—"

"It's the gloves," the mother said.

"The gloves?" Daniel said.

"Never mind," Leah said. "You're sure it's not too much? Just to the pier, then. There must be porters there."

"Of course there are porters," her mother said. "A Lloyd ship? Of course." She looked around. "So many. They're leaving? Like us? But maybe a holiday."

Leah didn't answer.

"And you. You're on the ship too?" the mother said to Daniel as they started. "Everybody leaving," she said vaguely. "Why should we go? Just leave everything? The flat. Am Modenapark," she said to Daniel, placing it. "How can we leave that?"

"It's not ours now. You know that." An exaggerated patience, talking to a child. "Herr Blauner owns it."

"And the factory."

"Yes, and the factory," she said, a glance toward Daniel, cheeks red, embarrassed.

"Your father would never have sold it."

Leah said nothing, not wanting to rise to this, an old argument. "Look, they're opening."

A loud clanging, the metal doors sliding across the entrance, the high vaulted shed behind filled with orderly rows of uniformed customs inspectors standing beside their tables. Daniel clutched the suitcases more tightly, expecting another surge, a fight for a place in line, but the doors opening had the opposite, calming effect. Lloyd Triestino was right on time, as it always was, the uniforms reassuring signs of order. They were boarding, safe.

"You sold it and we still have nothing," the mother said.

"We had to sell," Leah said, her voice low. "You know that. And now we have tickets for this boat."

"For all that. The furniture, the carpets—"

"It's not allowed to take anything." The voice taut again. "You remember at the station? How they took my earrings?"

Without thinking, Daniel glanced at her ear. Pierced, now just a faint pinprick in the lobe, bare, unexpectedly intimate. He imagined her taking the rings out at night, putting them on the dresser, a ritual.

She turned to Daniel. "My mother's not herself today. I'm sorry for this. Pay no attention." A private conversation, as if her mother weren't standing there.

"It's hard to leave," he said.

"She wanted to bring her dishes. The dinner set. She wanted to bring dishes," Leah said, almost to herself, a verbal shaking of the head.

"What does Herr Blauner want with them?" her mother said. "A man like that. The good dishes. How would he know? An—accountant. An employee."

"Herr Blauner knows the value of everything," Leah said. "Everything."

"Bah. He—"

"Enough. We'll talk later."

"When it's too late to go back."

She looked at her mother, eyes softer. "It's too late now." She took out a handkerchief. "Here, you're smudged." She dabbed the handkerchief at the corner of her mother's mouth. "You want to look your best. It's first class."

"First class. Such an extravagance."

"Yes, it is," Leah said, smiling a little. "You'll enjoy it."

They showed their tickets and the exit visas and were waved over to the inspecting tables near the wall. Daniel heaved the suitcases up.

"Open, please."

The inspector started pawing through the clothes, not a cursory check, thorough, just as the man in the café had predicted—feeling seams and hemlines, running fingers along the suitcase lining, tapping for false bottoms.

"If you have anything to declare— You know it is an offense to—"

"There's nothing," Leah said.

"No furs?" the inspector said, nodding to her coat. "Maybe lined?"

Leah shook her head. "Wool. No furs, no jewels. Nothing."

"Why so many gloves?"

"My hands. They get chapped."

"Delicate," the inspector said.

Leah shrugged, not answering.

The inspector ran through the clothes again, fingering one of her slips.

"Silk?" he said, a leer, still holding it.

"Yes."

"Good silk," he said, rubbing it again, as if there were skin underneath.

For a second Daniel thought the inspector might take it out of the bag, his commission, but he dropped it and closed the lid, marking the suitcase with chalk. "Welcome to the *Raffaello*, Madame. The bags will be sent to your cabin. Bon voyage." Even a stage nod, like tipping a hat. Leah stood there, slightly stunned, all the months of worry over with a simple nod. Madame. A passenger of the Lloyd line.

"Open, please," the inspector said to Daniel.

"Thank you so much," the mother said, suddenly grand, a *gnä-dige Frau*, extending her hand to Daniel.

Daniel took it and dipped his head, what was expected.

"Herr–?"

"Lohr."

"Ah. We are Auerbach."

"Yes, thank you," Leah said, watching this, a slight frown at the exchange.

"Look at them," the mother said, turning to face the crowd behind them. "If your father could see this. How it would all end."

"Nothing's ending," Leah said, curt. "Come. We're holding up the line." She touched her mother's arm. "Just look ahead, remember? Something new. Maybe you'll like it."

"They bind little girls' feet. What kind of people would do that to a child?"

"Thank you again," Leah said to Daniel, moving her mother away.

"Maybe I'll see you on the boat."

She turned. "No. It's not that kind of trip."

He raised his eyebrows.

"You know, moonlight on the water. Like in a film. But it's not a film."

She looked past him toward the city, then straightened and turned away, a full turn, her coat moving with her, closing a door.

———

His cabin was made up for one, no last-minute roommate, with a plate of fruit on the desk and a welcoming note from Lloyd's. A button by the lamp could summon a steward. Tea was served in the lounge at four. On deck, blankets would be neatly folded on reclining chairs. Best clothes for dinner. An orchestra afterward for those in the mood, or the dark smoky bar, gleaming ice shakers and bartenders in bow ties. Three weeks of this, not looking over his shoulder, not wondering if Franz had broken. Now there was laundry pickup at the touch of a button. But not for free. Somebody had paid for it all. Get the package.

The silent butler door was just outside the bathroom. Daniel slid back his side, half hoping it would be empty, a slipup for which he couldn't be blamed. One of the cabin boys or porters darting all over the deck, somebody who'd seen an opportunity and taken it. But it was there, a thick envelope, sealed, about the weight of some folded legal document—or a block of opium. How much did that weigh? But why bring opium to China, coals to Newcastle? He picked up the envelope, feeling it. Never mind, just expedite. Nobody gets hurt. He looked around the room. There were no niches on a ship, every inch put to use. Anyone looking would find it. If anyone looked. He'd already been picked clean. But an easy trap to spring at the last minute. Come with us, please. The trick was to distance himself from it— no jacket pockets or shaving kits, anywhere personal. He opened the desk drawer. A room service menu, a leather folder with stationery.

A rap on the door, making him jump a little, the envelope still in his hand. He slid it under the stationery, shoving the drawer closed just as the cabin door opened.

"Sorry, sir. I didn't think you were—"

A porter with the suitcase, barely out of his teens, glided smoothly around the room, setting up the luggage rack, opening the porthole. "Laundry through here," he said, tapping the silent butler. "Shoes overnight." He turned to face Daniel. "Is there anything I can do for you?" Expecting a tip.

Daniel took out some coins. How long would ten marks last at this rate? The boy pocketed the money without looking. "Just ring if you need anything. Dinner's at eight. 'A' deck. The maître d' has the seating plan. Have a pleasant trip." What he always said, all of it now surreal. Dressing for dinner.

When the boy had gone, Daniel looked around the room again. They'd check the stationery folder every day to make sure it was full. The extra blanket in the bureau may or may not be needed. The back of the hat shelf. Not a hiding place, somewhere in plain sight. What would a Lloyd passenger do, one who had dinner on A deck? Daniel checked the ship plan, then headed down the corridor, the envelope in his breast pocket. The purser's office was on the other side of the dining room.

"I wondered if I might put something in your safe. You have—?"

"Yes, of course. I should warn you, we can't take responsibility for any valuables once they're taken out. Some of our lady passengers like to wear their jewels and then forget to—"

"It's only valuable to me," Daniel said, taking out the envelope.

"I see," the purser said, looking at Daniel, wanting more.

"Takes weeks to replace, if the lawyers had to draw— Anyway, better safe than sorry. Could I leave it with you, then?"

"Of course." The purser filled out a receipt and handed it to him. Daniel smiled. "I'm always losing things, so that's a relief."

The purser took the envelope, attaching a duplicate ticket stub. "If you'd just sign here?"

On the promenade deck people were milling near the rail, some waving down to the pier. The air was fresh and clear, washed clean by last night's rain, and Daniel took in a gulp of it, feeling pleased with himself, as if he had gotten away with something. He checked his watch. Not long now. He imagined them tearing his room apart, looking for the planted envelope, their excuse to haul him off the boat, while it lay out of reach in Lloyd's safe. Whatever it was.

He looked at the people still coming up the gangplank, like animals into the ark, in pairs, hoping to outrun the flood. Who were they all? Couples holding each other, leaving their best dishes behind. Did they all have an Uncle Nathan, someone to pull strings? The bad boy, while the older brother made his parents proud. A judge. When Daniel thought of his father, he saw the starched collar, formal, even at home, even after he was dismissed and sat in the front room reading the newspaper, still in his collar, waiting to be called back, when the world returned to its senses. "You think they don't know who you are? A Jew in the Kammergericht?" Nathan had said. "They don't see under the robes?" "And what are you?" his father said, one of their arguments. "A disgrace." "To who? Your friends in the club who won't talk to you now?" "A disgrace to the family. A real crook. Not like before, a kid with the gangs. Something you grow out of. But you didn't. You got worse."

And then Nathan crossed a line. Years of running errands, collecting debts, working at the Black Cat in Nollendorfplatz, maybe selling drugs, elbowing his way higher in the rackets, as wild as Berlin itself in those years, the glint in his eye when he winked at Daniel, their joke, Eli as a starched collar, and then a man was dead and Nathan had to leave. Did it matter if it was murder or some grotesque misfire? A man was dead and he had to go. To America— that was the plan. "A good place for him, a gangster country," Eli said, but it was he who gave him the money, slipped it to him when nobody was looking, and only Daniel, in the next room, saw the good-bye, a hug so tight you couldn't tell the one from the other. And after all that, a few postcards, New York and then California, where the movie stars were, and then nothing. Until Kristallnacht, when the starched collar was clubbed by Nazis and hauled away and the bad boy, now in Shanghai, tried to save what he could. The last of the family.

A blast from the ship's funnel, a gush of steam, then the pling of a xylophone, a steward with the all ashore signal. Visitors scurried to the gangway. They were really going. Daniel looked down at the people on the pier, hats moving like a restless swarm of insects, handkerchiefs waving, then a sudden still point, the man from the café, eyes fixed on the gangway. Nathan making sure he got off safely. No, making sure the package got off.

Daniel felt a shuddering beneath his feet as the ship started to pull away. He was getting out. He looked at the busy street, trams threading into the city, the opera set square with its cafés, and he felt suddenly like one of the thick ropes being slipped off its mooring. He had never known anything else, unless you counted the year in London, and now he felt he would never see it again, Europe taken from him, someone else's property, like Leah's mother's flat. For a second he felt a stab of panic, no country, no money, but then as the boat began to slide away relief swept through him. Europe was going to destroy itself and he'd escaped. There was the rest of the world. He had English, what you needed in Shanghai to find a job. Everyone had said so. There must be money to make, if Nathan was there. Daniel thought of the package in the safe. No landing card needed in Shanghai, but smuggling put you at risk anywhere. Still, that was the price of the ticket and now he could be whoever he wanted. He looked at the receding pier, the crowd beginning to drift away. No one here knew him, even knew his name. He could arrive in Shanghai as anybody. Not part of Franz's group, not Eli's son, not anybody he'd ever been, someone new. Just part of the flotsam and jetsam that washed up in a place like Shanghai.

———

Daniel stayed on deck for hours, just drifting, until there was no more land. The water was oddly flat, as if they weren't on a sea at all but a toy boat in some god's bathtub, waiting for a hand to splash them and make waves. It must be rough sometimes—there were violent storms in Homer—but today it stretched to the horizon like glass. When the air turned cooler, he retreated to one of the deck chairs and sat, sheltered, watching the people. How many were Jews, feeling saved? Was there a look, some permanent wariness in the eyes? The *Raffaello* wasn't a refugee ship—the people at the rail might be traveling for reasons of their own. A job in Ceylon. A brother in Singapore. A business in Manila. None of them looked as if they were escaping anything. Down below, on the crowded decks, you might see worn, apprehensive faces but up here, in the first class air, it was just another Lloyd's sailing.

He saw her before she saw him. Away from the rail, near one of the storage bins, not actually pacing but restless, waiting for someone. Her heavy coat was open to the mild air and as she turned her legs came into view, the first time he had taken them in, long and slender, a dancer's legs. He stared at them for a second, imagining her sitting in a café a few tables away, crossing her legs, unaware that he was looking. Then lying next to him, stretched out, his hand running over her hip, turning her toward him. Nathan's voice at the Black Cat: It's all about the legs, when you're hiring for the line. You can work around everything else—push up the tits, lose a nose with some makeup. You know. But you can't do anything about legs, not if you're putting them in the line. Auditions. Looking at legs. Maybe not just looking.

She turned again, the same abrupt, tense movement he remembered from the pier, a motor idling. It's not that kind of trip. Now a woman was joining her, dressed for a bon voyage party, a smart suit and hat. Someone she knew, but not a friend, an odd formality. Then, to his surprise, Leah took off her coat and held it while the other woman slipped into it. He sat up, following the scene like a silent movie, everything perfectly clear without sound, the words acted out. Leah buttoned the front, then brushed the woman's shoulders, emphasizing the good fit. The woman walked a few steps, the coat flaring out, and nodded, then checked the seams. She looked up. How much? A price named, but dismissed. Now real bargaining, a pantomime of gestures. A counteroffer. No, Leah couldn't possibly let it go for– In this condition? The lining needed work. And anyway they weren't in a shop on the Graben. The situation was– You know what the coat's worth. I'm prepared to take a loss on it, but I'm not going to give it away. Feel the wool, it's best quality. Actually feeling it for her, rubbing the sleeve, and it was just then, looking up, that she saw him. A quick start, flustered, so that when the woman named another price, she seemed distracted, nodding just to be at an end with it. The woman opened her purse and took out some money.

More silent film. Not quite enough, she'd have to give her the rest later. Leah hesitated, her eyes glancing toward Daniel, then darting away. If you want cash. Yes, I want cash. Well, then. Shall I bring the coat to dinner? No, I'll wear it now. Daring her to object, imply that she was dishonest. All right, giving in, the rest later. It's a good price. Rallying, saving face, head erect. It's a fair price, the woman said. I'm surprised you got it out– They only look for fur, Leah said, staring at her. Well, then it's lucky for me, the woman said. A good Persian wool, that's not so easy to come by. Yes, Leah said, lucky. The woman looked at her, not quite sure how to take this, then let it go. What about the gloves? she said, touching one of her own, sign language. Another time, Leah said, a side glance toward Daniel. I have to sort them. Auerbach gloves, the woman said. Another piece of luck for me. To find them here, like this. Yes, Leah said, but so vaguely that nothing registered in her face.

After the woman left, Leah walked over to the rail, turning her back to Daniel, shoulders straight, a child's defiance, not looking when he joined her. For a minute they stared together at the water.

"It gets cold in Shanghai," he said finally. "It's not the tropics."

"I wondered what you would say. So I'll get another coat, a cheaper one." She turned to him. "She has marks. Not like us. Ten marks, then nothing. How are we going to live, on nothing?"

"So you sell your clothes?"

"What else do I have to sell? It's a good coat. My father bought it. He cared about things like that, how we would look. So, the best. And what do I do with a good coat in China? Who am I going to impress? While we starve. So sell it and get a cheap one and with the difference–" She stopped. "Anyway, it was something I could get out. The Nazis, I thought, they won't know what it's worth. Fur, yes, but a good Persian? So I'll sell it and we'll eat. You have to start thinking about that–how we're going to eat."

Daniel said nothing for a minute, letting things settle. "And the gloves?"

"My father made them. You don't know Auerbach gloves? No, why should you? Ladies' gloves. People in Vienna know. They kept the name on the factory–it sounded Aryan enough and people knew it."

"After it was sold."

"Well, sold. To the manager. All these years, my father thought–and in the end, what did it matter? So now it's his. Another fair price. They were going to take the factory anyway. So at least we got something." She looked down. "Herr Blauner."

Another awkward moment, staring out.

"Cigarette?" Daniel said, taking out a pack.

"I gave them up. They're expensive in China, someone told me." She looked at him. "Yes, all right." She leaned down toward his cupped hands while he lighted it for her. "Thank you," she said, a theatrical exhaling. "So first the suitcase, now this. But you should know– Nothing's going to happen. Between us. So you know."

"It's just a cigarette."

"Oh, yes? Maybe. But I can't afford it. I can't afford you, either. A Jew with ten marks." She looked away. "It's nothing personal. I have to think about–other things."

"What other things?"

"How we're going to live, my mother and me."

"You made it this far. You're here."

"And you think that's the end of it? You're like all the others. Get on the ship, we're saved. But now what? You know what I was thinking before? See the water–how flat? Like in those old maps, when the world was flat. Angels in the corners, blowing wind. And the ship goes right to the edge–and falls off. That's the ship we're on. And everybody's happy to be here."

"You think you're going to fall off the map?"

"No, I'm going to survive. I just don't know how yet." She flicked the end of the cigarette over the rail. "I can do office work," she said, as if it were surprising. "I helped my father, in the factory. The books. I could do that. There are German firms there. Except they would be Nazis, wouldn't they? So maybe a shop. Sell other people's coats." She shrugged. "A *vendeuse*. Imagine, a shopgirl."

"What were you in Vienna?"

"A daughter. The eligible one. My sister was already married. So, my turn."

"She's still there?"

"Holland. If you think that's safe. I don't think anywhere's safe. Not now. So, Shanghai. The end of the world. You know what they do there? Somebody told me. The Jewish charities meet you and take you to a *heim*. A dormitory. Otherwise you'd be on the street. Until you get on your feet and find a place somewhere. If you do. Can you imagine my mother in a dormitory? So I have a little money from the coat," she said, patting her pocket. "I can take her somewhere else. They help you find a place, the charities. If you have money. You haven't heard this?"

"No."

"Maybe it's different for a man. Dormitory life. Like the army." She tilted her head, looking at him. "What do you do? A doctor, maybe, something useful?"

He shook his head. "Journalist. Was. Not so easy in the New Germany. So this and that. I can translate from English to German. Sometimes a publisher gives me work. A friend from the old days, before the race laws. No name on the book, of course."

"So how do you live? This and that. Your family?"

"Not anymore. My father died in Sachsenhausen."

"They killed him?"

Daniel shrugged. "A sudden illness."

"Oh," she said, turning back to the water. "What did he do? That they would kill him?"

"Nothing. He was a judge." He caught her surprised look. "In the Kammergericht. But in the end—"

"A judge. So, a good family. But you still have to live. What will you do there?"

"Get a job. But right now? Enjoy the trip. Maybe tempt you with cigarettes."

"Tempt me. To do what?"

"Enjoy the trip too. There's plenty of time to worry later."

"It's not a joke." She gripped the rail. "You don't feel it? We're all going over the edge and there's nothing we can do." She held the rail tighter, a demonstration. "No way to stop it."

"If you really believed that, you wouldn't be here. You'd still be in Vienna. Now we have a chance."

"Well, Vienna. Not there. Not in Am Modenapark. With Herr Blauner. My father would die a second time."

He looked at her.

"First the business. Then the daughter. Maybe he thought I came with the flat. An extra."

"But you didn't," Daniel said quietly.

"No? How do you think I paid for these tickets?"

He glanced away, embarrassed, as if he had caught a glimpse of something through a door left open.

"I don't know why I'm telling you this," she said. "A stranger. Maybe that's why. It's easier." She looked directly at him. "Maybe it's because you saw me with the coat. I had to explain."

"Not to me. People do what they have to do."

"They say shame goes first. When you're poor. But I don't think so. You still feel it. You know up here," she said, finger to her temple. "It shouldn't matter, but it does. So maybe that's why. You saw me with the coat. The rest of it . . ." Her voice drifted over the rail. "All these things I didn't know how to do. My father's ashes, picking the urn. You'd think anybody could do that. Signing the papers for the factory. Knowing Blauner was stealing it. My mother. Pretending it's all nothing, just a trip. Nobody told me how to do these things. I have good manners. My father thought that was all I would need. Think what it's going to be like now. All the time. You can't survive on manners."

"You did a good job with the coat. From what I could see. Did you get what you wanted for it?"

Leah nodded. "If she gives me the rest."

"She might not?"

"Frau Mitzel? We know her a little. 'Look how I tricked these Jews. For once they don't get the better—'"

"She'd do that?"

"Maybe not. My mother knows people, her friends. She wouldn't want to look bad to them. But who knows what they think these days? So we'll see."

"Another?" He held out the cigarette pack.

"Then I'll owe you two."

"Let's not keep books. I have more."

She leaned in again for a light. "I promised myself, after Blauner, I'd never be obligated again. To anyone. For anything. And here I am—" She blew out smoke, then turned to face the water. "Look. You can't see it anymore. Europe. It's gone."

CHAPTER 2

Daniel was seated between Frau Auerbach and an American called Florence Burke, the only one at the table wearing jewelry. She was one of those women who used style to compensate for bad features, short jet-black hair swept back from her face to emphasize the beaklike nose and red wide mouth. Leah had come in a light jersey dress that could have used some dressing up–the sparkle of a brooch or some line of color–but the dull beige had the effect of drawing you instead to her dark eyes, shiny, full of light.

"Did you arrange this?" he'd asked her, nodding at the maître d'.

"Hah. They probably put all the Jews together. So we won't bother the others."

"There are Jews all over the boat."

"Not in first class. Just us. So here we are. Not making anybody uncomfortable."

"I had no idea you weren't allowed to bring anything out," Florence Burke was saying to Frau Auerbach. "It's just theft, isn't it? Pure and simple. I'm sorry. I should take these off–" She reached for an earring.

"No, no. They're lovely. It's good to see them. You're an American. It's a different situation for you. You have been in Germany?"

"For the music. But never again. What's going on there now—you don't feel safe. Even if you're American. Still, it's lucky for us in Shanghai. Do you know who's on the boat? At least I'm told he's here. Blumenthal. The violinist. Imagine having him there, not just on records. The evenings—"

"You live in Shanghai, then?"

"My husband's with Pacific Bank. Of course, he doesn't care one bit about my evenings. He's just there for the job. But why shouldn't we have a bit of culture, too? We're the fifth-largest city in the world. We should have more than just a racetrack."

"What's it like?" Daniel said. "Living there."

"What's it like?" she repeated. "Well, it depends where you are. The British pretty much run the Settlement and all they care about is keeping you out of their clubs. Very pukka. Big houses, lawns. Surrey with more gardeners. It's so much cheaper. I don't see the point of a house myself. You're always having to fix something, deal with the staff. We're in the French Concession, a flat in the Avenue Foch. Much nicer, I think, though of course *chacun à son goût*."

"Is there an American section?"

"There was. Now it's all merged in with the Brits in the International Settlement. Technically, it's Chinese territory, of course, but the concessions gave foreigners the right to trade there, manage their own affairs. So it's like a colony even if it isn't a colony."

"With extraterritoriality," said a deeper voice a few seats down, a Japanese who'd been introduced as Colonel Yamada but who was wearing a suit, not a uniform.

Daniel turned to take him in. About the same height, which made him tall for a Japanese. A soldier's erect posture, even the suit somehow military. Stiff hair, short on the sides.

"Yes," Florence said. "Whatever that means exactly. I've never been sure."

"In matters of law, you can only be tried in the courts of your native country. An American by American courts. The French by the French, et cetera, which means in practice they hardly ever get tried at all. Certainly not by the Chinese government in Nanking, whose laws are meaningless to them." His voice was patient, with an almost ceremonial politeness.

Florence looked at him, her eyes suddenly shrewd. "The government controlled by you."

Colonel Yamada dipped his head. "An occasional influence only." Casual, dismissive, as if the invasion hadn't happened and none of them had seen the pictures and newsreels, captured troops used for live bayonet practice, civilians buried alive, their heads sticking out as the Japanese soldiers trampled them into the ground.

Florence turned back to Daniel. "I don't know how much you know. About the war. You ask what it's like now. Like an island, really. Surrounded by the Chinese. Which is to say, the Japanese, since they won the war."

"Not yet," Yamada said. "Yes, we have protected our interests. But it would be premature to say 'won.'" Close-shaved, his face was smooth, shiny, a porcelain glaze.

"Well, I don't know what you call winning, then." She turned to Daniel. "They've got Chiang Kai-shek hiding out in Chungking pretending he's still running China and Mao up north somewhere. And a puppet government in Nanking."

"I would not use that term," Yamada said pleasantly, enjoying himself.

"You've got troops stationed in Ningpo and a big battleship just sitting there in the Whangpoo. Absolutely nothing to stop you taking over the city, which I guess you could do in a few hours, but you don't."

Yamada dipped his head again. "To march on the Settlement would be seen as an act of provocation, would it not? Japan has no wish to go to war with America. Or the British Empire."

"But everyone says it's just a matter of time."

"And yet you stay."

"Yes," Florence said, an airy sigh, oddly light. "Dancing on the rim of the volcano. That's what *Collier's* said. Literally dancing. Lots of clubs in Shanghai. Famous for it. Ciro's is probably the one now. Sir Victor's place." She caught Daniel's blank expression. "Sassoon. He built the Cathay Hotel. Where there's also a very nice club, by the way."

"But do you go to these places?" Frau Auerbach said.

"No. Well, once in a while. I enjoy a flutter at the tables. I draw the line at the Canidrome, though. Dog races. Really. And taxi dancers. But the men all go. They come out to work for Jardine or one of the banks, so plenty of money in their pockets and why not go out and spend it? Work hard, play hard. That's the excuse anyway. Mostly I think they work a little and the money just *comes*. That's what Shanghai's about. Which suits the Japanese," she said, looking at Yamada, "so why kill the golden goose?"

"Please?" Yamada said.

"An expression. I just meant the Japanese are making a lot of money in Shanghai without the bother of running it. So why upset things?"

"We have many businesses, yes."

"Ooh, champagne," Frau Auerbach said as the waiters started pouring. "How nice." A child at a party.

"First night out," Florence said. "I must say, Lloyd's still knows how to do things. Listen to that." An orchestra had started playing dance music at the other end of the room, the clink of silver at the dinner tables like grace notes.

"Yes, lovely," Frau Auerbach said, taking in the starched linen, the gleaming forks, the wine fizzing in the glass before her, the world as it should be.

"What were you doing in Germany?" Florence said to Yamada, direct, familiar.

"A liaison assignment."

"I suppose you can't say," Florence said. "Military things. Your new ally. How does that work? You meet with a vis-à-vis in the Wehrmacht? Hard to imagine. I can't think of two countries less alike. But maybe armies are always the same." Her hands fluttered, following her words.

"I'm not an officer in the Imperial Army."

"Oh, but I thought—colonel."

"I'm attached to the Military Police. The Kempeitai."

Daniel raised his head. Their Gestapo. He glanced around the harmless, festive room. People raising glasses, making toasts. Smiling with the Gestapo.

"Oh, well then, you really won't say. Never mind my asking."

"No, I can say. An exchange of information about methods. How the offices are organized. Meet colleagues. Put a face with a name. A liaison trip."

"Methods," Daniel said.

Yamada looked at him. "Methods of keeping files."

An awkward moment, filled with interrogation basements and blood, out of place in the bright dining room. Daniel felt a trickle of sweat at the back of his neck.

"And how did you find Germany?" Florence said, moving the table, or their half of it, back to dinner conversation.

"Interesting. Some remarkable things have been done. Of

29

course, not everything is as one would wish. As you say"—he nodded to Florence—"we are very different countries. Their ideas about race, for instance—"

"You don't agree?"

"How could I agree? I am not Aryan. I'm part of another race. So where does that put me in their theory? They seem not to be aware of this. They think only of the Jews. But if they believe what they say, then we must be inferior too. Like the Jews. Look where they've seated me tonight. Of course one doesn't say this there. And they have done remarkable things."

"Is that why you're allowing Jews to come to Shanghai?" Daniel said.

"A matter of Settlement policy, not ours. Maybe an absence of policy. A window that hasn't been closed yet."

"But the Japanese haven't tried to close it. You could make them—"

"We have some influence, yes."

"Don't misunderstand. We're grateful."

Yamada nodded. "It's not a matter of gratitude. There is a debt, you see. During the war with Russia, it was Kuhn, Loeb—you know Jacob Schiff?—who arranged for the loan that made our victory possible. These things are not forgotten. And I think it's still true the Jews can do things in Washington. Everyone says they have Roosevelt's ear."

Daniel looked at him, thrown by this. Goebbels's propaganda, actually believed. Jews in Washington, whispering in the right ears. International finance in their hands. What *Der Stürmer* wanted people to believe. Now believed, so a trapdoor was left open to rescue Jews. But what did it matter, as long as it was open?

"And you know, they are very hard workers," Yamada said. "The Chinese—" He opened his hand to let the thought out.

"Very different cultures," Florence said, moving them back again. "You know, they say the Chinese aesthetic is about adding, the Japanese about subtracting."

"I have heard this," Yamada said.

"I confess, I'm an adder—just ask Albert—but I love the *look* of Japan. The simplicity. Those exquisite kimonos."

"You have been there then."

"Yes. It's always different, isn't it, seeing people on their home ground. Everyone so polite, so friendly."

"I hope we are that abroad, too," Yamada said, a chess move.

Florence stared at him, checked, her hands still. "Of course it's very different in wartime," she said finally. "Terrible things happen."

"To both sides," Yamada said, another move.

She held his look for a second, then raised a hand to her hair, smoothing it back. "You know, I make it a rule never to involve myself in politics. Over here, I mean. We're guests, after all."

"Guests?" Yamada said. "Of the Chinese? I think they would be surprised to hear this."

"All I know is that once politics comes into it, somebody's bound to get offended and then there goes the evening. It's the culture that interests me. Think of it, hundreds and hundreds of years. The artistry you can find in a bowl. Of course when we first came out, you never met the Chinese. They still don't allow them in the English Shanghai Club. With the Long Bar. What's so special? So it's long. But bit by bit you bring people together."

"And yet," Yamada said. "If you have Herr Blumenthal play for you, you will not invite me. Or any Japanese. So, politics after all."

"There are certain sensitivities I have to respect. With my Chinese guests. And I think you would be uncomfortable. Do you really want to come? Or just want to make a point?"

Yamada smiled. "I think I've made it." He turned to Leah. "And what about you, Fräulein? Does the idea of a Japanese guest offend you?" A practiced charm, leaning forward slightly to glance at her breasts.

She had been quiet, following the conversation like a tennis match, exchanging looks with Daniel as the words gushed out of Florence. A private conversation, watching the others. Now, before she could answer, Yamada said, "But you're right. No more of this. Politics. We're all friends here."

"Yes," Frau Auerbach said, "all friends. Such a lovely room, isn't it?"

"Shanghai's like that," Florence said. "All business. So people have to get along."

"Much more easily done when the company is so charming," Yamada said, lifting his glass toward Leah. "Shall we be in Shanghai then? Would you like to dance?"

For a second everything seemed to stop, all of them frozen in a snapshot, the moment so unexpected that no one knew how to react. Leah's face went blank. Then a twitch as the table came back to life, flustered. And Daniel, watching Yamada's face, saw that it was the reaction Yamada had wanted, another test, their table, in the end, filled with Germans. Not Aryan, but not Asian either, Western. Yamada stood and walked over to Leah's chair, holding out his hand. A refusal now would be a public insult. Her eyes darted to Daniel, the rest of the table. Even another second would be too long. She got up from her chair, a slow, steady motion, pulled by a string. Yamada took her hand and started toward the dancing area, their presence causing the same reaction at the tables they passed, an awkward stillness. In a few minutes they'd be on the dance floor, a couple.

"Well, Frau Auerbach," Daniel said, getting up, "shall we?"

A sudden confusion in her eyes, then she saw his outstretched hand and smiled.

"Clara," she said. "Call me Clara."

Daniel nodded and glanced over to Florence, making eye contact, get the others, everyone on the floor.

"It seems we're pairing off," she said, catching it. She leaned across to a man Daniel hadn't met. "Herr Stern, you don't want me to be a wallflower, do you?" Standing before he could respond. "Come on, everybody. Show them what a table this is."

The others, bowing to her authority, got up, and began to fill the dance floor, Leah no longer dancing alone with Yamada but part of a group, her partner just someone else at the table, everyone having fun.

"I think she'd really rather dance with you," Clara said, testing.

"Oh, yes? Well, later maybe. When the good colonel's had his turn."

"I suppose it's all right," Clara said. "Do you think it's all right?"

"What? Dancing with—?"

"Everybody was looking. This wouldn't happen in Vienna. It just wouldn't."

"Well, we're not in Vienna anymore."

"No," she said, eyes clouding.

"Anyway, they weren't looking at her, they were looking at you."

She smiled, enjoying this. "I was right about you."

"Yes?"

"A charmer. I could tell, right there on the pier. Going to all that trouble. I thought, he's up to something. A Berliner. They're always up to something."

"I just want to enjoy the evening."

"Dancing with an old woman. Maybe a way to her daughter."

"She's already got a partner."

"Cut in," she said, practical.

"But that would leave you with—"

"I know. Then they really would look at me. Just as you said."

He smiled, a joke between them.

"Another minute," she said. "You don't want to appear too eager. Besides, I'm enjoying it. You're a good dancer."

"My uncle worked at a club in Berlin. Years ago. The girls there taught me."

"A club? How old were you?"

"Too young for them."

Another smile. "Oh, yes. A charmer. Practically Viennese. You remind me—"

"Of Herr Auerbach?"

"Oh, no. No, no." She laughed. "Someone else. Hair just like yours. No comb, just run your hand through it. My husband was almost bald."

"Well, I'm getting there. All the Lohrs. It's a family curse."

"The eyes, too," she said, not hearing him. "Everywhere at once. He was like that too." Her expression distant, following some memory. She looked around the room. "I didn't think it would be like this, the boat."

"What did you think?"

"Crowded. You know, a refugee boat. And here we are, dancing."

"Well, in first class anyway."

"Do you always travel first class?" Asking something else.

"Never. My uncle bought the ticket. I think first was all that was left."

"The uncle at the club? He's still there?"

"No, he left Germany."

"Everybody's leaving," she said vaguely.

34

"Years ago. Before the Nazis."

"So he knew. My husband said it would pass. And now look at us. I don't even know where we are. On the ocean somewhere, that's all. Your uncle was smart to get out when you could still take your things."

Daniel smiled to himself. There'd been a suitcase, he remembered. Small, traveling light. Two steps ahead of the arrest warrant. A different kind of refugee.

"Oh, there's Frau Mitzel," she said. In evening dress, not wearing the coat.

"A friend?"

"Not really," Clara said. "Someone we used to know a little. Not Jewish. Look, she's pretending she doesn't see me."

But she had seen Leah, stopping before she reached her table and looking straight out at the dance floor, her mouth tight with disapproval.

"You sure you won't mind if we change partners?" Daniel said quickly, moving them closer to Leah and Yamada.

"Don't take no for an answer," Clara said, almost a wink. "She wants to dance with you. I can tell."

He tapped Yamada's shoulder. A frown as Yamada pivoted to face him, unfamiliar with the custom, somehow thinking Daniel was objecting to his dancing.

"Change partners," Clara said, smiling at Yamada. "My turn."

Yamada stood there, not knowing how to respond to this, then collected himself and bowed politely. "Of course. My pleasure." He put his hand on her back. "You'll forgive my clumsiness. It's something new to me."

Clara smiled again, almost flirtatious. "Shall we?"

Daniel moved Leah farther onto the dance floor, away from them.

"What are you doing?" she said.

"It was your mother's idea, the cut-in. She thinks you want to dance with me."

A quick look. "I mean all this—" She waved her hand to take in the others on the floor.

"If people see you together, you'll be the talk of the ship. This way—it's a party."

"Because he's Japanese? I don't care."

"But other people do. There's a war going on in China."

"And he's the enemy?"

"He's not just Japanese. He's Kempeitai. Their Gestapo."

"Oh." She was quiet for a minute. "Then thank you, I guess." She looked up. "How do you know he's Gestapo?"

"He said so. The Military Police. That's what it means. At least this one isn't trying to kill you. He just wants to dance with you."

"Like a girl at a party. Dancing. My god. Look at Mother. Doesn't anybody see what's happening to us?"

"We're not dead. So why not?"

"You're enjoying it?"

"You know how I feel? I've been facing a firing squad and somebody stopped them in time."

"With a blindfold? A last cigarette?"

"But they didn't shoot. And now I'm here."

"For two weeks. And then what?"

"Two weeks is a long time. Depending."

"Yes, depending," she said, looking at him.

The band had taken a break between songs, turning the music sheets, checking their instruments. As Leah moved off the floor back toward the table, Frau Mitzel stood up and came over to her.

"Here," she said, handing her some money, lofty, giving someone a tip. Leah flushed. "I was surprised to see you making a spec-

tacle of yourself with your Oriental friend. Now your mother—"
She trailed off. "You people."

Leah looked down at the money in her hand. "It's not what we
said."

"No, but it's the fair price. I thought about it. Of course, if you
don't agree, you can have the coat back. Should I go and get it?"
Sure of herself.

"Give her the money," Daniel said, his voice low.

"Who are you?"

"Her lawyer."

"Her lawyer. Don't be ridiculous. Hardly a legal matter. I'm not
even sure it's legal to do this on board. What the Lloyd policy is.
But I don't think we want to ask, do we?"

"No, we don't. Just give her the money." His voice a little grav-
elly this time, so that she looked up, hearing a hint of menace.
"Now," he said, calmly, Uncle Nathan collecting for the gangs.

"Well, I don't have it with me, anyway. Even if—"

"Yes, you do. Give it to her."

"And if I don't?" Still sure of herself, playing.

He stared at her. "If you don't, I'll bribe the maître d' to seat
you at our table every night. The Jewish table. Even if you com-
plain, it'll take a day or two before the captain gets involved—
assuming he wants to get involved in something like this and upset
his maître d'—and by that time I'll have it all over the ship that
you're a Jew trying to pass, which might make the air at your table
a little frosty, but you'll be welcome at ours. Colonel Yamada
will probably ask you to dance." He took a breath. "Then you
can make a spectacle and see how well you do. Now give her the
money."

Frau Mitzel's face turned white. "You wouldn't dare."

"Yes, I would. It wouldn't take much. Maître d's always need a little cash. And Lloyd's, as you see," he said, gesturing back to their table, "likes to keep the Jews together. You'll fit right in."

For a second she said nothing, just stared, then opened her clutch bag and took out some notes, handing them over with a half sneer. "Thief."

Daniel took Leah's elbow, steering her back to their table. The band had started again.

"My lawyer," she said.

"I was a lawyer. Almost. Before my apprenticeship began, the Jews were dismissed. So that was that."

"A lawyer. You don't seem—"

"I didn't think so either. So it's just as well. My father was disappointed, though."

She stopped, looking at him. "I don't know anything about you, do I?"

"What do you want to know?"

"The fast talk, where does that come from? And then, underneath— she was afraid of you."

"Not much."

"Yes. She could hear it in your voice. I could hear it. Polite, but not really. So where does that come from?"

He shrugged. "Not a nice woman. Sometimes you have to— Anyway, you got your money."

"Yes." She looked down. "Nobody ever did anything like that for me. So why did you?"

He waited for a minute. "Maybe I wanted to make a good impression."

"So I would go to bed with you? To thank you?"

He looked at her. "Quite a conversation to be having. On a dance floor."

"You think I don't see it? How you look? I know what you're thinking."

"Yes? You can read my mind?" He started walking again. "I'd better clear it out then," he said, indicating his head. He stopped and turned to her. "I'm not Herr Blauner. You don't owe me anything."

She looked at him, then nodded. "No, not him. But who then? Tell me something. How were you going to pay? The maître d'."

"I wasn't. Ten marks, whatever's left. That's all we have. You know that. But she doesn't."

A faint smile. "So a little bit of a gambler, too. And where does that come from?"

"There you are," Florence Burke said when they rejoined the table. "You almost missed the fish. I love poached salmon, don't you? I was just telling your mother about Sir Victor. Sassoon. So generous to the refugees. Of course, there's so much, it's not a sacrifice, but still— People can be funny that way. Rich as Croesus, but you have to work to get it out of them, show where it's going. Sir Victor just writes a check. You'll like him," she said to Leah. "And he'll certainly like you. An eye for the ladies. But watch out. A harem mentality there. A night on the town, that's what he likes." She sat back a little, sizing Leah up. "You'd be the right age for the Kadoorie boy, the cousin. To tell you the truth, I always find him a little dull. But how dull can that much money be? And no Hardoons at the moment. All taken. They say the old man, the grandfather, still collects the rents himself. In the Chinese alleys. Knocking on doors. At his age. I suppose he must have a bodyguard with him. I know I would. Month after month, making his rounds. Imagine it."

"You should meet that cousin," Clara said.

"Oh, with my dowry?" Leah said. "People like that always marry their cousins."

"Well, that is the problem," Florence said, serious. "They like to keep the money in the family. And you know, the more there is, the more protective they are. No, we'll find you some nice young man from Jardine's."

"With marriage on his mind," Leah said, teasing.

"There are other arrangements," Colonel Yamada said.

An awkward silence, even Florence at a loss.

"Well, in that case," Leah said, her voice light, "we might as well start at the top. Do you know Sir Victor?" she said to Florence.

"He's not hard to meet. Just go to the club at the Cathay. He's usually there. Or at Ciro's. Holding court. Don't worry, he'll see you." She made a circle with her thumb and forefinger and held it up to her eye. "With his monocle."

"Really?" Leah said, amused.

"Really. He's very old school in some ways."

"Better stick with Jardine's," Daniel said, catching Leah's eye.

"Don't be fresh," Florence said. "This is serious for a girl."

"Especially if she's not a girl anymore," Leah said.

"You're still a young woman," Clara said.

"Mmm. For years now."

"The years become you," Yamada said, a slight bow.

Another look from Leah, trying not to laugh.

"You know a great many people in Shanghai," Yamada said to Florence.

"Well, we've lived there for years, so you meet people. And of course my evenings. I do think music brings people together."

"Do you know Madame Chiang? Is it true what they say? He listens to her?"

"I've met her. Years ago, when they lived in Shanghai. But of course even then—I mean, the generalissimo's wife. That's in another league from my little parties."

"A pity. I would like to meet her."

"Well, yes," Florence said, just to say something.

"An extraordinary family, the Soongs," Yamada said to Leah. "One sister married the finance minister, the richest man in China, they say. Madame Chiang married the generalissimo and the other sister married Sun Yat-sen."

"One loved money, one loved power, and one loved her country," Florence said, almost in a singsong voice, a familiar line.

"But how much power does she have now? A government in exile. Is it really a government at all?"

"Well, they think it is. And not exactly in exile. Chungking is still China."

"But the government is in Nanking."

"Yours, you mean," she said, then backed away. "Still, it can't be easy for her there. So far away. What do they do all day?"

"One is told they are frequently in bomb shelters," Yamada said, his idea of a witticism.

"Still? I thought it was hard to attack. That's why they went there."

"It is mountainous, yes, not so vulnerable as other places. But really, a matter of time."

"You're very confident."

"I've seen our forces in Nanking."

"Ah. Well, I don't know. It's all beyond me. Clara, do you enjoy music? Come to one of my evenings."

"We had a Bechstein," Clara said. "Such a beautiful instrument. The tone. Do you remember, when we were young, everyone had a piano? Someone in the family played. Often the daughter. It wasn't a real home without a piano. But the Bechstein, well . . ." Her voice rushed up, like champagne bubbles, then evaporated.

The waiters were changing the plates and pouring coffee. Colonel Yamada put his hands on the table, pushing back his chair.

"I will leave you to the music. The first day out—it's always an early night for me. The movement of the water perhaps." He took out a card and handed it to Clara. "May I give you my card? If you or your daughter should need my assistance—"

"Your assistance?" Clara said.

"Frau Auerbach, China is at war. With us. With itself. In such a place, it's good to have friends. Old dancing partners," he said, smiling.

"At war? Then why are we—?"

"Mother," Leah said.

"China's at war," Florence said. "Shanghai isn't."

Yamada looked at her, then bowed his head. "Enjoy the rest of your evening. And thank you for the dance." Another tip of his head to Leah.

"Imagine," Florence said, watching him pass between the tables. "'I want to meet Madame Chiang.' Just like that. They really are impossible."

But the mood had somehow changed, the music and the talk touched by war. I've seen our forces in Nanking. Florence kept the conversation going, but the gossip now had an edge. Everything's all right, really. Nothing has changed. But it was going to.

"Why don't you two dance again?" Clara said. "Such nice music."

"I'm sure Herr Lohr has better things—"

"Daniel," he said, getting up and extending his hand. "May I?"

But the dancing was different too. The band was playing "Easy to Love," a smooth, gliding number, and the other couples were passing in a circle around them while they scarcely moved, small steps, their own circle, not talking, aware of each other. He could feel her breath near his ear, the warmth. She pulled her head back.

"Say something. They're watching."

"There's nothing to see."

She glanced to her side, then back, as if she were looking for a topic. "Where did you get that?" she said, nodding to a faint scar under his left eye. "A fight?"

"I fell and cut myself when I was a kid. I thought you couldn't see it anymore."

"If you're close enough," she said, lowering her head, moving back a little.

"Anyway, why a fight? Do I look like somebody who gets into fights?"

"A bad boy? Maybe. I'm trying to decide," she said, reading his face.

"Should I be? Would you like that?"

She looked up. "Nothing's going to happen. I told you that."

"You did."

She leaned back again, their cheeks no longer touching, but the effect was to make them more aware of the space between them, the feel of their bodies moving, the air charged, the beginning, when you know it can happen.

"People see everything on a boat."

"And you care what they think?"

"No." She paused. "I didn't used to. My reputation? Hah. And then you don't have it anymore and men look at you differently. I want to get off the boat as a *gnädige Frau*. Respectable."

"For the young men from Jardine's?"

"There isn't going to be one. Not for me. You know that."

"What, then?"

"Maybe one of Colonel Yamada's arrangements."

"Stop."

"Who knows? It sounds like a place where you can sink fast."
She stopped moving and looked up. "But I'm not going to. I'll
work in a shop. But then you really have to be respectable. No gossip on the boat."

"Nobody knows you. Except Frau Mitzel. Nobody cares. They
have problems of their own. They don't even know where we are.
Somewhere in the Mediterranean. You can do anything you want."

"Go with you, for instance."

"For instance."

She moved her hand, touching his shoulder. "Look, this is nice.
Dance with someone my age. Flirt. You forget how to do that. But
I have to keep my head clear. Do something for me? Don't start
anything. Not now."

He waited a second, then nodded. "Maybe someday, then," he
said softly. "When I'm settled in at Jardine's."

"Oh, Jardine's," she said, smiling, patting his shoulder again.
"An answer for everything." She let her arms drop, no longer
dancing.

"Come out on deck."

"Oh, and then what?" She shook her head. "I'd better get
Mother to bed. She has trouble these days."

But Clara wanted a last glass of champagne at the bar, so they
were another twenty minutes, listening to stories of Vienna but
talking over them without saying anything, the way they'd talked
at the table, in a look, some private language. Leah had draped a
white sweater over her shoulders and in the dim light of the bar
it seemed to float around her like a moth, trying to settle. Every
time Daniel turned back from Clara he met Leah's eyes, her head
cocked slightly, as if she were working out a puzzle, down and
across. Then she'd look down and play with a swizzle stick, restless,

the air jumpy. Finally Clara began to flag and they said their good nights, Daniel seeing them out, then taking up a stool to order a final drink. It was only then, from this new angle, that he saw Yamada sitting in a dark corner.

"I thought I would not intrude," Yamada said, getting up.

"You should have joined us."

"No, I think it was better this way. But may I join you now?"

"Of course."

"I thought I might give you one of these too," he said, handing Daniel a business card. His name and a phone number, no address.

"Is it a custom in Japan? The cards?"

"A custom, yes. But not to everyone. Only persons of interest."

"That sounds like the police."

Yamada smiled. "No, it simply means worthy of interest."

Daniel's drink arrived and he took a sip. "And what makes me worthy?"

"So many people are sentimental about China. Mrs. Burke. A culture in a bowl. But you're not, I think, sentimental. You'll see China for what it is, a country that needs guidance. And then your response to the dancing, so quick. A man who's not sentimental and who can think on his feet—such a man would always be of interest. Maybe useful."

"Useful."

"Gathering information. Any number of things," Yamada said, almost airy.

"I don't understand. You're offering me a job?"

Yamada smiled. "I'm offering you a contact. Shanghai can be— Do you know anyone there?" A harmless question.

Daniel looked at him. Give nothing away. Franz's training. "No."

"And what will you do there?"

"I don't know. Dig ditches if I have to."

"In a country where millions are willing to do this." He paused, nodding at the card. "A contact might be valuable."

Gathering information. Informing. The bar suddenly smaller, warm. Daniel took a breath, then held out the card. "I don't want to mislead you."

"Mislead me?" Yamada said, expectant, almost a smile.

"Your new friends. The strategic alliance. I can't have any part of that."

"A matter of politics."

"Killing my father. That's their politics. You have the wrong friends for me. I'll never call. Here."

Yamada looked at him for a moment, the card between them, then nodded toward it and stepped back. "Herr Lohr, may I offer you some advice? Never close a door."

He stayed another second, motionless, a stage effect, then nodded and left.

Daniel went out on the open deck, thinking the air might help, gulps of it, but the night was so black, moonless, that he felt trapped in the dark. He was back in Berlin, waiting to be snatched, using up his nine lives with stories, a nimble jump at the last moment. But how many lives were already gone? The other end of the world wasn't far enough. So far his luck had held. He'd survived Berlin. He looked out into the dark. And he had Nathan waiting. The others were going to Shanghai because there was nowhere else to go. He had Nathan.

———

In his cabin the bed had been made up. Had anyone searched the room while he was out? But what was there to find? The bed neat, blanket stretched tight. What you should expect in first class. Relax.

The tapping was so faint that at first he thought he'd imagined it. Then another. He glanced around the room. Everything in place. But why wouldn't it be? He had to answer. Would Yamada come himself or send somebody? Maybe the purser. He jerked open the door, expecting a white uniform, anyone but Leah. She slid in, closing the door behind her.

"I took a chance you'd be here. No one saw." Slightly out of breath, as if she'd been running.

"What are you doing?"

"Do you want me to go?"

"No. No. What—?"

"If I think about it, I won't be able to—"

She took his sleeve, pulling him to her, so that they were up against each other, her back to the door, their faces now side by side, the only sound their breathing, air warm against his neck, then turning into each other, her ear, cheek, the side of her face. No sounds, just the breathing, louder now, his head filled with it. She reached up and put her hand behind his head, bringing him closer, kissing him on the mouth, then pulling away, excited.

"Turn off the light," she said, almost a whisper.

He reached up and turned the switch, the only light now a faint strip from the hall coming through the transom and the ship's lights reflected in the porthole.

"Are you sure?" he said, kissing her again, moving down to her throat.

She nodded, then started unbuttoning his shirt and then they were both doing it, kissing and taking off each other's clothes, pulling them off, some kind of race, touching each other's skin, falling against the door, then holding each other from behind, pulling up her slip, now naked, the wonderful feel of below, slick, then his prick in her hand, both of them stroking each other, in a rush, running out of time. He laid her on the bunk, looking at her now, all of her, falling down next to her, running his hand along her hip and then sliding it between her legs. She jerked, as if her skin were jumping and grabbed his hand away, pulling him on top of her, then holding him from behind as he slid in, faster now, an urgency to everything, panting, the sound in his ears, making their bodies smack against each other, going faster until he couldn't stop, the warmth of her overwhelming, and he came, feeling himself spurting. For a second they didn't move, then, feeling his weight on her, he began to slide back and she cupped him from behind, holding him.

"No, don't go," she said, short of breath. "Stay."

Quieting him, on his elbows now, until he felt her gripping him inside, keeping him hard, and he started moving, not fast, barely moving at all, his penis too sensitive, just a sense of moving together, a rhythm, moving back and forth and he heard what he hadn't heard before, some sound underneath her breathing, not loud, a faint gasping, being drawn out of her against her will and then a panting, the most exciting thing he had ever heard, and he went faster, following her lead until it felt that she was coming out loud, the sound of it racing through his head, so that when they came together, he had already been there, had already heard it.

For a while they lay next to each other, not moving, feeling the faint breeze on their skin, the laziness after sex. His eyes were now used to the dark and he could see the floor littered with clothes, like markers to the bed. He thought of her pulling him to her, the surprise of it, a jolt, instantly hard. And then after, the rush to finish, the way it always happened, but different, sex always something new.

"Are you cold?" he said and, not waiting for an answer, got up and took his bathrobe off the peg and covered her, then lay next to her again. "Why—"

She put her finger to his lips. "Another minute. Listen, you can hear the water."

But instead he heard his own breathing, slowing down. She pulled herself up on one elbow, her other hand on his chest.

"Why? You're not bad looking. And you asked."

He reached up, answering this by running his hand down the side of her face.

"I don't remember asking. Not in so many words."

"Not in so many words, no." She raised herself a little higher. "So why? When we were dancing. I thought, what if I'm right? What if we fell off the edge? How do you spend the last days? The ship keeps going. What if it's the last time? And we were dancing and I thought it would be good with you. So. And it was, wasn't it? You're the right one for this."

"This what?"

"Whatever we're going to call it."

"Not one night."

"No. But then we get there and it's over," she said. "Something that happened on the ship."

"That's what you want?"

"Don't you? No strings. That's what you like, I think."

"You don't know that."

"I don't know anything about you. Enough for this, that's all. I'll know you in bed. The rest—" She moved her hand to touch the scar under his eye. "It's exciting, not knowing. Maybe you really are a bad boy. A criminal."

He looked at her, disconcerted. "What makes you say that?"

"You're always looking to see who's there. I saw it on the pier.

49

And here, too. Always alert. Who's like that? At first I thought, a soldier. A soldier's trained to watch. But that doesn't seem right."

"You're imagining things."

"No, it's true. Always a look over your shoulder. Maybe somebody's following. Like in American films, when the gangster is on the lam. You know that expression? On the lam. That's what it feels like with you. You're here but you're always watching. We're on the lam."

"Who's following us?"

"I don't know," she said, no longer playing. "Gentiles. Everybody. I don't know why. I don't know what we did." She looked up. "But they can't get us here. On the ship. It's nobody's territory. It'll just be us."

She moved her hand farther down.

"Do you have to get back?"

"I gave her a sleeping pill. She doesn't wake up after that. We have time."

"And then what? You tiptoe down the hall carrying your shoes?"

She leaned over and kissed him. "We can worry about that later. We only have three weeks. Not even that."

"We can't do this all the time."

"No, not all."

He rolled over, facing her. "This is a funny—whatever it is. You keep talking about the end and we've just started. Maybe we won't want it to end."

"But it will."

———

Frau Auerbach slept in the afternoon, an old Viennese habit, and Leah was in his cabin by four. He could see her now as he undressed her, the light from the porthole bright against the wall, the berth in shadow. Afternoon sex was slower, exploring, running his hands over her skin as if they had all the time in the world. Nights were like the first one, furtive, rushed, one ear cocked toward the hall, half expecting footsteps. Every night. The sex fed on itself, their last meal, greedy for crumbs. Again and again, the hunger part of some larger defiance, outrunning whatever was chasing them. You can't get me. Not a romance, an escape.

Part of the excitement was the hiding. Nobody knew. People gossiped and read books and sat in deck chairs staring out to sea, while Leah writhed beneath him, her body slippery against his, sweating. Later, dry again, they would appear on deck and say hello. No private signals that might catch someone's sharp eye. Every afternoon. Their skin flushed with it, a fever.

Meanwhile the world slipped by. They went through the Suez Canal, a shallow trench with high banks of sand, just wide enough for the ship to pass. The sleepy docks at Colombo, where they loaded the tea. He imagined a misty upland plantation, one day folding into the next, no one chasing you, even sex taking its own time. When the boat had pulled into Bombay, passengers crowding at the rail to see the Gateway to India, they were in his cabin, his mouth on the soft skin of her inner thigh, the ship's arrival just noise through the porthole. Now, after Colombo, the long stretch to Singapore, day after day of water, but in the East finally, the conversation at dinner about what they would find. Somebody's niece had been out there for years, spoiled now by cheap servants. The Jews below had other things to think about. It was useful, everyone said, to have some English. Relatives already in Shanghai had started to apply for visas again, a back door approach to America, to Palestine, some place they really wanted to go. Most of the refugees had settled in Hongkew. The Chusan Road had bakeries and coffee houses and German-speaking doctors. Little Vienna. But still.

Colonel Yamada had managed to get himself rotated to other tables at dinner, but stopped by theirs to say good evening.

"You must know everybody on the ship by now," Florence said.

"No, no. I am not so social. A temporary arrangement only, I think. They changed the tables after Bombay."

"Not this one."

"And you, Herr Lohr, you're enjoying the voyage? I'm not surprised with such company," he said, including Leah. "I have your permission to ask her to dance?"

"Fräulein Auerbach doesn't need my permission."

"Ah. Then perhaps this time I'll be able to finish the dance," he said, offering his hand to Leah, as if she'd already accepted, something he'd settled with Daniel.

"The Greater East Asia Co-Prosperity Sphere," Florence said, watching them go, her tone unexpectedly grim. "Who's going to stop them, I wonder."

"Stop them from what?" Clara said idly, not really paying attention.

"Taking everything. All of it. The rubber, the oil, you know, their ambitions in the Pacific."

"He always seems such a gentleman," Clara said.

"No, he's not that," Florence said. "Anything but that."

Daniel followed her gaze, taking in the hand around Leah's waist, the other locked in hers, the shoulder leaning forward. All harmless. Then why the clutching in his stomach? Irrational, coming out of nowhere. Not jealousy, not even an instinct to protect. He had no right. Still, a disturbance in the air. A few hours ago she'd been naked in his bed. That had to count for something, some kind of claim. Who was she to him now? Yamada was smiling, his eyes oddly still and watchful as he moved, the deliberate grace of a predator.

"I wonder what he was really doing in Germany," Florence said.

"But he's not a Nazi, is he?" Clara said. "I mean, how could he be?"

"Maybe an Aryan of convenience," Florence said, smiling at her own joke. She turned to Daniel, lowering her voice. "Better protect your interests."

"My interests?"

"I don't miss much," she said, then glanced toward the dance floor again, leaving it at that. "You're like us, the States, I mean. You think the good guys always win. Because they should. But they don't. Keep an eye on him. He's just waiting to pounce."

Daniel looked at her. The same image, as if she'd been reading his thoughts.

"They're all waiting, the Japanese. And that'll be the end. Of Shanghai. Of course I can get out. I'm American. But think of all these people belowdecks. They'll be stuck, with the Japanese in control."

"Instead of you."

"Oh, I know, I know," she said, catching his tone. "We're nothing to write home about. But at least we're not making nice with the Nazis. The worst of it is we don't care. About any of it. Madame Chiang speaks English. So we think they're the good guys, she and the generalissimo. You might as well have the Manchus back. Nobody knows where the money goes. Anyway, not to fight the Japanese. The only one who wants to fight them is Mao, if Chiang would leave him alone. Which he won't. And meanwhile the Japanese just gobble up the country."

"You surprise me," Daniel said, the music still playing in the background.

"Because I read a newspaper once in a while? Don't worry, nobody else does. As long as the factories keep working and Jardine Matheson shows a profit, nobody in the Settlement cares what's happening in China. Now, anyway. But they will. If I had any brains, I'd get out now. Hop off when we get to Manila and take the first ship home."

"I thought Shanghai was home."

"It is. But it won't be when the Rising Sun gets its hands on it."

"So why–?"

"Well, I do have a husband to consider. And he's not going anywhere. Not with business like it is. And I can't leave him alone. A trip to Europe– He knows I'm coming back, so there's only so much trouble he can get into. But the States? Every chippie in town would be lined up at the door. Not that I mind that so much, but the talk. Everything out in public. Well, listen to me. How did we get started on this?"

"The Japanese."

"That's right. Protecting your interests." She looked at him. "It's good advice."

Daniel dipped his head. "Taken."

"What are you two talking about?" Clara said, leaning over to be nearer.

"China. The war."

Clara looked at her blankly.

"I don't know anything," Daniel said, "and Florence was giving me a scorecard, so at least I'll have some idea who's who."

"In other words, I was boring him," Florence said, her familiar voice.

"No, I was interested. You know the country and I don't."

"Hardly," Florence said. "You could spend a lifetime there and still not know China. But every once in a while you see something—it's like looking through a crack. It was there all along and you didn't see it. You know Chou En-lai? He's Mao's right hand. Maybe his brain too. He used to live in Shanghai. A very intelligent man."

"A Communist?" Clara said.

"One day, he took me to a factory," Florence said, ignoring her. "Well, he took a friend and I went along. A silk factory. I'd never seen one. No idea what they were like. Huge vats of boiling water to separate the strands, boules rising to the surface and you have to skim them off the top of the water. Children do this. All day. And their hands were bright red because sometimes you slip or you're not fast enough and the water gets them. Children with boiled hands. And Chou said, this is China. I never forgot that. Of course," she said, taking a breath, "there's more to China than that. Wonderful things too. But if you don't know about that, then you're just passing through. I think that's what most of us in the Settlement are doing, just passing through."

"It's barbaric," Clara said, genuinely upset. "Why would they show you such things? Foreigners."

Florence looked at her. "We own the factories."

Only a few people got off at Singapore, usually a major exchange point, rubber planters coming back from leave, junior officials off for a break in Hong Kong. Now all the berths below were crammed with Jews, ticketed to the end, no stops in between. In Manila there were a few new faces, businessmen in white linen suits and a gang of musicians carrying instrument cases. Gus Whiting and his Cincinnati Five, chewing gum, hats pushed back on their heads, cartoon Americans, all sharing a double room and expected to play in the lounge after dinner to pay for it. According to the woman next to him at the rail, who knew things. Behind them, a handful of men who looked like crew replacements—open shirts and work pants and soft canvas bags for what little they were carrying. Then, finally, a flock of girls, all blondes, all wearing white sailor hats, swooping up the gangplank, chattering, little squeals, trailed by a short man who seemed to be counting them to make sure they were all there.

"Who's that?" Daniel said.

"No idea," the woman next to him said, then to Daniel's surprise, took out a pair of binoculars for a close look, as if the girls really were birds. "Bert's Broadway Babies," the woman read off one of the suitcases. "Must be dancers, don't you think? All dressed alike. Where are they going to put them, the lifeboats?"

The short man, maybe Bert himself, seemed unconcerned, gathering them up for a group photograph. More squeals, then smiles, broad and eager, the forget-your-troubles cheerfulness of the movies.

"Chorus girls," the woman said. "I hope they're not planning on bringing them up here."

But Bert, now holding a clipboard, seemed to be giving out room assignments on B deck, safely out of first class sight.

The Cincinnati Five appeared that night and were good, a jazz combo that made the regular dance orchestra seem polite and faded. Gus Whiting had a patter of American slang that only some of the passengers could follow, but the spirit of the group was infectious—they seemed to be having a good time playing for themselves and whoever wanted to listen in. Nathan had booked bands like this in Berlin, making the Black Cat a regular stop on the jazz circuit. Could you do that in Shanghai? Evidently, yes. Here was Gus Whiting working the South China coast. Somebody Nathan would be happy to snap up. Assuming he was still running clubs. But what else would he be doing? What else did he know? America had been the dream, a jazz dream. Then why leave? A few postcards and then he was gone. On a boat to China.

"So now I know something else about you," Leah said. "You like this music."

Daniel nodded. "I had an uncle who was a fan. Had all the records."

"The same uncle who taught you to dance?"

"Not him, the girls in his club."

"Chorus girls?"

"No."

"Whores."

"They didn't see it that way."

"What else did they teach you?" she said, having fun with it.

"I was a kid."

"And now look," she said. "All grown up." She smiled, then looked away, a shift in mood. "About later. I can't, tonight. Don't wait for me. I have to stay with my mother. She's having one of her bad days."

"I thought she went right out. One pill and—"

"Not tonight. Not when she's like this. She forgets where she is. She wanders off. I have to be there." She looked at him. "Maybe it's just as well. We have to get used to it. We're almost there. Hong Kong and then—"

"We don't have to get used to anything," he said, suddenly feeling what it would mean, getting there, Leah disappearing, the trip just an erotic dream.

"Those are the rules."

"Rules."

"I know. But my mother isn't going to get better. She's going to get worse. And now her doctor is in Vienna and we're—"

"There are doctors in Shanghai."

"And how do I pay? Selling gloves? Maybe I'll have to sell something more. Maybe he's married. I'm used to that. You're not."

"Don't."

"I have a sick mother who's losing her mind. Who knows what I'll have to do? And what will you do then? Stand by and watch? Be my pimp? No. We're good for each other now, for this. But after?"

"It doesn't have to be that way."

"No? But it will be." She reached up and put her hand on his cheek. "Don't be like this. Don't ruin it. This is what we have."

"Before we fall off the map."

A weak smile. "Maybe it's already beginning. You know what I saw today? I was looking down at B deck, at the Broadway Babies. Rehearsing. A tap dance. You could hear the shoes all the way up here. Then a line, all kicking together, with those smiles. Having a good time. And who's the audience? Some men by the rail, in coats, because that's all they have, their Viennese clothes. The girls are in shorts, flirting, just to get a reaction. And the men are standing there looking, sometimes a little German. The language is like a prison for them now. No money, no English, what's next? And here they are, in the middle of the ocean, watching the Broadway Babies. Not smiling, amazed, the way you look when you fall off the map. Amazed."

"Leah—"

She touched his chest, stopping him. "What happened to your uncle? He's still in Berlin?" Changing the subject.

Daniel waited for a moment. "He went to America." Not exactly a lie. Who knew what Nathan was doing? Except it must be illegal.

"Then he can get you a visa. A relative in America."

"I don't know where. It was a long time ago. We haven't been in touch."

"Maybe it's him you're looking for. Over your shoulder."

"I thought that was because I was a criminal."

"No, I know you better now. You know someone in bed. Not a criminal. The opposite."

"A cop?" he said, smiling.

"Not that, either." She looked up at him. "Tomorrow's the last night. We'll say good-bye then."

But something had already happened, a sense of coming to the end. He could feel them being pulled down, like kites. There was a farewell party the last night, with streamers and champagne and promises to look each other up onshore, but the mood was apprehensive. The trip had been a time-out for everyone. Now they were there, back in their lives. Even the lovemaking seemed off. When she came to his cabin, after the party, she seemed distracted, her motor running again, her mind racing ahead. Her mother was fretful, the champagne had given her a headache, people, up late, were in the corridors—everything except what was really happening.

"I wanted it to be special for you."

"It was." She kissed him, a thank-you. "I have to go," she said, beginning to dress.

He watched her from the bed, her fingers deftly hooking her bra.

"Remember, tomorrow, no scenes. I'm a *gnädige Frau* again. Like Frau Mitzel."

"Just like," he said, smiling.

She leaned over, another kiss. "Tell me something. It's your real name, Lohr?"

"Yes," he said, surprised. "Why wouldn't it be?"

"I don't know. People do that sometimes. I thought, when you were so careful, maybe you were in some kind of trouble. So the name—"

"No trouble." Not anymore, not here. "Anyway, does it matter?"

She looked at him. "When I remember all this, I want to get the name right."

"Leah—" he said, starting to get up.

"No, stay in bed. Then I can remember you in bed."

She looked at him for another minute, about to say something, then turned instead and opened the door a crack. "It's safe now. I'll see you—" She caught herself. "I won't, though, will I?" Another second. "Well," she said, her voice low, then stepped into the hallway and closed the door behind her.

CHAPTER 3

The *Raffaello* was too big to dock at the city piers on the Whangpoo, so it anchored at the mouth of the Yangtze and sent the passengers ahead on smaller tenders. Daniel had been expecting the photographs he'd seen in magazines, the sweep of riverfront lined with skyscrapers. Instead there were miles of mudflats with warehouses and factories, the workaday back end of a port, dingy buildings behind chain-link fences, rusting piles of scrap. Then suddenly, beyond a broad curve of the river, there it was, the European waterfront, neoclassical banks and office towers, art deco hotels, all lining the Bund in a show of commercial swagger, Liverpool maybe, even parts of Trieste, all faithfully re-created here, as if the workers in the offices hadn't really left home. Department stores and trams and sleek Western cars. Like anywhere, Berlin even, except the buses were filled with Chinese, the stores advertised sales in incomprehensible lettering, coolies in straw hats pulled rickshaws. Not Europe after all. Old men in long silk robes and hair queues; girls in tight *qipao*s, necks covered but thighs visible through the slit skirts; beggars; food stalls with wisps of smoke; children racing through the crowd for no apparent reason, a stage set in motion.

The river seemed as busy as the street. They maneuvered past a Japanese warship, anchored there as a reminder, then dodged a string of flat-bottom barges that swept past them like schools of fish, sampans bobbing in their wake. The rickety piers stretching on the mudbanks were now filling up with passengers from the tender, people in European winter coats waved through customs to keep the lines moving, no questions asked, then herded onto the backs of trucks by people holding signs from the Jewish Relief Agency, standing up to save space, a livestock crowding. Daniel thought of the trucks in the streets after Kristallnacht, snatching up people for Sachsenhausen, the same herding. Leah had disappeared into the crowd, the polite pushing to get off. But now he caught a glimpse of her, standing in the truck's flatbed, holding on to the rail, jutting forward like a ship's figurehead, heading toward the edge of the map. The Relief Agency must keep records. If she and Clara spent the night in a heim, there'd be a way of finding her. You didn't just disappear, not even in Shanghai.

But first there was Nathan to find, in a pier full of people looking for one another, calling names and holding signs. His uncle must know which ship, he'd arranged it. Or someone had. Daniel felt the package in his pocket, then walked past the customs tables, the indifferent inspector, the opposite of Trieste. No hand on his arm, come with us. At least he'd got the package through. Up ahead he could see Florence handing luggage to a uniformed driver, slipping back into her life. My evenings. A culture in a bowl. Where was Nathan? If Daniel left the pier, he'd be swallowed up by the city. He looked at the street. Potsdamer Platz, buses and cabs and crowds. Even a traffic policeman on a stand, this one in a Sikh turban, an import from the Raj.

"Mister Lohr?" A stocky man with a fighter's face. No tie, a jacket stretched by wide shoulders, not an official.

"Yes?"

"Your uncle's in the car. This way."

"The car?" Daniel said.

"Safer," the man said. "No crowds. I'm Sergei." As if this explained something. No attempt to take Daniel's suitcase. A bulge in his breast pocket. "Nice trip?" The ordinariness of it slightly surreal.

Ahead of them a line of cars, most with drivers, waited in the sun.

"You work for my uncle?"

"I look out for him. I'm Irina's cousin."

Daniel glanced at him. A world he knew nothing about. Had Nathan married? Did he have children? That seemed improbable somehow. But it had been ten years. People change.

But Nathan hadn't. The smile came first, the way he used to walk into a room, following his smile. A shiny Buick, Nathan stepping out, still wiry, quick, but completely gray, the face fuller, like Daniel's father's, in fact.

"Duvey, thank god," he said, hugging him, a clutch so unexpected Daniel felt light-headed. What Nathan always called him, a nickname for David, but Daniel's anyway. "My god, look at you." Clasping his arms, taking him in, eyes watering. "Just like Eli. I can see him in your face."

"Uncle Nathan," he said, at a loss.

"My god, you were just a kid. So who wasn't. And now look."

"Better get in the car," Sergei said.

"They killed him, didn't they? Eli."

Daniel nodded. "They said an illness."

"Bastards," he said, his eyes teary. "Eli. Rabbi Lohr." His father's nickname, at least to Nathan. "So now it's just us."

"Thank you for—"

Nathan waved this aside. "We're blood. So you're here." He

raised a finger. "English only, yes? No German. It's an English city here." He looked over at Sergei. "And a few Russians. Great dancers. The girls, I mean."

"Who's Irina?"

"You heard about her already? Oh, from big shot here. She takes care of me."

"You're married? I didn't know."

Nathan shook his head. "My bookkeeper. She takes care of my business. And me, once in a while." A wink in his voice. "You'll see. We go back, you'll meet her." Another look at Daniel. "So, my Duvey, all grown up. And now what? At least you're out of that hellhole. Nazis. I used to miss Berlin, but what was I missing? The Black Cat? I got another one. You remember Schildkraut? How he had clubs all over the city? Well, that's me now. An impresario. Nate Green."

"Green?"

"What the hell, what's a name? You want to start over, start over. I get to Shanghai, I thought, who the hell knows who I am? Plus, in those days, maybe better not to know. So—Nate Green. Why not? You want to change your name? You can do it right now. Just say."

"Then I'd have to be Green."

"You're a nephew, so maybe you're my sister's kid. She married a Lohr. If you want to be a nephew. Maybe you don't want. There's a lot comes with that. I'll explain things. The point is, you don't have to be anything you don't want. Work with me, don't work with me. We'll figure it out."

"Work with you?"

"At the clubs. Don't say no until you see what it is. Then you say no—okay, no. You don't want that life. But first see what it is. You bunk in with me, until we get you something. I know, a man your age wants his own place. But right now you stay with me, all right?"

"Of course."

"We've got a lot to talk about. Everything that happened. It's a story, you'll enjoy it. Not everybody likes this life. But you'll listen, yes? Not like Rabbi Eli. Everything I did—it was always wrong to him. He didn't even want me to see you, did you know that? Maybe he was right. Anyway, we'll catch up. I don't even know—"

"Why did you leave America? Let's start there. You always wanted to go there."

"And I was right. Maybe someday, you'll go, see for yourself." He paused. "Why did I leave? The truth? It was like before. I got a little greedy. Just a little. But you don't take from the Italians, not even a little. So, a friend, he says there's a boat for Manila and I take it, what the hell, I'm marked, you have to go somewhere. The same friend, he sets me up with a job in a casino there, helping with the slots, and I get there and I'm thinking why is he doing all this for me. Maybe to prove a point. You can go all the way to Manila and they can still get you. I'm going to be an example. I don't know if it's true, but what the hell? You have to trust your gut. So I turn around—I never got to the slots—and I go right back to the docks and there's a boat for Shanghai and I get on it. And then—" He made a ta-da gesture. "Nate Green."

"So you can never go back? To America?"

"Not if I want to keep breathing. I don't know, who remembers? Maybe they forgot. But they never forget. You don't want to chance that. That's all your luggage?"

"That's all we're allowed to take out."

Nathan turned, stopped by this, and took Daniel's arms again. "My god, to see you. I thought maybe I'd never— You know, you become somebody else and you have to go with it. Forget about things. And then I'm hearing things, what's going on over there and I think, I have to get them out. Eli, he won't even talk to me, but I have to get them out." He gripped Daniel's arms more tightly. "I'm sorry he didn't make it. You know they used to say there was bad blood between us, but there was never bad blood. Never."

"I know."

Nathan looked away, then took a breath. "So, the trip was good? For that money–"

Daniel nodded.

"It's a good place to meet women, a boat. They got nothing to do. But maybe not this one."

"No, I met somebody."

Nathan looked up, a slightly crooked smile. "Jesus Christ, flat broke and you're chasing skirt?" He turned his head, taking Daniel in from a different angle. "You were always a funny kid. Just like Eli–and then not. I used to think, he's got the devil in him, too. I always wondered how that would work out."

Daniel shrugged.

"I'll say one thing for you. You always knew how to keep your mouth shut. You'd see something and I'd think, uh-oh, he'll go right to the rabbi with this one, but you never did. It's a good thing to know, how to keep a secret." He glanced up. "Somebody meet up with you in Trieste?"

Daniel nodded. "I got it," he said, putting his fingers on his pocket.

"Any trouble?"

"No. They didn't check." He tipped his head toward the customs shed.

"It's all at the other end," Nathan said, familiar with it. "You take a look?"

"No. It's still sealed."

Another glance, amused. "All that way and you don't look? Me, I would've gone nuts. Curiosity killed the cat, though, right? So who's smarter? You got a good head on your shoulders."

Daniel moved his hand to his pocket.

"Not here. In the car."

"What is it? Dope?"

"Dope," Nathan said. "Is that what you think? I'd have you do that? No, it's all on the up-and-up. Well, mostly. You'll see."

"Then why all the—"

"I said mostly. Sergei, we ready?"

"I'm waiting."

But at the car door, Nathan heard his name called.

"Nate Green. In the daylight, too. I thought you slept days."

"I don't sleep at all. What are you doing here, Gus?"

Daniel turned. The Cincinnati Five.

"You were on the boat," Gus said, recognizing him. "I saw you listening."

"My nephew," Nathan said. "My sister's boy." The lie as easy as breathing, the story now, if Daniel kept his name. "So what brings you back? I thought you were playing Hong Kong."

"And Macau. You should see what they're doing there. The casinos. But we got a split week here at the Canidrome."

"Now you're playing at the dog races?"

"Very funny. The ballroom. They got the Broadway Babies between sets. You see them on the boat?" he said to Daniel.

"Christ, Gus. That's shit. You're a serious musician."

"I'm a serious eater too." He turned to include Daniel. "Your uncle's what they call careful with a dollar."

"The Cat isn't that kind of club."

"I know. No dog races out back. Craps, either. Just the music.

67

People you want to play for. That's what he says every time but you don't see his hand going into his pocket." He turned back to Nathan. "I've got five people to think about now. So the Canidrome, okay. It's a living."

"Stop by the club. We'll talk. I may have something for you if your dog doesn't come in."

"I mean it, Nate. I can't afford the Cat."

"Not the Cat. A new place opening out in the Badlands. Everything first class. Roulette tables, dice, everything. And the music. We're talking the Ciro's crowd, not the Cat. Serious punters. A real floor show. Sir Victor'll be there first night, I got a bet on it."

"And this is your place?"

"I'm a partner."

"The kind where somebody else puts up the money and you put in your valuable expertise?"

"No, I have money in it. And I hire the talent. So come out to the club. We'll talk."

"When's this?"

"In a few weeks. The paint's drying now. It's going to be the biggest thing in town. Bigger than Farren's. You know I always liked your playing." He turned to Daniel. "He used to play with Teddy Wilson." Then back to Gus. "Come out, see the room. A spot right over the piano. You got the whole room watching."

"What are you calling it?"

"The Gold Rush. Which is what's going to happen. So why shouldn't you pick some up too? We could talk about a regular thing. I mean, you're going up and down the coast, over to Yokohama, how long are you going to be doing that? When you've got the perfect gig here."

"And how long are the Japs going to keep the clubs open?"

"The Japs have nothing to do with it. They *go* to the clubs.

Besides, the Badlands, nobody knows for sure who's in charge. The Brits don't have jurisdiction, not once you're out past Avenue Haig, and the French just take envelopes and look the other way, the way they always do. The Japanese don't want to step on any toes. You could say it was made for us, the partners. No raids. No Special Branch. No Chinese gangs—if the peace holds. Just money waiting to be picked up. The best of everything. If I thought Teddy Wilson would come out here, I'd hire him. But you're the next best thing, so I'm going to hire you."

"And where'd you get all the money? For a place like this. The best of everything."

Nathan smiled. "I put some by. I'm careful with a dollar." He reached behind and fished out a wallet, then slid a bill out and held it up. "Here's a hundred on account."

"Jesus, Nate, you're walking around with hundred-dollar bills?"

"I'm protected," Nathan said, nodding toward Sergei.

"You'd better be. Out there. From what I hear—"

"It'll calm down. Too many people with interests now. Gus, take the money. Come see the club. You don't want the job, give the money back. It's earnest money, between us."

Gus looked at him, then pocketed the bill.

"Just don't bet it on the dogs, okay? Comp me and I'll come catch your show."

"Comp you?"

"The way I'm going through money these days," he said, spreading his hands, the Nathan smile like a punch line.

"Watch out for him," Gus said to Daniel, then turned back to Nathan. "I'll think about it. Right now I better round up the guys before they get into any trouble. That's the part of the job they never tell you about."

"Then let the club do it for you."

Gus looked at him, then waved this off, melting back into the crowd.

"You think he'll give it back?" Daniel said, watching him go.

"He'll want to. But he loves the pipe. And that's a hard thing to get ahead of. So I think I just got a piano player. Hopheads. You don't do any of that, do you?" he said, suddenly parental. "You know what it does to you? That's why the Chinese tried to keep it out."

"What, opium?"

"Any of it. Keep off it."

"You ever try it?"

"Once, to see. Smooth. Everything gets smooth. But I like it a little scratchy. I like to know what's going on. Anyway, let's get you home." He put a hand on Daniel's shoulder. "Irina's cooking something. Pelmeni. Which she only does about twice a year, so tell her they're great."

"I don't want to be in the way."

"What, way? There's nobody else now. Just us. Way."

Nathan opened the back door, holding it for Daniel. "How do you like the Buick? Nice, huh? Practically cleaned me out. But after the club opens—" He stopped, seeing someone coming from the crowd on the pier. "Oh, the Rising Sun. He was on the boat?"

Daniel turned. Colonel Yamada, this time in uniform, about to get into another car. A surprised flicker of recognition, then a smile.

"Yes. You know him?"

"We do business. He wants to do business." Correcting himself. "Colonel," he said, greeting him.

"You surprise me," Yamada said to Daniel. "I thought you'd be with the others. In the heim."

"The heim?" Nathan said. "He's family. My sister's son." The story real now.

"You never said," Yamada said, looking at Daniel, assessing, "that you knew anyone here. So maybe there's an answer to the mystery. How does a Jew have something so valuable he puts it in the purser's safe?" He caught Daniel's expression. "Of course it was reported. A man who's allowed to bring out nothing. I was curious. I made a mental note," he said. "A person of interest. But now I think here's an answer. It wasn't yours. A courier only."

"Daniel has nothing to do with the business," Nathan said.

"Yes. So let's do it this way." Yamada looked at Nathan. "He brought something for you. No doubt a house present. I won't ask what. I will leave it to you to decide what the squeeze should be. Let's say sometime this week? No need to take this any further. I'm sure you'll know exactly how much it would be. If I knew."

Nathan stared at him for a minute, saying nothing, then nodded. "This week," he said.

"An interesting family," Yamada said to Daniel. "I hope you kept my card. But of course now I know where to find you. A drink one day, perhaps."

"He's not part of the business," Nathan said again.

"Ah. A social drink then." He turned to Nathan. "This week," he said, then headed back to his car.

"What was all that?" Daniel said. "Squeeze."

"His piece off the top. Everybody gets squeeze out here. Settlement police. Xi Ling, for protection. Jack Riley, he runs the slots. You have gambling, you have squeeze. It's the way it works. Now the Japanese want a piece too. The new clubs, outside the Settlement. They've got the French in line ahead of them. But they're working on it."

"You going to pay him?"

Nathan nodded. "I have to. I don't, he'll come sniffing around for something else."

"I'm sorry."

"No." He looked at Daniel. "The safe, huh? I never thought of that. It should have— Anyway, it's worth a little squeeze. And once he takes it, what does that make him? Not that I didn't know."

Daniel reached for the package. "What's in it anyway?"

"In the car," Nathan said, letting Daniel get in first.

When Sergei pulled away from the curb, Daniel handed the package over and watched Nathan slit the seal with his fingernail. Money. Two stacks of bills, pressed tightly together. One-hundred-dollar bills.

"Currency's king out here," Nathan said. "You want dollars. Sterling. Even yen. You know how much this is worth in yuan? As far as money's concerned, there is no China. You want dollars."

"And it's illegal to bring it in?"

"No. But it's illegal not to tell. You move it through a bank, they like to take a fee. So why should they have a squeeze? You pay to exchange it, but you're getting so much you can afford a little off the top. Just one of these, you can do all right for months. And nobody has to know. The clubs, it's a cash business anyway. Taxes, you have separate books. I'll show you. Irina, she can move cash around like a three-card monte dealer. But you want hard currency. Here, you'll need some walking around money to get started. Your cut." He peeled off two bills and held them out, a tip to a waiter. Daniel looked at the bills. *Your cut.* Not a loan. Earnest money.

———

Nathan told Sergei to take the long way home so Daniel could see some of the city. The department stores on Nanking Road. Wing On. Sincere. Bigger than Wertheim's. Soochow Creek, so crowded with boats you could walk from one side to the other on them.

Hotel doormen whistling for taxis. The racetrack, the girls in Thibet Road.

"Don't go to places here. Your dick will fall off. You want, I can recommend a place. Anything you want. A doctor once a week checks them out. Same one we use at the Cat. And none of the girls at the club, understood? They're for the customers."

Billboards for Hollywood pictures. Bubbling Well Road. Chinese alleyways.

"You go in there, take somebody with you who knows. Otherwise, you never come out. Like hinterhofs, but not in a row, any which way."

Daniel leaned closer to the window. A clump on the pavement. "That's a man. Over there."

"They pick them up at night. It's worse in the winter. You know, in the cold. They got a wagon that collects them."

"Or they just lie dead in the street?"

"People die. You want to see something? Go to Soochow late. You see candles on the water. You know what they are? Paper coffins. They can't afford to bury them, so they put them in these paper coffins and let the tide carry them out. With a candle. They're paper, so they don't last long. But then the water takes them."

Daniel said nothing. They were turning a corner, the clump now out of sight.

"You see things here," Nathan said. "I saw a kid eat someone's puke."

Daniel turned, facing him.

"Some sailor, blind drunk, he pukes all over the road. And the kid eats it. Like it's the first thing he's had all day. I know. You think you can't do something and then you're starving and you do it. A kid."

The Black Cat was in the French Concession, off Avenue Foch, a converted house with a small stage and room for tables, the living quarters and office above. The hallway to the restroom was lined with slot machines, but otherwise the club looked like any backstage, dingy and shadowy, sensitive to sunlight. Irina was in the office, a big open safe behind her, and smiled politely when she took Daniel's hand, her eyes frankly looking him over. Nathan had said she'd been a dancer and although the body was fleshy now, the blond hair mostly out of a bottle, she still had a dancer's posture, head held back. She stood behind the desk with an air of possession—her office, her house—but her movements were tentative, self-conscious, eager to do the right thing.

"You don't look like each other," she said, her voice direct, Russian. "The trip was good?"

"He met Yamada on the boat. They had a little dance. Duvey and the Kempeitai. So maybe we're more alike than you think."

She rolled her eyes, tolerant. "Listen to you." Then, to Daniel, "Be careful with the Kempeitai. Everything's serious with them. Not a joke, like with Nathan." She thought for a second. "But maybe it's useful."

"He wants squeeze," Nathan said.

"Give it to him." The direct voice again.

Nathan nodded. "But not the Gold Rush."

"I'm sorry," Irina said to Daniel. "I know you've just arrived, but Nathan—" She turned to him. "You should know. Sid Engel's dead."

"Dead? How?"

"How do you think? Shot. I told you it's serious this time."

"Sid doesn't have a piece of the Rush."

"No, the Glass Slipper. What's the difference?"

"Xi Ling, that's the difference. He didn't have Xi."

"Well, Sid's dead. Esther called. The funeral's tomorrow. She's—well, how she would be." She turned to Daniel. "I'm sorry for this.

Your first night. We wanted this to be a celebration. I made up the old office for you. It's a daybed, but it's all right. I didn't know how long you were staying." A question.

"Staying," Nathan said. "It's his home."

"I don't want to be any trouble."

"It's no trouble," Nathan said. "So we'll celebrate anyway. What, we're going to bring Sid back if we don't eat?"

"Watch yourself," Irina said, "talking like that. A friend. Here, sit," she said, moving them to a table in the adjoining dining room. Dark furniture out of czarist Russia, deep burgundy chairs, lace doilies, and a samovar in the corner. China miles away. "I'll bring some glasses. I made pelmeni," she said, suddenly shy, a girl's smile.

"Wait till you taste this," Nathan said. Then, to Irina's back, "They're sure it's the Japanese? It could be—"

"Of course it's the Japanese. I told you this would happen. They're sending a message. Anybody can hear it. Unless they're too thick up here." She tapped the side of her head. "You don't go anywhere now without Sergei, it's a promise?"

"Then what the hell am I paying Xi for?"

"So he doesn't shoot you himself, that's what."

"He's a partner. That was the idea."

"I told you when this started—" Her voice trailed off, pre-occupied now with setting out the vodka and pelmeni.

"This make any sense to you?" Nathan said to Daniel. "It's like I was telling Gus. The new place in the Badlands. Sit. We have a million things to talk about and here we're talking about the Badlands. But, what the hell, you have to know sooner or later. What's going on. If you're going to be in the business." Then, catching Daniel's look, "If you want that."

Irina stopped, hovering, glancing at Daniel, then poured out drinks.

"Welcome," she said, raising her glass. "Better times. Safe times."

"You listen to her you wouldn't do anything," Nathan said. "Nobody's going to bother you. But if you're worried, I'll get you a gun." Daniel looked up. "For carrying around. It sends a message," Nathan said, looking at Irina, echoing her. "You know how to use a gun?"

"Yes."

"You do? In Berlin?"

"Lots of people have guns in Berlin."

Nathan was looking at him, working this out. "You weren't with a gang. Eli would have dropped dead. So something—political maybe. You're taking potshots at Nazis?"

Daniel shook his head. "The idea was to protect yourself."

"You know how politics works here? Chiang wants to get rid of the Communists? He calls Big-Eared Du. You like the name? He ran the Green Gang, And the Greens ran Shanghai. The real government. So Chiang tells him he wants the Communists gone and Du gets his people to take them out. Thousands and thousands. Just like that, takes them out. Before, it's a Communist town. You know, with all the factories. Now, nothing. Unless a few crawled into a rathole somewhere. So Chiang's problem's solved. And he stays out of Du's way. They look out for each other. The Nationalists set up a drug force. Let's clean it up once and for all. And who does Chiang appoint to run it? Du. Who runs the drug trade. So that's politics here."

"They shot the Communists?"

"Thousands. The Greens have informers all over, so it was easy to pick them off, make sure you're really getting Communists, not just anybody. Of course, this is years ago now, but that's how it worked. And what's the difference between Chiang and Du? You tell me." He poured another round. "These pelmeni are something, aren't they? So, the Badlands."

Irina stood up. "This I already know. I'll get dinner."

"There's more?" Daniel said, patting his stomach.

"Flatterer," she said, but pleased. "So you're like him that way."

"When the concessions were laid out," Nathan said, already in the story, "they were a little fuzzy about the western boundaries. Nobody cared. It was country, nobody's living there. Some Brits with horses. Goyim and horses—it's a weakness with them. No clubs, just the Del Monte. Then the city started filling up and they extend the roads out there and somebody notices it's technically Chinese territory, not the Settlement's. Every few years the Holy Rollers here want to crack down on the gambling and what have you and here's the Western Roads District that turns out to be outside the jurisdiction of the SMP. Shanghai Municipal Police. So people use the opportunity and start building clubs. You go out there now—Great Western Road, Edinburgh Road—you'll see. They're still building. And after '37, the Japanese see *their* chance. They're closed out of squeeze in the Settlement and Frenchtown, but here's new money, on Chinese territory, which means Japanese territory because they won the war and Wang Ching-wei takes his orders from the Kempeitai."

"Wang Ching-wei."

"The Chinese puppet. He's taking on the gangs for the Kempeitai so they can have everything to themselves. And who's caught in the middle? You open a club now and everybody has a hand out. So far it still works, there's enough to go around. But you start with the Japanese and the whole thing tips. They think they're going to pay for their Occupation with squeeze."

"There's that much?"

"Enough. Why do you think everybody's building out there?

Joe Farren's going to open a new place in Great Western Road, a monster, even for him. Big floor shows. A Ziegfeld. He thinks. The Gold Rush—look, it's our chance. To get the real players, some real money. Who comes to the Cat? People who like Teddy Wilson. We don't even have a dance floor. That's the difference. A jazz club, you listen. A nightclub, you're pushing some skirt around and trying to cop a feel. I got pieces of clubs like that. The Montecito. Good money, even with squeeze. I'll show you the books." Glancing at Daniel for his reaction. "But the Rush. Place that size, the liquor alone covers your nut. So the tables are gravy. Not poker—I rent out a room in the back here for that. Roulette. Real money. But not if the Japanese get their hands on it. They're not like Xi, even Wu Tsai, they don't see the give-and-take. The French, they're smiling at you while they do it. But the Japanese just take." He held up a finger. "But not from me. I've been doing this a lot of years. I know how. So, no, thank you. You want to shake someone down, go somewhere else. Squeeze Farren, I don't care. But not the Rush. They don't even know what they're getting into. Wu Tsai has a piece of it. Xi. You don't want to mess with that. The Japanese think it's just me. That's my fault probably. I'm the front guy. So they think it's all mine. They wouldn't be in such a hurry to make trouble if they knew about the others. That's why I set it up this way. It would be a favor to them to know." He paused. "And maybe that's where you come in."

"Me?"

"You take him the squeeze for the currency. You're old friends, you show up at his office, nobody thinks anything of it. And while you're there you have a little chat, one pal to another. Who really owns the Rush. Who he'd be crossing if there were any trouble. Sid's problem, he never let anybody in. Everything's Sid Engel, his way. So he runs into trouble, nobody's got his back. But you make trouble for the Rush, you're making trouble for Xi. For Wu Tsai. And who does that? A crazy person. Then a dead person. Just something Yamada should know, one friend to another."

"Slow down," Irina said. "He hasn't even unpacked yet and you have him doing business with the Kempeitai."

"Somebody he knows."

She looked at Daniel. "You don't have to do this. Get involved. There is no debt here. You don't owe this one anything."

"Who's talking 'owe'? Of course you don't owe. A little favor, that's all. But if you don't want—"

"Little favor," Irina said to Daniel. "Little. Big. You're working for him, you're part of it. You want this life?" She faced Nathan. "How do you know he wants this life? Just off the boat and you're handing him a gun. Give him a little air, so he can breathe."

"This life. I don't see you packing up and leaving."

"I'm used to it."

Nathan started to say something, then stopped. "All right. Maybe it's too soon—"

"What did you do in Berlin? For a living," Irina said, practical.

"Lately, hiding out. Before that I wrote for newspapers."

"Newspapers," Irina said. "So introduce him to Loomis."

"That putz," Nathan said.

"Who works for the *North-China Tribune*." She turned to Daniel. "Is your English good enough? Could you write for an English paper?"

"The *Tribune*?" Nathan said. "A monkey could do it."

"And he owes you a favor."

"A bookkeeper," Nathan said, looking at Irina. "Who owes what to who. She keeps track."

"So you'll meet and see what you think. Maybe he has something for you. You don't have to decide right away."

Daniel nodded. "But the sooner, the better. I don't want to sponge– You've done so much already."

Irina looked at him, a half smile. "It's a daybed. It's not much."

"And while you're going through all your job offers," Nathan said, "don't forget to look at what's right under your nose." Meant to sound offhand, indifferent, but the voice throaty, giving him away, as if he had just touched Daniel's hand. Irina looked down, not saying anything.

"Okay," Daniel said finally, one step, nothing beneath him.

"I mean, it's right here, right under–"

"Nathan, I don't know anything about the club business."

"You'll learn. Anyone can learn."

"Not everyone has the instinct for it. I'm not you."

"A crook, you mean."

"I didn't say that."

"No. Eli. Over and over. Crook. He thought you had to be a crook to be in this business. And that's when it was still the old Cat, down in Nollendorfplatz. Just kids drinking beer. Not Big-Eared Du. So maybe he was right. In the end. But not in the beginning."

"He never said it to me," Daniel said, an easy lie, protective.

"No? Well, thanks for that," Nathan said, tipping his glass to an unseen Eli. "All right, an instinct. Maybe you have it, too, and you just haven't used it yet."

"Leave him alone," Irina said softly. "Here he is, out of Germany. We should all be happy, not talking about–"

"Okay," said Nathan, genial again. "And who started it, talking about Sid Engel? There's a funeral? I suppose I have to go."

"Of course you have to go." She looked over. "With Sergei."

"That's one way to meet people," Nathan said to Daniel. "They'll all turn out for Sid. He's been around, what? Forever."

"Well, now he's not," Irina said. "So go. With Sergei."

Nathan waved his hand. "All right. Enough about Sid. We have a million things to talk about," he said, this time actually touching Daniel's hand.

But what he wanted to talk about was Eli, the other presence at the table, circling back to him again and again, through the beet salad, the whitefish, another toast to Daniel's arrival.

"But what did he do? After they fired him."

"He read the newspapers. He got dressed every day, a suit, what he wore to court, and he read the papers in the sunroom. After Mother died, he stopped going out. Lunch with Siegel, another judge, once a week."

"And you. You came to see him."

"And me."

"You have a child, you always have—" Nathan stopped, a quick glance at Irina. "So Katia—what was wrong?"

"Her heart. He said she died from worry. That the Nazis—"

"But she was gentile."

"She thought that's what protected him. That if she weren't there, they'd come for him. And they did."

"So he was alone. In that house. To think of it that way. When it was always Katia and you. Everybody busy. It was the same growing up. Busy. You know, the oldest, everything revolves around him. You're the younger one, you always want to be doing what he's doing. His games. His friends. Especially when he doesn't want it. 'Play with your own things.'"

"Did you fight much as kids?"

"No, that was later. When he became the rabbi, the good one. A judge, even before he's a judge. This is wrong and that's wrong and I'm— But that was later. Now you look back, you see what it must have been like for him. He's a judge, he's the *law*, and his brother—well, his brother was me. So that was hard for him. But when I had to get out, he didn't say anything, he just did it, got me out. So now Germany's going crazy and I thought I can do something for him. But I couldn't, I couldn't get him out. Just you. But maybe he knows. He sees you're all right."

"Maybe he knows," said Irina, dismissive. "That's the drink talking."

"Well, so we can think it. Why not? I hope he can see us. See this," he said, opening his hand to take in the room, his life. "How everything turned out."

Irina stood up. "I'll clear. He gets like this."

"You have no imagination," Nathan said. "A bookkeeper."

"And you're tired," she said to Daniel. "And we've all got a long day tomorrow."

"Who's taking Esther?"

"Stan Klein. He's a cousin."

"Yeah, and maybe something more."

Irina ignored this. "You know, I was thinking. She's going to want to sell the Slipper. Maybe go home. The way she sounded on the phone. Somebody could pick it up for a good price."

"Somebody who?" Nathan said, sober again. "We're overextended as it is."

"No, we're not. I'm careful about that."

"What would we do with the Slipper?"

Irina shrugged. "I'm just saying it might be going cheap. If Esther wants to clear out. It's a good business."

"Or maybe somebody marries her and gets it for free."

"Who, for instance? You?" Having fun with it, the way they talked to each other. "You're such a prize."

He looked at her. "What are you thinking?"

"I'm thinking if Xi owned the Slipper he'd have to make a deal with the Japanese. And while they're doing that, it might take the heat off us. At least until we open. Buy some time."

Nathan said nothing, then smiled and turned to Daniel. "You see why I'm keeping her around?" He thought for a minute. "You know, if they even thought Xi was interested–the Slipper's already up and running. Money now. The Japanese would want to take care of that first. Not the Rush."

"And why would they think he's interested?" Irina said.

"Because I'm going to tell them he is," Daniel said. "When I deliver the squeeze." He looked at Nathan. "That's what you're thinking, isn't it?"

Nathan nodded slowly.

"You can't just send him–" Irina said.

"I can do that much," Daniel said. "A message." Another step.

"We'll go over what to say. The point is, Yamada will know you're speaking for me. Family."

Later, when he couldn't sleep on the lumpy daybed, Daniel went to the bathroom, then followed a dim light downstairs. A stage light, so low it was barely visible in the shadows, but keeping the tradition going. A kind of yahrzeit candle for Sid Engel. Who didn't see things as they were. What Irina did. While Nathan saw something else, not the beat-up stage, the dull finish on the piano, but something glowing in a cone of light. Wisps of smoke turning blue, Gus Whiting gliding his hands over the keys, pinpricks of light around the room, from cigarettes, table lamps, nothing as it was, better. Eli might be looking down, finally approving. Daniel might be a son. Du was a political figure.

Nathan's whole life, Daniel now saw, was a kind of romance,

seeing what he wanted to see. Not things as they were. A nephew running errands for a gangster. A business partner who wiped out rivals, just like that. Someone who hadn't turned out so bad in the end, had he? Running whores in a club. But the hug when he said good night wrapped around Daniel like a blanket, the blood rushing to his ears. Not things as they were. But all he had.

CHAPTER 4

Sid Engel was buried in the Jewish cemetery out on Baikal Road in Yangpoo.

"I thought the burial was family only," Nathan said in the car.

"There is no family," Irina said. "Not here. Esther feels close to us."

To Daniel's surprise it was a traditional Orthodox service, rending clothes and scooping earth to toss into the grave. At home, Esther would have mirrors shrouded and chairs with their legs cut down, everything by the book.

The reception afterward, however, back at the Silver Slipper, was purely secular. A band played Sid's favorite songs and the crowd talked over it, the room loud with voices and tinkling glass. Just what Sid would have liked, everyone said. A good turnout, a busy evening at the Slipper. No one mentioned the cause of death. A sudden illness, like Eli. Daniel noticed several Sergeis in the crowd, guns bulging in their jackets, eyes alert, but none of the guests seemed apprehensive. Funny stories about Sid. One of a kind. What people would have said anywhere. If Sid had had a heart attack. Daniel looked at the crowd again. Men from Berlin or

Chicago or Hamburg who'd come in the '20s to find their fortune and mostly found it, or at least enough to keep them here. Not everyone had been running away from something. But they were businessmen with bodyguards.

"Isn't it wonderful?" Esther said. "Everyone's here. If Sid could see it—"

"They're here for you, sweetheart," a man said, kissing her cheek. "You need anything, these next few days, you let me know, okay?"

Esther nodded.

"It's not easy. I know. The thing is, there's no hurry. You don't have to decide anything until you're ready."

"About the Slipper you mean."

"About anything."

"Listen: 'Moonglow.' He loved that."

"You get an offer, check with me before you do anything, right?"

"That's what Stan says. But nobody offers."

"They will. It's early days. Anybody wants it, he has to raise some money first."

"Better hurry, then, before I'm on a boat back to the States. I only stayed for Sid. And now look. You're afraid of your own shadow these days."

"It'll pass."

"That's what Sid said. Nathan," she said as he came up. "Al, you know Daniel? Nathan's nephew. You meeting people, honey?"

"Everybody, I think."

"What are you, just off the boat?"

"Daniel, Al Klein. The Mayfair."

What Nathan had done, too, add the club to each name, the real identifier. Sol Greenberg, the Casanova. Fred Stern, the Elite.

86

The Little Club. The Cathay Tower. Nathan had circled the room, beaming, Daniel beside him, turning Sid's funeral into a welcome party.

"Al, you look good," Nathan said.

"Clean living. So you're bringing in some new blood?" he said, nodding to Daniel. What everyone thought now. "You could use it."

"We could all use it. It makes you think, Sid being gone. What's next? You have to think ahead." Nathan took a breath. "You have any little visits from the Kempeitai lately? You know, they make a deal with one, it makes it harder for the others. We act together—"

"Don't shit me. When did we act together? It's business. You do what you can. The Japs aren't going away. Look at Sid. He said no and where did it get him?"

"He said no to a lot of people. We don't know—" Nathan stopped. "Just tell me if they visit, that's all. So we know what they're up to. We've all been here a long time."

"You know what I think? The Badlands, it's a new game. They take out Sid, we know it's them, and what can we do? It's a new game."

"Well, hail, hail the gang's all here." A voice behind them, high-pitched and American, with the lazy vowels of the South. "Klein and Green. A new partnership in the making? The *North-China Tribune* wants to know."

"Selly," Nathan said, wary, oddly uncomfortable, but moving aside to include the man. "What brings you here?"

"You know I never miss a party. Even a wake," he said, drawing out the word. "You never know what you're going to pick up once people have had a few." He held out a hand to Daniel. "Selden Loomis, the *Tribune*." Name, club.

Nathan, catching up, started to introduce Daniel, but Loomis cut him off. "Oh, I already know all about him. He's your nephew and he just got out of Germany and he's a genius, a big newspaper-man back in the Fatherland and I should hire him. Or at least give him a trial run." He looked at Nathan. "Irina. And like a dog with a bone." He turned to Daniel. "That pretty accurate?"

"Maybe not the genius part," Daniel said, looking more closely. A rumpled white linen suit, thinning hair, and a cigarette in his hand that looked as if it was always there, part of him. His posture matched his accent, languid and slouching, his jacket hanging from his shoulders as if it were over the back of a chair.

"My god. An honest man. In Shanghai. I suppose we'd better talk." He turned to Nathan. "Can I pry him away? If you've fin-ished showing him off." He looked back at Daniel, a tailor measur-ing. "Very presentable. Good. That's important in the job."

"Which is what, exactly?"

"May we?" Loomis said to Nathan, leading Daniel away. "Walk with me," he said, lighting a new cigarette that had appeared out of nowhere, like a magic trick. "Quite a party. You'd never think he'd been *shot*. Not that that's news lately. Very Dodge City. I hardly go out. Which is a problem, since that's what I do, so I get other people to help out. Legmen. I usually sit tight in Ciro's, maybe the Cathay, and let you come to me. My legmen. Of course there's the phone. But there's nothing like being on the spot. And since you're club royalty, you won't have any problem with access. People know you even before they know you, so you can get around. Which is why I told Irina I'd give this a shot. Otherwise, even for a genius, I wouldn't have anything. Am I going too fast for you?"

"Just keep going."

Loomis smiled. "God. Somebody who listens. So let's start at the beginning. I'm the Merry-Go-Round column in the *Tribune*. We're twice a week, sometimes an extra column on the weekend, depending on what's going on. Race week, for instance. Celebrity in town. We're the nightlife column. Who's where with whom? Who shouldn't be? Who threw a drink in whose face? We do not cover politics or crime—I mean, this little incident with Sid, that's somebody else's department. If Esther shot him, maybe, and if she shot him in the club, yes. But not as it is. A new act opening at the Canidrome? Yes. Your uncle's new place? Very much yes. I'll go to that opening myself. But mainly I send you. You make the rounds, see who's out, check in with the bartenders—usually we have an understanding, but you'll want to develop your own people. I don't know how good your English is, but it doesn't matter because I write the columns. You just bring in stuff. You don't need to write to be a snoop. You'll probably think all this is beneath you. I know. It's beneath *me*. But you might as well know now—it saves disappointment later. I pay by the item, but there's a draw to get you through the week. You can do all right. Half the foreign press is in Broadway Mansions, by Garden Bridge, but go around the corner and you can get something for half. Once in a while, there's the chance of a bonus. A big divorce, something like that. But mostly it's what you can pick up. You could make a lot more working for your uncle, but Irina said you'd rather do this. Or she'd rather you do this," he said, a sly arch in his tone. "So would you? It's not much to be proud of, but it's a job."

Daniel turned to him, suddenly back on the *Raffaello*, his last marks in his pocket, Leah selling her coat. Then in the Buick, Nathan peeling off two bills. Your cut.

"What's the favor you're paying back?" he said.

"Dear heart, what a question. And we've just met."

"Just curious. What the job's worth. Nathan fronting the draw?"

Loomis peered at him, intrigued. "No."

"I'm not worth it to you. So what was the favor?"

Loomis drew on his cigarette. "Let's just say Irina's a helpful person. And leave it at that. Do you want this or not?"

89

"I'm just trying to figure out how it works for you. I tell you who's having dinner at the Cathay and you pay me for that?"

"Depends who's having dinner. And if I print it."

"And that's worth money to you."

"Actually, it's the items I don't print that pay the rent."

Daniel looked at him.

"People like to be in the papers. Until they don't. Sometimes it's worth it to them not to be. We don't like to run embarrassing items in the Merry-Go-Round. We want people to be happy."

"If they pay."

"You're a quick study," Loomis said, a wisp of smoke coming out of his mouth. "And with your connections, my bet is you'll come across items we like."

"Items you don't print."

Loomis nodded. "Sometimes they're more valuable that way."

"How much do you make? Not printing things."

"Well, that would be telling, wouldn't it? Better to be discreet. People expect it," he said, confiding, a question of good manners. "So I take it you're interested?"

Daniel nodded. "It's not exactly what I had in mind."

"It never is, is it? For any of us. We're on the Bund. Just down from Jardine's. I'm there from ten on. You'll want another suit," he said. "Something a little more out-on-the-town. Oh, and no expenses, so the liquor's your own lookout. Learn to sip. Tricks of the trade."

———

It was agreed, finally, that Daniel would do both: work nights for Loomis to support himself and spend time with Nathan to learn the business.

"It's going to be yours. You sell it, you run it, whatever you decide, you should know how it works."

"You're leaving it to me?"

"It's in the will."

"I didn't know."

"How would you know? I'm not dead." He paused. "To tell you the truth, I never thought you'd be here—you know, to run it. I figured Irina would sell it and send you the money. Something out of nowhere from your old uncle. Drive your father crazy. But then you did come, so now things are different. You could—" He stopped. "If you wanted."

"What about Irina?"

"Don't worry about Irina. I give her a share and she puts it away. She's a saver. She's all right."

"You never married?"

He shrugged. "She said no. This way she can walk whenever she wants. What would she get out of it she doesn't have already?"

"She'd inherit. Your wife."

"No, I want you to have it. That was always the idea. You know what I wondered? Maybe she didn't want to because she's already married. Some Russkie from the old days, she doesn't know if he's still alive."

Daniel looked at him. A melodrama on a gaslit stage. "Why don't you ask her?"

Nathan shrugged again. "She'd say no. Then what do you believe?"

———

Daniel made the rounds of four clubs his first night, reporting back to Loomis with the items he collected from the bartenders on the payroll.

"Harry and Edna," Loomis said, looking at the list, bored. "*Quel surprise*. It would be real news if they stayed home some night. You see why it's the Merry-Go-Round. The same people going round and round. Until one of them falls off. Then we have something. I heard about a room, by the way, if you're interested. Ed Dillon. Going back to the States. Right behind the *Tribune*. You can practically roll into the office."

To Daniel's surprise, Nathan didn't object. "A man your age wants his own place. I know. Maybe I'll start reading the newspaper, you'll come visit me, like Eli."

"I'm here every day."

The apartment was in Kiangse Road, a block away from the Bund, and came with Ed's furniture and a houseboy who cleaned and would cook if you asked. You could live this way if you had a little money, since most people had none at all. What had shocked him the first day was becoming familiar, the bodies on the pavement, women in evening dresses in rickshaws, the drivers in little more than rags. One night he stood on Garden Bridge and saw the candles Nathan had described, the paper coffins floating out to sea. Something you shouldn't get used to, but did.

Nathan's house was in a quiet stretch of the French Concession, but here, near the river, the streets were livelier, packs of sailors looking for a good time at the brothels. Even in Kiangse Road, with its respectable offices and apartments. Daniel had noticed the men coming and going one evening, all the usual signs, and wondered what it was like inside. Red flocked wallpaper and get-to-know-you divans? Young girls from the countryside bought from their hungry families? Or old pros, hard as nail polish? Houses had specialties. Men came back wanting the same thing. So what did they come back for in Kiangse Road? Not opium, anyway, not even a hint of the sweet smell. He could see what the house was like for himself, just walking next door, but it was a passing interest, without heat, sexual urgency. It was easier to go back to the *Raffaello* in his head, the cabin with the moon through the porthole, skin slick with sweat, gasping breath. The only sex he wanted now, not a grunting ten minutes in Kiangse Road.

The day he got his first money from the *Tribune* he went to find Leah. I'm going to survive, she'd said. Not fall off. And he had. Now they both could. He imagined appearing at the heim, a figure of rescue, something out of an opera, come to take her away. And Clara. He'd need a bigger place. But there was his money from Nathan, too. So a bigger place, why not? The point was, they could do it, survive. Her breath in his ear.

Most of the refugees had been settled in Hongkew, a fair hike from the Bund, along Broadway, but it seemed wrong to take a taxi to a heim, so he walked. The next neighborhood over, Chapei, had seen the worst of the fighting in '37, and whole stretches of it still looked like a bomb site, rubble and fragments of buildings, but Hongkew had been cleaned up, only a few reminders of the shelling in pockmarked walls. Instead there were signs in German and Hebrew, coffeehouses, doctors' offices, women in hats, a giant dentist's tooth, kosher butchers, Vienna in a Chinese slum.

Everyone knew the heim—some were still living there—so he had no trouble finding it. He had imagined a kind of boarding school dormitory, with neat lines of beds, but instead found a crowded barracks, unmade beds and clothes hanging on pegs, toilet and slop buckets at the end, people sitting around, a few playing cards in their undershirts, their winter jackets too heavy for the heat. The air thick and used up, not enough to go around. The women's section was a little better, tidier, but had the same listlessness, people waiting to be told what to do, unmoored. No one had heard of Leah or knew where she was.

"Ask at the Agency, they keep a record. When they check you in. I'm new here myself, so I wouldn't know. A girl and her mother?"

But the Agency office didn't know either. A secretary in a starched cotton blouse, crisp as a nurse.

"Auerbach? Two nights, the dates match, so it must be them. But they left. They must have found a place."

"But no forwarding address?"

"For mail? We're not Cook's."

"If people want to find them."

"But nobody does. They don't know anybody here. Maybe she found a job, a place comes with it. It happens sometimes. And sometimes they come back, it's not what they thought. But I don't see anything here," she said, touching the page in the binder. "You know, it's not a prison, people can come and go. We just like to know how many to expect at meals. Sorry."

"Could I leave a message, in case she comes back? A number?"

"You could," she said, a trace of weariness now, "but honestly it'll just get lost in all this. You might come back in a few days. They come and go."

"Minna." A voice at the door behind him. "Oh, excuse me. I was looking for Dr. Markowski. He said he'd be—Daniel, is that you? I was wondering what had become of you."

"Mrs. Burke." Now in a tailored women's suit, hair swept up, out of the way, all business, holding a clipboard.

"Florence. How *are* you?" Then, to the secretary, "We're old shipmates."

"You work here?" Daniel asked her.

"I volunteer two afternoons. You should too. We could use more men. There's so much to do and the men think we're bossy. They'd listen to you. Mostly I'm out trying to find jobs for people.

And asking for money. That's really what would help. But you—are you staying here?"

"No, I have a place. I was looking for the Auerbachs. They seem to have disappeared."

"But they were here. I saw them."

"Two nights. Now—we don't know."

"Oh dear, it was probably the embarrassment. Clara and her—People do feel that and they shouldn't. It's nobody's fault. I should have looked in on them, see if things were all right. But you know, you get distracted and then—you can't do everything. There are so many. Leah must have found a job, if they could move out. So that's something."

"But where?"

She looked at him, her face softer. "She didn't leave word?"

"No."

"Well, she'll be in touch," she said easily. "I'd bet on it. What's your number, in case she calls me? I told her to. And I'm in the book, easy to find."

"The best way to reach me would be at the *North-China Tribune*." Not the Black Cat, slot machines next to the men's room. "I'm working there."

"Well, you've landed on your feet."

"If you can call it that. I'm working for the Merry-Go-Round column."

"The Merry-Go-Round. Selden Loomis?" she said, her face clouding.

"I know, it's just gossip. But it's a job."

She looked at him, about to say something, then shifted her attention over his shoulder. "Oh," she said, a little flustered. "Dr. Markowski. Just the man." Patting Daniel's arm, excuse me, then turning to the other man, which meant she missed Daniel's face when he saw him. Don't freeze, that sends its own message. Franz's training. Polite interest, someone you don't recognize. Make eye contact, then look away. Anybody, not a face you knew instantly. The flat in Berlin, only a few people. Tomas, then. Called what now? Dr. Markowski. Had he been a doctor? But how would Daniel have known? No personal information, nothing to give away.

"I talked to Hawkins at St. Joseph's. It's only part-time, so they can keep it off the books. Night duty. He can't do more, they're overstaffed as it is, with everyone coming now, but it's something. You share it. They have to, because of the license problem. Somebody has to sign off on things officially. But you're there and they can see what you can do. You're not an orderly."

"Thank you," Markowski said. The same voice, calmly handing over the gun.

"I wish I could do more."

"No, no, I can't thank you enough. I know what things are like." Telling him how to use it. Get to know the feel of it so it's comfortable in your hand.

"Florence is a miracle worker," Minna said from behind the desk.

"Hardly that," Florence said, handing Markowski a card. "Hawkins. He'll be expecting your call. No German, I'm afraid, so it'll have to be in English."

"I understand." Glancing at Daniel now, working something out.

"What an awful time this is. We just have to get through it." Florence looked at Daniel, aware of him again, then took another card out of her bag and handed it to him. "You promised to come to one of my evenings. Wednesday, if you're free. Seven."

Daniel nodded.

"Well, Minna, I should fly. Do you have a minute, though?" she said to Daniel.

"May I offer you a coffee?" Markowski said to Florence. "At the Wienerwald?"

Daniel looked at him. An obvious overstep, not really expecting Florence to go, a message to him.

"Sorry, can't," Florence said, slightly taken aback. "Good luck at St. Joseph's. I'm sure it'll all work out." She picked up a folder from the desk. "Homework. Daniel?" As if he were the driver.

Outside, she waited until they reached the car, away from the office.

"Can I say something to you? I know it's none of my business." She stopped. "But it is my business. All of us. Your friend Mister Loomis. Do you know about him? Not the Merry-Go-Round. I mean the other stuff he writes. Little love notes to the Greater East Asia Co-Prosperity Sphere."

"Loomis?"

"He thinks the West has had its day. That we're all as corrupt as he is. Asia's the future and it's Japanese. A strong hand on the tiller. And so on."

"He says this in the Merry-Go-Round?"

Florence shook her head. "On the radio. The column's too silly. Or maybe you don't shit where you sleep. If you'll pardon my French. The Japanese station here. The British Empire's sun is setting and guess whose is rising? And the States? We're just a bunch of kids who don't know what we're doing. Except being led around by the nose by the oil companies and—wait for it—the Jews who have Roosevelt's ear. Or so says Mister Loomis."

"He believes this or he's paid to say it?"

"Does it matter? Either way it attacks us. You've just been in Europe. You know what they're doing there. They can do it here, too, if enough people listen to Loomis." She looked away. "Well, that's today's sermon."

"I didn't know."

"And you still need the job. I know. What can any of us do. Here in Island Shanghai. But we'd better do something. Anyway, a word to the wise." She looked at him. "I'll let you know if I hear from the Auerbachs. Nobody just disappears."

But Tomas had, in Berlin. When he missed two meetings in a row you had to assume— Then avoid the meeting place, in case they'd broken him, the last tie cut. But now here, alive, the same face.

———

He was at a corner table in the Wienerwald, a coffee in front of him. Daniel began the charade of looking for a place, asking if the other chair was free.

"It's all right. It's not Berlin here," he said.

Daniel sat. "So you're Polish now?"

"I was always Polish. I just wasn't Markowski."

"It's your real name?"

"It's a common name. In Warsaw nobody would think anything of it."

"And you're a doctor? Were you before?"

He smiled. "It's good to see you. Still with the questions."

"It's still Tomas?"

"Karl." He looked up. "That one's real. You don't have to be that careful here. And you?"

"Daniel."

"Ah," he said, looking at Daniel as if he were trying on a coat, seeing if it fit.

"What are you doing here?"

"I take care of people in the heime. You know, in conditions like that, the crowding, you worry about disease. One case, then two, then everybody's—anyway, it's a worry. Some of them are weak. Nobody's starving, but nobody's fat, either. The Agency does what it can but it's a lot of people to feed and they keep coming. So it's a gift for them, a doctor on call. Our licenses aren't good in the hospitals so we have the time."

"And now you're at St. Joseph's."

"With someone to sign for me. But not an orderly," he said, Florence's voice. "But yes, it's something. She's a friend?"

"Not really. We met on the boat. You know, friends at dinner."

"For me it was the train. To get here. Tea and black bread, that was dinner. Maybe a little salami. Anyway, it's something. Even part-time. I'm grateful to her."

"They don't pay you at the Agency?"

He shrugged, then looked toward the window. "They feed me."

"They feed a lot of people."

"And I should take somebody else's food?" He turned back to Daniel. "The truth? I treat whores. Abortions. That's my living. They don't ask to see a license. Sometimes exams for the clap. Most of the houses, the good ones, have a regular doctor for this. I fill in. That's what I do. And you?"

Daniel looked at him. A man who'd once put a gun in his hand.

"I collect gossip for a newspaper."

Karl nodded. "But here we are. Are you still so serious?"

"Collecting gossip?"

"No, the way you feel about things. Are you still a Communist?"

Daniel looked around, a reflex. "I was never in the Party."

"No. Franz said it would be better if you weren't. That your father had influence and it would be easier for you—"

99

"Franz never said this to me."

"No. But that was the plan. He had plans for all of us."

"And I was going to influence my father?"

"He thought he could be useful."

"He was wrong. They killed him."

"It's still there in your voice, how you feel. I remember that. What did he do? I never knew."

"He was a judge."

"Ah."

"What did Franz think? That he'd go easy on Communists because I asked him to?"

Karl hesitated. "I think it was more—if we knew what he was thinking, we could work with that, maybe apply pressure if it was important."

Daniel stared at him. "Spy on him."

"It's not exactly like that."

"Well, he's dead, so it's not exactly like anything now. And I'm still not in the Party."

"You were in your head. You don't leave that. You still see the logic."

"In Germany. To do what we were doing. To stop them. But now we're here. Doing what we're doing." Daniel looked up. "What was the plan for you?"

"To go to Moscow. Work with the Comintern."

"And did you?"

"Yes, still."

"Still," Daniel said.

"What has changed? Except things are worse." Karl stirred his coffee. "You know, in the end, Franz gave everyone away. Except you. He died before he could give them you."

"And you."

"No, he told them," Karl said. "That's why I had to disappear, why I missed our meeting. You must have guessed—"

"I thought you were dead."

"Good. That's what I wanted. Close the file. But you, it's even better. There is no file. There's no record of you. Nobody knows. You're in a perfect position to—"

"To what? Go back to that?" Daniel shook his head. "I'm retired. I collect gossip, that's what I do now."

"Nobody retires."

"Yes, they do. Me. I got out of Germany. We're somewhere else now."

"It's all connected."

"Oh, the better world argument? No more. I just wanted to kill Nazis. Now I'm here." He looked around. "We should probably go. It's a long time to share a table."

Karl smiled. "It's easier to operate here. There is no Gestapo. But nice to see the old instincts are still there." He looked up. "You know where to find me. Where do I find you?"

Daniel shrugged. "It's not a secret. The *North-China Tribune*."

"As Daniel . . ."

"Lohr. But you won't need to find me. I'm retired. I don't have a file. And I'm not going to start one here." He looked over at Karl. "I'm glad you're alive, though. I'm glad you're still in it. Whatever it is." He held up a palm, a traffic cop. "I don't want to know." Another pause. "Was he really going to use me that way? Franz?"

"If it was good for the Party. That was the rule."

"And he thought I'd do it. To my father."

"For your father. For everybody."

CHAPTER 5

Irina did more than keep the books at the Cat. It was she who dealt with the linen supply service, the liquor distributor, Jack Riley's share of the slots, the cleaning staff—everything that kept the place going day-to-day. Nathan managed the talent and the security arrangements and "looked for opportunities," spending afternoons at auditions or meeting with Xi Ling to plan jobs that suddenly came up—a warehouse in Pudong that hadn't paid its protection money and whose inventory would be hard to trace. But opening the Gold Rush made new work for everybody. The Rush was a mock Tudor mansion whose estatelike lawns and driveway required a new layer of security, staff to protect the grounds and guard the parking areas. A casino could survive anything except violence—once past the gates, customers had to feel safe—but the question was how many more men Xi would need. Meanwhile, Gus Whiting had signed for the opening, along with Rita and Carlos, the exhibition dancers, and a full chorus line to fill the Rush's much larger stage. So Nathan's days were suddenly busy and Daniel had most afternoons to himself.

He spent them in Hongkew, just walking, sometimes sitting

in a café, expecting to see her. Little Vienna was compact. If she were there, she might easily pass him in the street, picking up a cake for Clara at the bakery, running an errand. If she were there. She hadn't returned to a heim, not according to the Jewish Relief Agency secretary, but she might be living somewhere nearby. It would be easier, certainly easier for Clara, to stay in a German-speaking neighborhood. She'd still be in Shanghai—there were no visas to anywhere else—so why not here? Any day now he'd look up from his coffee cup and she'd be coming down the street.

He even went to Florence Burke's evening, on the off chance that she might turn up, and found himself stuck in a room of folding chairs, listening to a Chinese poet read from his work, first in English, then Chinese. Apparently a new magazine was being launched, featuring the poems, another effort to bridge the cultures. Afterward a string quartet played and champagne was passed and Florence fluttered around the room introducing people, another bridge. Daniel thought of her at the Agency office, holding her clipboard, ready to get down to work. Someone who'd gone to a factory with Chou En-lai. Now asking maids to refill glasses, a diamond brooch flashing on her dress. More Shanghai pieces that didn't fit. But Leah wasn't there.

Nathan wanted Daniel to meet with Yamada on his own, a kind of trial run for acting on behalf of the Rush.

"First of all, he's already in a good mood—you're handing him squeeze. A nice envelope, too, so he's a kid with candy he didn't expect. Then you tell him how it is with the Rush, who owns it. It's not that *we* have any problem with squeeze, he's sitting there with it, but the others— Nothing has to be decided then and there. He expects you to be a messenger, back and forth, so it's not the last word. See how it goes."

"He'll want something, no matter what," Irina said. "If he'll take half of that—"

"Just see what he says. You're his friend. Not Jessfield Road, though. People go there, they don't always come back. Anyway, who takes squeeze in the office? With people around. You want somewhere neutral. Let him pick."

"Let's go over the percentages again," Irina said. "So he knows you know."

———

Yamada picked the Barbary Coast, a jazz club out near the race-track, close enough to the Park Hotel to have an arrangement with the concierge. No dance floor, just a performing stage, wallpaper with San Francisco landmarks, probably drawn from postcards. A place you went to for the music, like the Cat. The singer tonight was a Chinese girl with a skirt slit up the thigh and a flower in her hair. She was still finishing her first set when they arrived, so they took seats at the corner of the bar, which gave them a view of the stage.

"You've been here before?" Yamada said when she finished, looking around, as if he were counting the house.

"Once," Daniel said.

"That's what you do now, I hear. Go to such places. Every night."

"It's work."

"For Mister Loomis. So I hear. But you enjoy it. What do you think of him?"

"He's all right."

"It's a useful job."

"Useful?"

"You hear so much in such a job. So much information."

"Well, you can read it in the Merry-Go-Round."

"Not all of it, I think."

"You'd have to ask Selly about that."

"Oh, I do. From time to time. It would be helpful if I could ask you. From time to time. And, you know, this would be useful for you, too."

"How so?"

"The current situation—" He opened his hand to take in all Shanghai. "Things won't always be this way. It will be good to have Japanese friends."

"I hope I will," Daniel said, dipping his head. He took out the envelope. "I brought this," he said, sliding it toward him.

Yamada opened it just long enough to see the bills, then slipped it in his breast pocket. "Very generous."

"My uncle's a generous man. He likes to buy a little goodwill, too."

"Goodwill?"

"For times when he can't be so generous. When it's not up to him."

"I assume you're talking about the Gold Rush? Do you speak for him?"

"Sometimes."

"But not this time?"

"No, I can speak for him. But I can't speak for the other partners. He wants you to understand the situation."

"I think I understand it well. Is something not clear? The Western Roads District is outside the Shanghai Municipal Police's authority. Which means it falls to the Chinese. We sometimes act for them. In the collection of fees. The Gold Rush is in this district—a dangerous district. The owner will have to protect his property. He will need someone to guarantee security. As well as so many of the little things. Licenses. Permits. We both understand this, yes? The only question is what the protection fee should be. We have suggested a percentage. Have you come with a counteroffer?"

"I wish things were that easy. Unfortunately arrangements have already been made. For security, the things you mention."

"Then they will have to be unmade."

"They can't be. The security's being provided by the owners themselves. My uncle isn't the sole owner. If he were—" Daniel let this lay for a second. "But he isn't. And the others would never agree to such an arrangement. It's the business they're in. You know them. Wu Tsai. Xi Ling. You've shared squeeze before. But this time they're the owners. They'd be squeezing themselves."

Yamada took this in. "What figures are they proposing?"

"None. No squeeze." He thought of Irina. Take half. "This is just the Rush," Daniel said quickly. "The other clubs in the District—I can't speak for them."

Yamada stared at him, quiet for a minute. "What makes you think I would accept this? This special arrangement?"

"Because otherwise you'd have a gang war on your hands. Who wants to fight Wu's men? Xi's? Nobody. They'd turn Shanghai into a war zone. You don't want that. That's what I wanted to explain." He nodded to Yamada's pocket. "Why the extra squeeze now."

"So for this tip—this generous tip—the Gold Rush pays nothing."

"They don't need to pay anything. They already have protection."

"Not from me. You know I could have people arrested there. It's not the Settlement. It's Japanese."

"Chinese, I thought."

Yamada waved his hand, dismissing this. "Don't. One of your

virtues is that you're direct, I thought. Cards on the table. But this time you're overplaying your hand. When you sit down at the table always ask, what do the others want?"

"And what do you want? Squeeze."

"Of course, squeeze. For now. But when Shanghai's Japanese, I want things to be different. Not as they are. A criminal city. Something better. No Wu. No Xi. No vermin. So you see, the gang war doesn't frighten me. That war will come sooner or later. And we will win it. You think the Japanese city will be the same city. With different people collecting envelopes. But it won't. There will be a new order. So it doesn't matter to me what Xi thinks of our arrangement. Or Wu. You don't believe me?"

"I'm just trying to figure out how much of it you believe. A new order. There's a new order in Germany, too. That hasn't stopped the envelopes." Daniel took a sip of his drink. "You don't want to go to war with Wu. Or Xi. Not yet, anyway."

Yamada looked at him, then nodded. "I agree the timing is not ideal. So, cards on the table. What do you want? A smaller percentage?"

Daniel shook his head. "No percentage. What do I want? I want you to leave the Gold Rush alone. It's my uncle's chance to make some real money and I want him to have it. He saved my life. I'd like to do this for him."

"A sentimentalist? I don't think so. We both know you're not that."

Daniel shrugged. "But that's what I want."

"And what do I get? While your uncle gets rich?"

"You get rich too. Not the Kempeitai. You."

Another stare, trying to slow things down. "Do you have a proposal to make or are you thinking on your feet again?"

"How much is the Gold Rush squeeze worth, anyway? You're

gambling the place will be a hit. Otherwise you'd go for a flat fee. Rent. You collect, whatever happens. But a percentage? There are a hundred ways to skim off money before we get to the profits you're going to divide. You'll still do fine, but you can do better."

"Go on."

"Forget the Rush and go into business for yourself."

"Business."

"Stop taking envelopes. Own the place. Take all the profits."

"What place? Your uncle's?"

"No, he's out of it, remember? You buy the Glass Slipper. Sid Engel's place. In the Settlement, not the Western Roads. It's already up and running. The cash starts right away."

"I'm an officer in the Kempeitai. I can't buy—"

"I know. I'll buy it for you. I can get it cheap, too. At least get it for a good price. Sid's widow would sell it to me. It would be like family."

"With my money."

"With your money. A private arrangement, between us."

"And what do I do with this prized possession?"

"You let me run it. In fact, you pay me a management fee. I'd like to say 50 percent, but then we'd start haggling. I'd take 25 percent for running the place—soup to nuts, with my uncle to help. And the rest goes to you. I've looked at the books. That would be a hell of a lot more than you'd be squeezing out of the Rush. And that would go to the Kempeitai. This would go to you."

"And what would I say to my colleagues, if there's no arrangement with the Gold Rush?"

"That you're keeping the peace. Well worth it to the Kempeitai to keep Wu and Xi friendly. Strictly speaking, you don't have to explain anything. And this other arrangement is your business, nobody else's."

"Except yours."

"It's not going into the Merry-Go-Round, don't worry." Daniel paused. "It's business, that's all."

"This is your uncle's idea?"

"No, mine."

"What an interesting man," Yamada said slowly, his eyes still on Daniel. "We meet, you have nothing. And now we're business partners?"

"It's just another envelope. Think of it that way. A thicker one."

"That's what you want? To do business with the Kempeitai? That doesn't offend your—what? Scruples?"

"I'm not doing business with the Kempeitai. Just you."

"Because we trust each other," Yamada said, amused. "And where do I get the money? For such an investment."

"No bank is going to turn down a colonel in the Kempeitai. Not here."

"To buy a nightclub."

"To buy a company. With several things in its portfolio. I'll have it set up for you. You won't own the club by name, the company will."

"An answer for everything."

"That's what you pay me 25 percent for."

Yamada looked up. "You know, what you're really asking me to invest in is you. Are you a good investment?"

Daniel spread his hand open. "You decide. If you're nervous about the banks, you can always get the money from Wu Tsai. He has a history of working with the powers that be. When he was with Big-Eared Du."

"With the Nationalists."

"One hand washing the other. Well, you're the other hand now."

"Are you seriously suggesting I become indebted to a gangster?"

"It's one way to stay alive. He won't want to lose his money."

Yamada leaned back. "Where do you come from, I wonder."

"Berlin. It's a lot like here. Or was. And now I'm in business here. Or do you want to think about it?"

"I'd like to see the books, see what I'd be buying."

"Of course."

"And I still have to decide—"

"What?"

"What you want."

"Leave the Rush alone," Daniel said steadily. "And I'll pay you to do it. Nathan makes more. You make more."

"And the Kempeitai makes nothing. And you?"

Daniel glanced over. "I'm taking out a little insurance."

"For what?"

"The New Order. Friends in high places."

"Ah," Yamada said, just a sound, then turned toward the door. "Your boss."

Daniel made a half turn and saw Selly Loomis barreling toward them. "Well, look what the cat dragged in," he said, the drawl even broader tonight. He nodded to Yamada. "Colonel." Then to the bartender, "Felipe, one of your martoonies. Anybody here tonight?"

"Just us," Daniel said.

"Well, you got yourself a hell of a source. The colonel knows everything that goes on. He give you anything yet?"

"Mister Loomis, you know with the Kempeitai information only flows in one direction." Smiling but making a point.

"As it should, as it should," Selly said, reaching for his glass. "You two old friends?"

"We met on the ship."

"Mister Lohr was very popular," Yamada said. "An excellent dancer."

"I'll bet. You catch Mei-ling yet?" Loomis nodded toward the empty stage. "She's supposed to be good."

"She's on in a few minutes," Daniel said, looking at his watch.

"Well, one number, then watch my dust. Sir Victor's got a party going at the Tower Club and that's always good for a picture. You hear what happened out on Great Western Road? A drive-by shooting. Broad daylight. It's getting worse out there, in the Badlands. Can't you just go in and clean it up?"

Yamada bent forward, slightly formal. "Unfortunately, disputed territory, it's very difficult without giving offense."

"It's the opium, not the gambling. 'Course, the two go together, don't they? Well, pick your poison." He took another sip.

"Who was shot?" Daniel said.

Loomis shrugged. "Some Chinese. How do you identify a Chinese? It was Xi's gang, though. The way he always does it. The bodyguard melts away and—well, you know. All it takes is one shot. And now somebody will want revenge, so back and forth. Maybe you're right," he said to Yamada. "Stay out of it and they'll take each other out. Like Chiang and Mao. And you walk right in." He checked his watch. "She's late and I've got a party to get to. Stick around for the next set, will you?" he said to Daniel. "If she's any good, give me an item on it. We haven't plugged the old Barbary Coast in a while. Got to keep the sources happy, right, Felipe? You hear anything, just give it to Daniel here. He's learning on the job. Colonel, show him the ropes, yeah?"

"Mister Lohr shows them to me," Yamada said, smiling. "The Berlin way of doing things."

"Not anymore, not from what I hear. You have to say that for them—they cleaned up the place. No more vice squad, not there. Right?"

"Different vices," Daniel said.

"Yeah, well," Loomis said. "Speaking of which, Colonel, word is your boy Nomura's racking up some debts at the tables, so a word to the wise. You don't want the Kempeitai to get a reputation—"

"Thank you," Yamada said.

Daniel watched the look between them. So that's how it was done. A word to the wise.

"God, I hate to see that," Loomis was saying, looking toward the tables. "The Chinese don't like it, either, not really. If you're going to go with them, do it in a room somewhere. Not parade around so everyone can see. It just makes everyone uncomfortable, mixing like that."

Daniel followed his gaze, then stopped, suddenly light-headed, as if he were in a dropping elevator. Leah and a Chinese in a Western suit, older, clearly together. As he pulled back her chair she looked up, her eyes meeting Daniel's, surprised, then flustered. He could feel himself not breathing. She was dressed to go out, her scalloped neckline cut low enough to show her skin, the soft white he remembered in the half dark. Now she was sitting, but restless, looking up at them, then away, not smiling, pretending they weren't there.

"Well, I'm off," Loomis was saying, but in an echo chamber, background noise, like the clink of cutlery. "Let me know if she's any good. We'll run something."

Daniel felt himself nod, felt Loomis slipping away from the bar, all of it happening somewhere else. Leah. He was starting to get up from his stool when Yamada put a hand on his arm.

"She's with a client. It will be awkward for her."

Daniel looked at him. A client. Everything clear in an instant. Another elevator drop.

"Did you know?" Daniel said quietly.

"We're supposed to know things. No, don't look."

But his head wouldn't move. A businessman, probably. Who else could afford a club? Could afford her. No longer in the heim. A place of her own.

The Chinese ordered a bottle, sitting next to her, their shoulders touching. A Western couple at the next table stared at them, then went back to their drinks. It makes everyone uncomfortable, Loomis had said. Do it in a room somewhere. Somewhere like Kiangse Road? But maybe it wasn't like that. Maybe just an evening out.

"It would be a kindness not to interfere," Yamada said. "Some other time. When she's not— Will you have another?" Drawing Daniel's attention away. "You know, your proposal tonight? I could have you arrested for attempting to corrupt a Kempeitai officer. You're aware of that?"

"But you won't. Not in the International Settlement. I can only be tried in the courts of my native country," Daniel said, half his mind still elsewhere.

"But you have no native country, not anymore. An interesting legal dilemma. So, you'll stay in Shanghai?" Making conversation.

"I can't go anywhere else."

"You're not going to apply for an American visa? Many of the others—"

"The waiting list is years. Don't worry, I'll be here to run the Slipper, if that's what you're asking."

Yamada nodded. "That's reassuring. So you think I'm going to accept this offer."

Daniel said nothing, willing his head to face Yamada. Was she looking up? Clinking a glass with the Chinese? Thinking what?

"Is she in a house?"

Yamada looked up. "No, I don't think so."

"But you don't know?"

"Mister Lohr, we don't have time to investigate such things. Does it matter?"

"What does it mean here, to go with a Chinese?"

"It means she's not like your Mister Loomis. Maybe something better. We all have to do things to survive. You work for him. You make deals with a man who shoots people in the street. You take advantage of a widow to get a good price–"

"To go into business with the Kempeitai. So who are we to say."

"Exactly. Ah, at last," Yamada said, almost drowned out by the applause as Mei-ling took the stage. "Am I Blue?" In a tempo too fast for the song. Daniel turned, now facing the stage and the side tables beyond, a direct line to Leah and the client. Sitting closer, the man looking at Mei-ling, then down into Leah's dress. Her eyes darted toward Daniel as he turned, then to the singer, then back again. Yamada had retreated into his drink, listening, everyone now focused on the stage. Except for quick side glances, neither of them able to look away, but not talking, either, the way they had on the boat. "Them There Eyes." The businessman shifted slightly in his seat so that Daniel imagined the hand resting lightly on her thigh, then more heavily, moving, stroking her, anything he wanted, what he had paid for. Daniel felt his skin jump, the air itself prickly. When the song ended, he turned to Yamada.

"She's terrible. I've had enough."

Yamada looked at his watch. "I'll drop you." He placed some money on the bar and headed quietly toward the entrance foyer.

Daniel followed. Show nothing in the face, not the disturbance racing through him. That first night on the boat, pressed up against the wall, her mouth on his, his mind blank, just the touch of her. Now someone else with his face in her neck, paying for the wine.

They were at Yamada's car when Felipe came out of the door in a hurry.

"Mister Lohr. A minute. I have something for you."

Yamada smiled. "More items for Mister Loomis. You'll have to give up this job when you're running the club."

"That's a deal," Daniel said. "Be right back." Meeting Felipe halfway, but still far enough away so that Yamada couldn't see the matchbook in his hand, hear him say, "The lady said to give you this," or see Daniel's face finally move, crack open. The Horse and Hounds Bar at the Cathay. She wanted to see him. The rest was not important. She wanted to see him.

———

At first he thought she wasn't coming, had run away again, but then there she was, crossing the art deco lobby, past the shopping arcade, the Lalique lamps. He had forgotten the walk, a motor turning over, in gear. The Horse and Hounds was deliberately dark and Leah stopped for a second to adjust to the light, scanning the tables until she spotted him, then hesitated, not sure what to do next. He stood and pulled back a chair for her.

"I got your message," he said.

"Yes," she said, to say something. No embrace, not even touching hands. "I'm glad you got here first. They don't like to serve a woman on her own. They think it looks like—well, what it is. Mostly. A brandy," she said to the waiter who had appeared out of the dim light.

Daniel was looking at her, moving his eyes across her face. She turned aside, self-conscious.

"How do I look?" she said.

"I thought you weren't coming."

"It took a while. To get away."

Daniel looked down at his drink. "What are you doing?"

She said nothing, the question hanging between them.

"You don't have to do this," he said, still looking down.

"What do you know about it?" she said, abrupt, a reflex.

The waiter set down her drink. "Thank you," she said, but didn't pick it up, letting it sit there. "No lectures, okay? I'm really not—"

"I mean you don't have to do this," he said again, the emphasis now on "don't." "I have some money. I can get more."

"And set me up at the Cathay? Hot and cold running water and all the room service I want? I wish you'd told me earlier."

"I mean it."

"You don't have enough." She looked away. "Anyway, I wouldn't take it from you."

"Why?"

"Because then you'd be like the others. I don't want you to be that."

"Leah—"

"It's not as bad as you think. I'm all right."

"Are you?"

"Well, that depends, doesn't it? On what you think is all right."

"How did it happen? I mean, what—?"

"Oh, you want the story. Men always want the story. As if they had nothing to do with it. It's exciting to them, I guess. I can't think why. How do you think it happens? Somebody offers you—something. You take it. And here we are."

"I'm serious. What happened?"

"So, where to start? At the heim, probably. Have you been there?"

"Looking for you."

She sat back for a second, stopped by this.

"Well, then you know. The toilets at the end? Always a wait. And my mother couldn't wait. And wouldn't use the buckets. Did you see the buckets? She wet herself. And then she cried. I think she's been waiting to cry, for months now. She couldn't stop. And even when she did— I knew if we stayed in that place, she'd die. I still had the money from the coat, so I found a room. In Yangtzepoo, not far from where the Jews are. Mostly Japanese. But she started wandering off, so someone had to be with her all the time. Not Chinese. They frightened her. I don't know why. Just the look of them. And I didn't want to hire someone from the heim— then everybody knows—so I found a Russian. A widow, she's got nothing, so even my mother looks good to her. But still, I have to pay her something. And we have to live. So a man I met in the heim notices this—there are men who look for this, it's what they do—and says he knows a job for me. I don't know what he gets, maybe a free drink for bringing in the girl. You know what a taxi dancer is?"

Daniel nodded.

"A man buys a ticket and you dance with him and he tries to feel you up. And you let him. And sometimes, if they like you, they see you after and take you somewhere. You don't have to go. It's not like a brothel where they just come and pick and you have to do it. But if you go, it's money. Sometimes more than once, if they really like you. A regular. Which is what everyone's hoping for. And then maybe one tells a friend about you and so on and it's a business. You don't have to dance anymore. They call. They make appointments. Sometimes they take you places. The Barbary Coast." She looked over at him. "It's not so bad. My mother has someone. Her own toilet. Her own *room*. One for each of us. I can afford that."

"I thought you were going to work in a shop."

She smiled a little. "This is easier to get, this work. Especially if you're willing to go with the Chinese. They like Western girls. With them you get dinner—they want to show you off. So." She took a sip of her drink. "I don't know why I'm telling you these things. I don't tell anyone else. Only you." She looked up. "I'm all right. You know, before, on the ship, I was afraid. I thought something terrible would happen in Shanghai. But nothing did. My mother's going to die here, but you can do that anywhere. I guess we're going to die here too." She made a wry face. "The last stop. So. So now you're rich? How are you rich?"

"Not rich. A job. The *North-China Tribune*."

"Really?"

"It's nothing to brag about. Gossip. But it's a job. And I work for my uncle."

"Your uncle? You never said."

"He's a crook. I didn't know what he'd want me to say. He has a new name."

"What do you mean, crook?"

"Crook. He runs a nightclub and he's got his hands in a bunch of pockets. Things fall off a truck. Some gambling. Not opium but he's got friends in the business." He looked over at her. "Girls."

She didn't move for a second, taking this in. "He runs girls?"

"He has an interest. In a house."

"And you help him?"

"Not with that."

Another moment, looking at him.

"So. I'm a whore and you're a crook. A fine pair."

"That's not who we are."

"Yes, it is. It's who we are." She smiled to herself. "So my mother was right. She said you must be a crook. A Jew from Berlin. They're all crooks there, not like the Viennese. Crooks or department stores. That's how they think in Vienna."

"Is she better? Now that you're in your own place?"

Leah shrugged. "She's afraid to go out. It's confusing to her—the way people look. Sometimes I take her to Chusan Road and she sees the German signs and it's a little better. At least she doesn't wander off and get lost, the way she used to."

"You could get a place in the French Concession. It's more like home." He stopped. "I could help you."

She looked at him for a second, then shook her head. "It's not the ship anymore."

Daniel waited. "Do you ever think about it? The ship?" His voice lower.

She turned her head. "It's another time. Now it's—something else."

"It doesn't have to be. I have money. I can help."

"How much does he take from the girls? Your uncle."

"I don't know."

"Maybe it's that money."

"Leah—"

"Never mind. I don't want to quarrel. Thank you for the offer. I'm all right."

"You're not all right."

"No? Well, let's just say I'm getting by. And I know where the money's coming from. So that's one thing anyway. It's late. I should go. My beauty sleep," she said, touching her face. "They like pink cheeks." She stood up. "What you said before—you were looking for me? At the heim. You found me. So now you know. You didn't even have to pay me for my time." She looked down at the table. "Well, one drink. But no more. It's a memory now, that's all."

She turned to go.

"Leah," he said, throwing some bills on the table, starting to follow.

"I'm all right. There's always a taxi on Nanking Road."

But for some reason there wasn't, maybe a large party that left all at once and took the waiting cabs. She wouldn't use a rickshaw. "Look how thin they are. You can see they're dying from it. I'm just over the bridge. I'll walk." She touched his hand. "I'm sorry for—well—"

"Alone? At night? I'll walk you."

"It's safe."

"People get shot in the street here. I'll walk you home." He took her elbow and headed toward Garden Bridge, the lights of Broadway Mansions just ahead.

"Like a boy after a dance," she said, half to herself. "A little gentleman. You know the balls in Vienna, before Lent? It's January and no one walks in the cold. But the taxi pulls up and he has to walk you to the door. Why? A kiss? It's never more. I think it's just the custom. Were you like that? Before you were a crook?"

Off Broadway the streets got narrower, branching off into alleys, only a few streetlamps, the air heavy with the smoke of cooking fires, stale grease.

"This is where you live?"

"It's not so bad. The houses have courtyards inside. And the Japanese are clean, so the streets—here, I'll do the key. Nina will be up. Can you find your way back?"

He nodded, then pressed forward, her back against the building, the way it had been, everything instinct now.

"Leah, for god's sake. All this—" His head against her neck, then kissing her, not a gentleman's kiss, hungry, the way they kissed, her mouth open to him, kissing back, both of them pressing against each other. For a second the street became the stateroom again, the bunk waiting for them to fall on the crisp sheets.

She caught herself, putting her hands on his chest. "Stop. We can't."

"Why not?" he said, kissing her again.

"Because we can't." She pushed him farther away, drawing in some air.

"I think about it all the time. You."

"Don't."

"Come back with me. I'm just behind the Bund. No one's there. Not your mother. Not Nina. Just us, the way we—"

"We can't," she said, another gulp of air. "I've just been with someone. I can't—"

He drew back, some blow to the head.

"Your face," she said. "If you could see your face. What did you think? It was dinner and a show? That's why I was late. Oh, don't look that way." She turned her head. "That's what I'll see, that look. Not the memory." She dropped her hand from his chest. "This is who we are now."

CHAPTER 6

Esther Engel sailed back to the States the day war broke out in Europe. A group from the Slipper had come down to the Bund to see her off and at first Daniel thought the men pouring out of the office buildings were other farewell parties. But no one was smiling or waving at the tender. Instead they had the slightly dazed and aimless look of people at a traffic accident. Was it true? What was the BBC saying? The local stations? Did it mean Hong Kong was at war? Singapore? But Germany was far away. Too far away for the Luftwaffe. And yet looking at the crowds, Daniel could feel the vise closing, Europe clutching its throat. The men in suits in front of Jardine's would be called up soon, soldiers. The *Raffaello*, the refugees, would stop coming, all gates closed now. Still, today Esther was blowing kisses and smiling, going home, her future safe in a wire transfer to Wells Fargo.

Everyone was happy with the deal except Irina.

"The others pay, but not us? It makes trouble. To have an exception."

"Trouble for whom?" Daniel said.

"The Japanese. To do business this way."

"But it's in their interest. To keep the peace."

"You think that's what they want?"

"It's what Yamada wants. So he can count his money."

"No, he's not like that."

"Everybody's like that."

"Not everybody," she said, looking over at him. "You. You're not like that." She hesitated. "You know Nathan wants you to take over the business. Is that what you want?"

"You think I can't do it."

"No, you can do it. We'll show you. I don't want him to be disappointed, that's all. He's a good man."

Daniel looked up.

"Not perfect. Good. He brought me here from Harbin. You know what it was like there? He got me out. You don't forget something like that."

"You paid your way. He couldn't do this without you," Daniel said, spreading his hands.

Irina nodded. "But you're the son."

Daniel said nothing for a minute, letting this settle. "And you think it's a bad deal," he said finally.

"Pay half. Something. Then nobody notices."

But Nathan had no qualms.

"Xi wants to meet you. He says you have balls. Coming from him—"

"Irina thinks we're asking for trouble. We should pay something. Then the others—"

Nathan shrugged. "She's a bookkeeper. Cautious. Yamada agreed, that's what matters. The others don't like it, that's his problem. He wants the take from the Slipper, he'll make them fall in line. It's a sweet spot for him. His name's not on it. Even your friend Loomis has no idea—which is the way we want to keep it. It's a nice piece of information to have."

"As long as the take keeps coming."

"Sid knew what he was doing. The talent stinks, but the slots are steady. And the tables. He ran it clean—no opium, no girls. Just a nice little turnover week after week. Which is all you promised Yamada, so we don't have to reinvent the wheel. Just keep it going. You'll save if you buy your liquor with the Cat. Irina can do that. Maybe later you want to make changes. We'll see. Right now we have to think about the Rush." He looked up at Daniel. "And no squeeze. Jesus Christ, Sid would pee in his pants."

The meeting with Xi felt like a royal audience, formal and respectful, watched over by an interpreter.

"He speaks English," Nathan said. "But this way it gives him an extra ear, if he doesn't understand something. Just be careful what you say."

But as it happened, Daniel didn't have to say anything. Xi greeted him, looked him over, and talked to Nathan about the security arrangements for the Rush.

"The driveway is the choke point. We search for guns there. The grounds are swept by the guards, but nobody's getting over that wall anyway. The layout favors us."

"Opening night you're going to have a crowd. You hold them up at the gate, you're going to have a traffic jam in the street."

"I'm not worried about opening night," Xi said. "Too many people." He nodded to Daniel. "Your boss. Press photographers. No one pulls a job in a crowd like that. But the next week, that's another story." He turned to Daniel. "Tell me. What would you have done if Yamada had said no?"

Daniel looked straight at him. "Paid the squeeze."

Xi dipped his head. "Good. We don't want to give people

ideas. In the Settlement, they expect to pay *us*. The Badlands, that's something new. The Japanese want to control it, but the Japanese don't understand yet. How to do business. You took advantage of this. But only once. People should expect to pay."

"He didn't say no. He made a deal," Nathan said. "Who else has made a deal with the Japanese?" Proud, handing out cigars.

Xi looked at Daniel again, a slight bow. "And I am most grateful. All the partners. But only this once."

Xi provided the muscle, the guns at the gate, the bodyguards, but Wu, rarely seen, seemed to have a hand in everything else. The backup generator, stuck in customs, was released overnight. Roulette wheels disappeared in Manila, then reappeared in a Pudong warehouse. The painters finished on time. The electricians hung the outside sign, a white neon light moving across gold bars.

"All he has to say is 'do it,'" Nathan said. "You say no, maybe you get an arm broken, just for talking back. So who says no?"

———

The closer they got to opening, the more Nathan needed to do—approve the matchbook design, watch the chorus line run-through, hire the extra croupiers. Irina watched all this with a kind of wry amusement.

"What's the hurry? You're late a week, so what? Nobody's asking for money back."

"Who knows how long we'll have? They're in Poland now. Just like that." He snapped his fingers.

"But not here," Daniel said.

"No. The Japanese. Waiting."

"We have Japanese friends."

"Friends can change. Look at the Russians. Friends with Hitler all of a sudden, so they get a piece of Poland. But wait."

"It's the radio," Irina said. "Every night with the radio." Something Daniel had noticed, too, an exile's need for news.

"You want to pay attention to what's going on. You wake up some day and there's a Nazi with a gun on you."

"So meanwhile, take a look at the ad. You like the dress? Big night out, that's what it says to me. All the English papers, yes?"

"Can you get it in the *Tribune* for free?" Nathan said to Daniel.

"No, but you'll be all over the columns. Loomis is hiring an extra photographer. Don't pinch pennies. Not for the opening."

"Couple of weeks on the job and he's telling me what to do," Nathan said, a smile, fond.

Loomis, in fact, was planning more than a column.

"We've got a full page, if I can fill it," he said. "So for once you'll be useful. Can you get me the reservation list?"

"It's only for the floor show. They don't have one for the casino."

"It beats standing on Avenue Haig and guessing who's in the car. Be interesting if the Germans show up, given what's going on. The consul likes a good time."

"They won't. Nathan won't let them in. No Nazis."

"It's China, not Germany."

"His club, his rules."

"And the Jews wonder why—"

A look from Daniel.

"It's starting. Warsaw, it's the start. I just hope when it's time, we come in on the right side here."

"The right side."

"You don't have to like everything about the Japanese to see they're going to win. China, then the rest. If we're smart, we'll get out of their way."

Daniel started to say something, then stopped. An argument that would go nowhere. "Meanwhile, I'll get you the list."

———

Irina, who never went anywhere, was making over an old dress for opening night.

"She doesn't buy, she saves. With all the money I give her," Nathan said.

"You wear it once. Where's the sense?"

An evening gown with a haltered top held up behind the neck, leaving the shoulders bare. Still white and smooth, but showing their age, like the dress. A fake white ermine jacket to cover, flashy, something a showgirl would have liked ten years ago.

"You'll look great," Nathan said, meaning it.

"I'll look like the maid."

Daniel sat back, half listening, outside. She must have been striking then. He got me out of Harbin. Just one string in a web of attachments, things no one else knew. Keeping Nathan's books, sharing his bed. And now what? A gold rush of money. But not enough to feel safe. Never that much.

Leah had moved. Daniel stayed away from Yangtzepoo and then last week he didn't, finding his way from Broadway all right, retracing the route they'd taken that night, the twisted alley. But she'd gone, a new family already in place in the courtyard. Back to the heim on Ward Road? More likely a service flat on the Avenue Foch, a view of the plane trees out the window, Clara shooed into her bedroom when whoever it was came by for his afternoon. Anyway, no longer in Yangtzepoo.

———

The night before the Gold Rush opened there was a shootout in one of the side streets off the Great Western Road, a gang dispute in a makeshift brothel that had been put up to catch the new casino traffic. There had been another the week before and neither had anything to do with the Gold Rush but Xi, taking no chances, doubled the guards and put an extra gun with Nathan's party, wedged in front between Sergei and the driver. An advance car, just in case, ran ahead of the Buick.

"It's like sardines in here," Irina said.

"Better safe than sorry," Sergei said from the front seat.

"At this time of day?"

They were going early, to check on last-minute details and, Daniel discovered, avoid photographers.

"I don't get my picture taken," Nathan said. "You never know who might see it. In the States, I mean."

"He thinks they're still looking," Irina said. "Nathan Green, Man of Mystery."

"You don't know what you're talking about," Nathan said, but nicely, too excited about the evening to be distracted. "Remember the old Cat, in Nollendorfplatz?" he said to Daniel. "Who would have imagined? A place like this."

The Gold Rush had begun life as a grand English estate, a Tudor pile that Sir Victor or one of the Kadoories had put up years ago when the Western Roads District was still country. There was an entrance gate and a driveway that swept in front of the house and continued around back to the parking area, where the stables had been. The nightclub had been carved out of the original hall, with the same high ceiling still in place. A broad staircase, divided at the top, led to the old bedrooms, now the gaming rooms, one flowing into the other, all with roulette wheels and blackjack tables, public and intimate at the same time. The old servants' quarters on top had been converted into private party rooms, card games that could go on for hours, with food brought in. Elevators now connected the floors, but the staircase guaranteed an entrance, crowded tonight with flashbulbs and people waving to friends, like a film premiere.

Daniel had been here before, but Sergei insisted on doing a walk-through, so he finally got to see the place with all the lights on, the sound of Gus Whiting's band rising up to the higher floors. Waiters floated by with opening night champagne. In the main casino room, one wall lined with slots, people were already gathering at the long bar, like the one in the Shanghai Club. Downstairs, food trolleys wheeled in and around the tables, then back to the kitchen behind the bandstand. Everyone had dressed up—long skirts and jewels, men in black tie, just like the movies. The dance floor, polished to a shine, was filled with reflected light. He thought of Florence Burke on the boat, Shanghai dancing on the rim of the volcano. This was the rim.

"He hasn't stopped smiling," Daniel said, nodding toward Nathan, who was greeting people at the foot of the stairs as if he were in a receiving line at a wedding. Irina, shyer, had skirted the photographers and instead huddled in a small group, presumably old friends.

"I told Xi to put another man in the parking area," Sergei said, looking around the room. "You know, they check for guns at the gate, but what if they had them in the car? They're not searching cars. What's to stop someone going out to the lot and picking up a gun there?"

Daniel glanced at the room. The last thing anybody seemed to be thinking about.

"The only guns you want in a place like this are yours," Sergei said. "Nobody carrying but you. You, me, Xi's people."

"How would they do it, though—and get away," Daniel said. "You get your cash, jewels, whatever you're taking, then how do you get out? Guards at the gates. Maybe the police already out there, waiting. You can't just walk out. Not to mention, you've got a slew of witnesses. You'd be crazy to try it. Especially tonight. Unless you want to get your picture taken while you do it."

Sergei looked at him, not smiling. "It doesn't always make sense. Look at last night. Where was the sense in that? But you've got two guys dead in the street. It scares the customers. They like it safe and quiet."

They walked through the casino area, Daniel looking at everything differently now, ignoring the tables but taking in the bulging pockets stationed around the room, Chinese in suits that looked borrowed. The dance floor was filling up. They walked through the noisy kitchen, whose back door led to the parking area.

"Just one driveway? No separate gate for deliveries?"

"Just one."

Back to the front, where cars were still pulling up, past the trimmed shrubberies and lighted walkways. In the distance, behind the wall, the tall plane trees the French had planted. Over by a bush, quick as a firefly, the flicker of a match, one of Xi's men having a smoke. Safe and quiet, even the air soft, maybe something else Wu had arranged for the opening.

"I'm going to check with the gate," Sergei said. "Keep your eyes open."

Daniel raised two fingers to his forehead in a salute.

Loomis had taken up Nathan's old position at the foot of the stairs.

"Working hard? If you want to know who anybody is, just ask Chen at the bar."

"They're still coming in," Daniel said.

Loomis nodded. "It'll make Farren crazy. How's he going to top this? More girls, I guess. Well, good for Nathan. I suppose this means you're going to quit the Merry-Go-Round."

"Why?"

"The son also rises. I hear you're going to run the Slipper. Cut your teeth on it, so to speak."

"My teeth are all cut. I'm just going to help out. Maybe pick up some items for you, who knows?"

"No, they all leave. So will you. Not that I blame you. Something better comes along, why not take it? It's touching in a way, the two of you, this reunion. Nathan's beside himself. How long has it been, anyway?"

"I don't know," said Daniel, deliberately vague. "Ten years. A long time."

"What was he doing in Berlin?" Loomis said, really asking now.

"What he's doing here. Clubs. He always liked the music. I'd better go check in with Chen," Daniel said, turning. "You have a whole page to fill."

"Surprising he didn't stay in the States. I always wondered why he left. Ended up here. Well, how did any of us end up here? You want to be careful, turning over that rock." He looked over Daniel's shoulder. "Well, my goodness," he said, his attention fixed now on the staircase behind them, a couple coming down.

Daniel glanced up and froze. Yamada and Leah, together, hand on her arm, her eyes on the stairs, careful in heels, then looking up, taking him in, startled, not expecting this. Yamada, however, had begun to smile, a cat in cream.

"Colonel," Loomis said, nodding, almost a bow.

"Mister Loomis," Yamada said. "Does this mean we'll be in the newspapers? Do you know Fräulein Auerbach?"

"I haven't had the pleasure. Fräulein."

"Miss," she said, uncomfortable.

"Of course you know Mister Lohr," Yamada was saying. "A dancing partner on the boat," he explained to Loomis, but staring at Daniel, daring him to respond, things coming full circle, no cutting in this time.

Don't react. But Daniel could feel the dismay creeping into his face, a door slamming. They were Yamada's afternoons on the Avenue Foch. And looking at her, the blood rushing into her cheeks, Daniel could see something break in her, too, the defiance, the running motor suddenly gone. Instead, an unexpected shame. This is who we are now.

"Everyone seems to have been on that boat," Loomis was saying.

Yamada looked around. "So. It's a great success. Your uncle must be pleased."

"Your uncle?" Leah said.

"Yes," Yamada said. "Mister Lohr's uncle owns the place. With a few partners." This with a sly nod, a look between him and Daniel.

"You knew he'd be here then," she said, a kind of thinking out loud.

"I hoped he would be."

"And see us," she said, finishing the thought.

"A happy surprise," Yamada said blandly. "It was a friendly time on the boat."

"Yes, a happy surprise," Leah said, trying to cover, but her voice flat, some will slipping out of it.

"How is your mother?" Daniel said. Get through it.

"Thank you, well," she said, a line in a play. "We've moved to the French Concession."

"A more comfortable situation," Yamada said, knowing, each word like a razor nick, enjoying it.

"How did you do at the tables?" Daniel cocked his head toward the stairs. "Any luck?"

She shook her head. "I don't play. It makes me nervous. What if you lose?"

Daniel took a chip out of his pocket. "Here, play this. Don't think of it as real. Just found money, a good luck piece."

Yamada intercepted the chip, stopping Daniel's hand. "It's not allowed, Mister Lohr, for the Kempeitai to accept–" Yamada said, another way of claiming her, the rules of possession.

"Oh, well, maybe you'll permit me to cut in once more? A dance?" he said to Leah. "Just one? It's allowed?"

"I really don't think–" Leah started.

"Of course," Yamada said, with a quick glance to Loomis, no polite way out.

Daniel walked behind her to the dance floor.

"Not so close," she said when he put his arm around her. "He won't like it." She took a step back. "Is that a gun? Why do you have a gun?"

"For show. So nobody gets any ideas."

"What ideas?"

"Taking the house's money. Upsetting the customers."

"So you work here. He knew you'd be here."

"How long have you–?"

"Since he saw me at the club. And knew he could–"

"And now it's just him?"

She nodded, looking down at the dance floor.

"That must make it easier for you. Less turnover." Unable to stop himself.

Her eyes flashed, a second of the old spirit, then dimmed again. "No. Different. It means something to him. Ever since the boat. Like Herr Blauner. He wants to take care of me."

"Leah—"

"He's looking. Smile. He'll ask what we were talking about. Nothing. One of your jokes. Frau Mitzel maybe."

"I'll come see you."

"No. There's a houseboy. He reports everything." She paused. "You don't know him."

"You must be alone sometimes."

"You mean when he lets me out of the cage? Where do I fly? Around the room. Then back." She made a weak smile. "But it's a nice room. I picked it. My choice."

"Your choice."

"Yes, why not? We have to live somewhere. You don't approve." Daniel said nothing.

Leah looked away. "Nobody does. Even people I don't know. When we're out. He likes that." She stopped, dropping her arm. "The music's finished. We have to go back." She looked up. "Don't make trouble for me."

"I want to help."

She ignored this, starting back off the dance floor. "Who's that with him?"

"My uncle." Huddled with Yamada and Loomis, still the life of the party.

"Look at you out there," Nathan said to Daniel. "Who taught you?"

Leah had gone to Yamada's side.

"You know Miss Auerbach?" Yamada said.

"I do now," Nathan said, dipping his head. "The colonel says you were on the *Raffaello*. Did he behave himself?" Pointing his thumb at Daniel.

"A perfect gentleman." She looked up at Yamada. "All of them."

"Well, you're lucky I wasn't there," Nathan said, a mock leer in his voice.

"Don Juan," Irina said, joining them. "He doesn't mean anything by it," she said to Leah. "You must be Colonel Yamada. I'm Irina. We spoke on the phone."

Leah looked at them, puzzled.

"The colonel and we have business interests."

"Business interests?" Leah said, thrown by this.

"Some advice," Yamada said, dismissing it, not looking at Loomis. "Well, shall we go? An early evening for us, I'm afraid. We don't gamble." Speaking for both of them. "But yours paid off. Congratulations. Gold Rush. So aptly named." He looked around.

"There's a lot of money in Shanghai," Nathan said. "Plenty to go around."

"So I've been told."

A flashbulb went off, two. Yamada and Leah.

"No, no," Yamada said, holding up his hand, about to grab the camera. He whirled around to Loomis. "He's one of yours? Take care of this." His voice ice, an order.

Everyone stood for a second, stunned, as if they had all been caught in the flash.

"It's done," Loomis said, shooing the photographer away. "Don't worry."

A silence, everyone uneasy.

"Well, I'm dead on my feet," Irina said to Nathan. "And I'm up with the chickens. You stay. I can go back with the Rosens."

"We'll drop you," Yamada said, then turned to Nathan. "Don't worry. She's safe with us. Kempeitai, after all. Everyone knows the car."

Daniel took in the circle of faces, backed into a corner, unable to say no, what Yamada had done all evening, some personal getting even. The driver, smoking near the waiting cars, was signaled.

"It was good to see you again," Leah said, formal as a handshake, aware of Yamada.

Daniel looked at her and felt his stomach twist in a sudden panic, something being taken away from him, unable to stop it, powerless, Eli being loaded on the truck.

"Well, when the cat's away," Loomis said, watching them get in the car.

Daniel, still distracted, looked at him, a question mark face.

"The wife in Tokyo. Assuming she minds. But she'd have to, wouldn't she? A cathouse visit, that's one thing, but actually setting someone up in a flat—"

"You're not going to use this, are you?"

"Dear heart, do you think I'm crazy? The Kempeitai? As pure as the snows of Hokkaido as far as I'm concerned. Just a little something for the favor bank."

Another question mark.

"Like a real bank, but no money. Put a favor in, let it collect a little interest, then trade it. Like currency."

"How does he know it's there?"

"I don't know. They do, though, somehow. They just assume, I guess. Well, I'm off to the Cathay. See what Sir Victor's up to. Congratulations, Nathan. You'll die rich."

"I like the rich part."

"Ha," Loomis said, heading down the front steps to the cars.

"Man's a snake," Nathan said.

"But he lets you know he is. So no surprises. Just watch where you walk."

"Look at you. Making deals with Yamada. Keeping the snake happy." Nathan paused. "What did you think of Xi?"

"What did he think of me?"

"You're right, that's the question. He doesn't give a fuck what people think. As long as they pay. But I'll tell you something, he's the one you want to work with. Wu, he's got the opium, so what more does he need? And he's got Chiang in his pocket. But Xi. He says something, pay attention."

"Okay," Daniel said, his mind still on Yamada. Turning the screw, enjoying it.

Nathan put his hand on Daniel's shoulder. "You'll be fine. You're quick. Look at this place. But you know what? I like it better at the Cat. The music. You pay the squeeze and no aggravation. But there's no money in it. Real money. Now you'll have something." He looked at Daniel. "Work with Xi. The others? Watch your back," he said, patting it.

"Okay," Daniel said again, only half listening, Nathan's voice like static, scratching the air. "I think I'll take a walk around, make sure everything's—where's Sergei?"

"Over there. He's like a shadow. You don't see him but he's there. You worry too much. Anybody wants to pull a job, they're going to do it outside. Where they can get away. Not in here. I ought to know."

"Ought to know why?"

Nathan looked over at him. "Not what you think. I just drove the car." A difference to him. "You learn things."

Daniel nodded. "I think I'll take a look anyway," he said, stepping onto the gravel driveway, passing the drivers waiting by their cars.

The air seemed thicker than before, the grounds quiet, so quiet you could hear the traffic in the street. Xi's men were still in place by the gate, the Gold Rush still blazing with light, all the same, as if no one knew that something had happened, his mind churning with it. He saw Yamada's face, turning up at the Avenue Foch at five. His *cinq à sept*. Clara in the other room. Did they make sounds? Her breath in his ear.

He took out a cigarette. Go home and write up items for Loomis. But his head was somewhere else. He kept seeing the room. Yamada taking off his uniform. Did he undress her or watch as she did it? Money left on the bureau. The houseboy who reported everything. Business interests. Running the Slipper for him. Daniel's own idea. Yet Yamada had somehow bought them both. And Daniel could feel, walking over the grass, that he'd pull the strings tighter, that they'd belong to him. And one day Shanghai would be Japanese and there'd be nowhere else to go. Except to fly around the room.

———

With Irina already gone home, there should have been more room in the back, but Sergei insisted on sitting there with Nathan, as if he really were a shadow, so they crowded in and let Xi's extra man have the now roomy seat next to the driver. The band was still playing, light pouring out onto the lawn, but Nathan had had enough.

"They'll start losing upstairs now," he said. "The drink gets to you and you're not careful."

"Well, that's when the house makes its money," Sergei said. "And you're the house."

"I know, but I don't like to see it."

Xi's extra man, glancing at his watch, seemed relieved they were leaving, his shift almost over. Up ahead, at the gates, the guards stood on either side, like sentries. Wrought-iron gates, like a big villa in the Grunewald. Except the faces were Chinese. Sergei took out his gun.

"What's that for?" Nathan said.

"Once we're in the street, you want to be ready for anything."

They were at the wall, the end of Xi's protected island.

"You're like an old woman," Nathan said.

"I'm here."

"It's no way to live," Nathan said, mostly to himself.

Daniel looked at him. The way he'd lived for years. Now the way Daniel was going to live. Instinctively he felt for his gun, too, just making sure.

The car slowed as it reached the end of the driveway. The guard on the passenger side leaned over to look in, checking. A flicker of the eyes from Xi's man to an empty car parked outside the gate. Just waiting. Like a getaway car. Getting away from what? The guard took a step back. Daniel felt the hair on his arms bristle, ears up, the way animals sense a storm. A flicker he wasn't supposed to see, some signal. Or imagining things, like Sergei.

Xi's man twisted around in his seat. A gleam of light on metal, then the metal itself, a gun pointing toward them, fast, the speed of surprise. Daniel pushed Nathan against Sergei as the gun fired, the sound of an explosion, loud, as if the car was blowing up, a grunt from Nathan as he was hit. A second bullet, to follow the first, finish the job, hitting Nathan again, but now Daniel's gun was in his hand, a quick jerk up, not thinking, firing into the man's head, which seemed to come apart, pieces of something flinging back, sticking to him.

"Down!" Shouting at Nathan, his chest now covered in blood, eyes startled.

Another shot. The other guard firing at the driver, whose body twitched from the impact, then fell over the wheel. Both guards now firing at the car, shooting through the window. Not a heist, a massacre, a back seat of sitting ducks. But Sergei had started firing back, bullets they weren't expecting. A simple hit, before anyone had a chance to react, then dive for the waiting car, disappear. The guard on the driver's side went down. A bullet whizzed by Daniel's head, the passenger-side guard still firing. A thunk as Daniel felt something punch his shoulder. The next one would do it. He held the gun with two hands, aiming, and fired. The guard staggered back, then fell. Shouts coming now from the lawn.

"He's hit," Sergei said, holding Nathan.

"We have to get him out of here," Daniel said, hearing Franz in his head. Get away.

"He's bleeding."

"We can't stay here. We don't know who else—" Daniel said. Nathan opened his eyes. "Hold on. We'll get you out of here. Sergei, drive!"

Sergei looked up, blank.

"You know the streets. Quick."

"What's on your face?"

"Him," Daniel said, poking his thumb toward the front seat. "Get the driver out. I'll get the other one. Nathan. Here, lay him down. Jesus, we'd better get him to a hospital."

Nathan staring at him, not saying anything.

"Move!" Daniel shouted to Sergei. "Before anybody—"

He got out of the car, then opened the front door, Xi's man falling. Daniel pulled him out and flung the body away from the car. Only part of his head. The front seat was covered in blood and what must have been pieces of his brains. Daniel took this in for a second, dizzy, his arm shaking, a tremor. I did this. But he would have killed them all, back seat ducks, an easy job. A moan. Daniel swirled around. The passenger-side guard, still alive. Another moan, fainter this time. He stepped over the guard, looking down. Leave him. Let Xi's men deal with him. What he was supposed to be. Xi's man. And what if he was? All of them. He looked down again. Not self-defense, not this time. Franz's voice. No witnesses. Daniel fired, a shot straight to the forehead.

Sergei had started the car. Daniel slammed the passenger door shut and jumped into the back.

"Okay, drive."

Sergei raced the motor, then pulled into the street. "We shouldn't move him. He's losing blood."

"We can't stay here. They could try again."

Nathan opened his eyes, registering this, then closed them again, his hand moving to clutch Daniel's. Holding on. Daniel looked down at it. If it went slack, he'd be gone. He could die. Like this, the way Eli had predicted. His high forehead just like Eli's now, something Daniel had never noticed. His hand clutching again. Daniel took off his jacket. "Here. Can you hold this on it? Where it's bleeding? Never mind, I'll do it. Just hang on. We'll get you to a hospital. Anybody behind?"

Sergei looked in the mirror. "I don't think so. More lights, though."

"Fast as you can. Let's not take any chances."

"The other guard. You kill him?"

"Yes."

"And Xi's man. That's going to put a price on your head."

"There were no witnesses. Except you."

Sergei looked up again in the mirror. "What's on your shoulder? Blood? You hit?"

"It's okay. If it were serious, I wouldn't be able to move it. Anybody now?"

"No. The car's a mess."

"Let's just get to the hospital. How far?"

"Country Hospital on the Great Western Road has an ER. Not far."

"That's the closest?" Daniel thought for a minute. "That's where they'll look. You know St. Joseph's?"

"Out in Hongkew? That's a lot farther."

"But you know where it is? Go there."

"With him like that?"

"We go to Country he could end up dead. That's where they'll go."

A sound from Nathan, his eyes still closed.

"Why St. Joseph's?" Sergei said.

"I know somebody there. He'll keep it quiet if we need him to. We don't know what we're dealing with yet. When we get to the hospital, call Irina. Tell her to get out—stay with the Rosens, somewhere she'll be safe. Don't tell her where we are."

"You think they'd go after her?"

"We don't know who 'they' are yet. But we're supposed to be dead and we're not. So they might want to ask her where we are. If she doesn't know anything—" He felt Nathan squeeze his hand. "You all right?" Nathan nodded his head.

"They were Xi's men," Sergei said.

"But why would he do it?"

"Take out Nathan, there's a lot more to go around."

"And how does the other partner feel? Wu Tsai just sits there and waits? Who's next? Unless they're in it together. That sound right to you?"

"No. But Wu—being a partner is something new for him. You don't have partners in the opium business. You have control."

"There's only one way to find out. Can you set up a meeting with Xi?"

"You want to meet with him?"

"We have to stop it. Before he tries again. If this was his idea. If it wasn't, we'll have something else to talk about."

"He could kill you at the meeting."

143

Daniel shook his head. "Too many people would know. After, maybe. But then I'd have you. Protection."

"It's too risky. I'll go."

"No, it has to be me. He knows I speak for Nathan." He looked down. "He'll be meeting with Nathan."

The traffic picked up after Bubbling Well Road, the usual stop-and-go stream of trams and rickshaws and cars trying to move past them.

"Can we go through Chapei?"

"It's longer."

"We don't want to sit in traffic in Nanking Road. Somebody spots us—" Daniel squeezed Nathan's hand. "Don't worry, we'll get you there. Just hold on."

"You know, St. Joseph's, it's mostly Chinese," Sergei said.

"So what? They bleed the same way."

"I'm just saying. It's not as nice as Country."

"We're not planning to stay."

"No?"

"No. Eventually they'll check all the hospitals, so we have to be gone."

"Then where?"

"I'm thinking. Not my place. They'll look. Not the Cat. Well, let's get him patched up first."

Nathan smiled faintly, opening his eyes, his hand gripping Daniel's more tightly.

"You're me," he said, almost a whisper. "Not Eli. You're like me. I knew."

Daniel looked at him, disconcerted.

"What'd he say?" Sergei said.

"Northing. He's rambling."

Another smile from Nathan, their secret.

Markowski, miraculously, was there, just beginning his night shift, and got Nathan on a gurney with the help of two aides, the Buick almost as big as the ambulance on duty in the garage.

"My god, what happened?"

"Shot. Twice. A lot of blood."

"I can see that," Markowski said as the aides began wheeling Nathan in. Swinging doors. "Who is he?"

"My uncle."

Markowski looked up. "Gunshot wounds, we have to report. It's the law. I'd get fired."

"I know. It's a big favor." He looked at Markowski. "I'd owe you. Anything. Just save him."

"God, the car– What the hell happened?"

"He wasn't the only one. Who got shot. I know, it's a mess."

"And all over you," Markowski said, nodding to Daniel's face. "You better get washed up before the nurses get a look at you. I'll get somebody to clean up the car. It's a specialty we have here. You should see the ambulance sometimes. Not so pretty, the way people die. What name?"

"John Doe."

Markowski looked over at him.

"I know. It's a big favor. I'll get him out of here as soon as we can move him."

"What about your shoulder?"

"Just a scratch. They missed."

"Come on. We'll take a look."

"Him first. He'll die."

"They're already working. Stabilizing him. It's the protocol." He turned to face Daniel. "I'll do what I can. But if he needs major surgery–"

"We'll find someone. We're not going to let him go."

"What was the shooting about, if I'm allowed to ask."

"Gangs. Out in the Badlands. He got caught in the cross fire."

"The cross fire."

"That's right," Daniel said, looking at him.

"You brought him all the way here from the Badlands? Why?"

"Nobody's looking for him here. And you're here."

"It's nothing–political, is it? Old times. I can't get near–"

"No, nothing like that. He runs a nightclub. Other things. Come on, we're wasting time. He's tough, but he's been shot. Do this for me, Karl. Please? I'll owe you."

"I don't do it for that. I'm a doctor. So."

Nathan was already out, hooked up to an IV drip.

"He's lucky," Markowski said, bending over him, examining the wound, his face now covered by a surgical mask. "A few more inches and the heart– All right. Let's get it out and see if we can stop the bleeding. You wait in there." He nodded to another room. "Orders. I've got an open wound here. I can't risk sepsis. Li, take a look at his shoulder. Make sure it's clean. He'll need a dressing. Look at this, right near the artery."

Sergei came back while the nurse was swabbing Daniel's shoulder with antiseptic. An examining room with cabinets of bandages and metal trays of tongue depressors, an old EKG machine in the corner, sprouting wires.

"We have to stay here," Daniel said. "You get Irina? How is she?"

"How is she. The end of the world. She wants to come."

"What did you tell her?"

"We're with a doctor. Not where. I'll call later, when we know how he is."

"You tell her to go somewhere safe?"

146

"Then how do I call? I sent some Russians over. To stay with her. She'll be okay. God, the smell here."

"All hospitals smell like this." Blood and urine and disinfectant.

"Chinese hospitals."

"That just means it's clean."

"What did he say?" Sergei cocked his head toward the ER.

"That it missed his heart."

"That was you," Sergei said, mimicking Daniel pushing Nathan.

"No. Luck." He looked up. "Now what?"

"Wu and Xi go after each other."

"Not if they think he's alive. They need to hear that."

Sergei looked over at him. "One of them tried to kill him."

"And might try again. I know. But what else can we do? If Nathan's dead, they'll eat up the place. Kill each other maybe, but take the Rush down with them. If Nathan's alive, at least we've got a kind of checkmate situation. They block each other. How many Russians could you get, if we needed them? Real protection."

"Enough."

"So Nathan has his men and they have theirs. Let's say we never know who tried to get him tonight. What matters is the truce. Before things get out of hand. So they have to know he's alive. That they're all still in it."

"You want me to call Xi."

Daniel nodded. "They were his men. Either he ordered them to do it or Wu got to them. Either way, he has to know it didn't work. And now we've got men of our own. So the smart play is a truce." He looked over. "Tell him I want a meeting. The sooner the better."

"Why better?"

"It only works if Nathan is alive."

After about an hour, Daniel began to pace, like an expectant father. It shouldn't take this long, not if it were going well. How good was Karl anyway? The group had relied on him, but the group had no choice. No hospital was safe from the Gestapo. Everything that had to be done had to be done privately. The room felt like a cage, the white fluorescent lights meant to keep him awake, a test animal. Next door, the footfalls of nurses' shoes. Nathan on a table. Sergei had been on the phone in the nurses' station, speaking Russian, organizing enough men to turn the Cat into a fortress. But that wouldn't happen overnight–they'd have to keep Nathan somewhere safe until everything was in place. Somewhere nobody would think to look.

"Xi said all right, tomorrow," Sergei said. "But his place. And why doesn't Nathan come himself?"

"What did you say?"

"I said he wasn't taking any chances. Not after tonight."

"So he knows."

Sergei shrugged. "He's got three men dead in the street and an army on the grounds–he'd be the first call to make. So he knows people were shot, but not what happened."

"He doesn't think Nathan was hit?"

Sergei shook his head. "Who's going to tell him? His men are dead. He said, is he all right? You know, concerned. I said why wouldn't he be? I was with him."

"And he bought it?"

"We're all supposed to be dead. But I'm on the phone, you show up tomorrow–who's to say Nathan isn't walking around?"

"And he agreed to the meeting, so that's something. I wasn't sure he would."

"You know why? He knows Nathan isn't planning any funny business if he's sending you. You're the crown jewels." A small, crooked smile. "He thinks you have balls."

"You think I'm crazy to do this."

"Maybe. I don't think he'll try anything. We're still one big happy family. With a problem. He said he'd do the mopping up."

"What, the bodies?"

"No, the car outside the gate. Maybe it tells us something. Anyway, you don't want the police all over it, so he moved it."

"The police."

"People shot in the street, the police are going to be called. You can't just throw them in the bushes. But the police blotter doesn't have to say where the bodies were exactly. Avenue Haig covers some territory. You don't want them near the Rush—it looks bad. So you move the bodies down the street. On paper."

"The police blotter," Daniel said. Something he hadn't thought about.

"Xi has somebody in the police who can make a little adjustment. Keep the Rush out of it." He paused. "Mopping up."

"Part of the service," Daniel said idly, thinking. When Xi talks, listen, Nathan had said. "Protecting the Rush. And setting us up." He looked at Sergei. "What if it wasn't him?"

"Then you'll need the balls. Wu is worse."

When Markowski finally came out of the operating room, nodding an okay, his forehead was shiny with sweat.

"There was tissue damage," he said. "So it took a while."

"But he'll be all right."

"I think so, but you'll need to watch him. Strictly speaking, he shouldn't be moved at all, but he can't stay here. We don't have much time. My supervisor's on the next shift and then we'd have to report it. Which I take it you don't want to do, right?"

"We can't. They might try again if they know where he is."

"They. Well, he's not going to just disappear. You have to move him."

"Isn't there somewhere else in the hospital? Not here, they'd look here. Somewhere nobody would think to look. A room in another wing, a supply room or something? Out of sight. Nobody knows."

"You ever work in a hospital? That buzzing you hear is all the little bees knowing everything. There is no such room. Anyway, I can't risk it. Can you take him home?"

Daniel looked at Sergei, who shook his head no.

"Tell me this," Markowski said. "The police. Are they looking for him? Is that who—?"

"No," Daniel said. "No police. Friends of his."

"Ah," Markowski said, not saying more.

"Franz used to say hide in plain sight. He's a patient. Can't we put him in a room with other patients? Bandage him up, something like that?"

"You're asking me to use the patients as decoys?"

"You just saved his life. Now we need to protect him. Think of it as—the Gestapo after him. Where would we hide him, where nobody would think to look?"

Markowski thought for a minute. "You swear no police?"

Daniel nodded.

"Let me make a call. They finish your car yet? Check if it's cleaned."

"You want to put him in the car? The way he is?"

"No, I'm going to put him in an ambulance. On a stretcher. You're going to be in the car. Clean as new. No evidence."

"We were never here," Daniel said.

"That's what I'm going to say."

———

Nathan was still unconscious when they wheeled him into the ambulance.

"He'll be out for a few hours," Markowski said. "Until the morphine wears off. He won't feel the ride. I'll go with him. You follow."

"It's okay for you to–?"

"I'm a doctor. Nobody questions a doctor. As long as I get back before the next shift."

"Where are we going?"

"Frenchtown. This hour, there shouldn't be any traffic. Just stay close."

Daniel nodded toward the driver, a silent question.

"Chang? He's all right," Markowski said, surprised to be asked. The Shanghai mind–the Chinese weren't there, invisible.

Sergei didn't want to leave Nathan but Markowski brushed this off. "I can use a gun, too, don't worry. And if we're stopped, how do I explain you?"

The ambulance pulled out of the receiving bay first, Sergei and Daniel following.

"How do you know him?" Sergei said.

"From Berlin. We used to work for the same man."

"Doing what?"

"Things," Daniel said, closing it off.

"Huh," Sergei said, a grunt. "I'm not supposed to leave Nathan. You trust this man?"

"He got us this far."

They were passing over Garden Bridge, the Bund curving ahead of them, still lighted, like a stage set.

"This man you worked for–what happened to him?"

"He was killed."

Sergei turned to look at him, then went back to the window. "Things," he said to himself.

They had reached the line of plane trees on Avenue Foch.

"Who hides out here?" Sergei said.

"Well, that's the point," Daniel said. A familiar block, the tall apartment building with the deco trim. Where nobody would think to look.

Markowski and the driver were lifting Nathan out of the ambulance, moving quietly, the sidewalks empty.

"Don't park in front," Daniel said to Sergei. "Around the corner. It's the top floor."

"You know this place?"

"Yes. But I never thought– Let me out here. There's a buzzer. Top floor. Burke."

He caught up to Markowski in the elevator. "What's going on?"

"She helps me sometimes."

"Florence?"

"She's more than you see." He looked at Daniel. "She helps us."

Florence was at the door with a houseboy, another invisible witness. Her hair had been pinned up for bed and she was wearing a floor-length Chinese robe, thrown on to cover a nightgown.

"In here," she said, all business, leading them across the large room where the Chinese poet had spoken. Ceramics on end tables, an old lacquered apothecary, a long Chinese scroll stretched out on the far wall. The guest room was at the other end of the apartment, curtains drawn, the bed already made up.

"What do I need to know?" she said to Markowski.

"The wound will be sore when he comes to. Probably some pain. Do you know how to use a hypodermic?"

"Yes."

"I'll leave this then." He put a small leather case on the bedside table. "Easy on the morphine, though. A little will go a long way." He looked at both of them, one to the other. "Stories. In case. You," he said to Daniel, "came and forced her at gunpoint to hide your uncle. You knew the apartment—you'd been here. She refused, but there was the gun. You," he said to Florence, "were scared. He always had somebody with him, so you couldn't get help." Then to Daniel again, "Make sure there *is* somebody with him. We don't want him leaving that room and surprising the neighbors. Florence can't keep him for more than a night or two, so get things ready at home. We all clear on that? She's sticking her neck out for you."

"I know," Daniel said.

"And I was never here. I'll come tomorrow to check on him. You came down with something and asked me to make a house call."

"I'll cancel lunch. I had people coming. Last minute, but everybody's always getting sick here. The air, probably," she said, her old voice, patter.

"Don't come and go," Markowski said to Daniel. "You know each other, so you might pay a visit, but that only works once."

The buzzer sounded, startling Markowski.

"Sergei," Daniel said.

Florence spoke in Chinese to the houseboy, presumably orders to let Sergei in.

"He's going to want to stay. They're joined at the hip."

"Oh, I know how that is," Florence said. "Wing is *devoted*."

Daniel looked at her, back on the ship.

"I can have a cot brought in for him. But what do I do with you?"

"If Sergei's with him, he won't need me anyway. I'll go calm Irina down."

"And show yourself?" Markowski said.

"They want Nathan, not me. I just got in the way before. You'd better go. Before the shift changes."

Markowski looked at his watch. "We're all fine then?"

"If you mean, do I have strangers with guns camping out in my apartment and I'm not supposed to know why, yes, fine. Well, not strangers. Imagine seeing you here. And in a dinner jacket yet. Very grand. What was the occasion?"

"A casino opening."

"Really," she said, drawing it out, looking at Markowski.

"Tomorrow," he said, evading this, passing Sergei on his way out.

"Ah," Florence said to Sergei, "and you're Mister–?"

"Menkinov," Sergei said, the first time Daniel had heard it.

"Well, let me show you where you'll be and where everything is. I must say, it's something of a comfort to have a bodyguard on the spot. Mister Green's just through here."

Sergei bowed, formal, taken in.

When she came back, she said nothing for a minute, lighting a cigarette.

"A faithful old dog."

"Who bites. If Nathan's in trouble."

"It looks like he's in trouble now."

"But he's going to make it. Thank you. For doing this. I don't know how to say it."

"I didn't know, on the boat, you worked with us."

Daniel raised his head. "Or you."

"It's useful, being a frivolous woman. No one takes you seriously. Or thinks you're ever serious yourself. They look right past you. Of course the cover doesn't work unless you really are frivolous, but I am, so it does."

"It's not politics, with Nathan. I don't think he has any."

"I know. Karl told me. Something about the gangs. I suppose that makes me a *moll*, hiding him. That's a first." She looked at him. "But you do. Have politics. You worked with Karl. And now so do

I. So we need to help each other. Oh, that look. I know. I really do see the contradictions, how ridiculous it makes me seem. I've got a banker husband who's in Nanking, probably making loans to Wang Ching-wei, the Japanese puppet. Imagine working for the Japanese after what they did in Nanking." She raised her head. "He doesn't know, by the way. That I'm hiding fugitives in the guest room. He'd have a heart attack. We don't share the same politics. I'm not supposed to have any. But you'd have to be blind not to see it. So you do what you can. Even when you see the contradictions. I still love beautiful things. I'm not hiding out in a cave with Mao. The Long March would have killed me. Which is what they'll want to do to people like me when they get in. And then make a mess of things, anyway, because people always do. I do see all that. But—well, a few more people might get to eat. You do what you can. And I have a spare room, so I hide people who need to be hidden."

"I'll never forget this."

"You'd better. If it comes out, I'll deny it. What would people think?"

"Thank you."

"Oh, all right," she said, stubbing out the cigarette. "Have a peek—make sure he's okay and off you go. It's going to be some morning. Canceling people at the last minute. The other one's Sergei, is that right?"

The guest room was quiet—no glaring hospital lights and footsteps running down the hall. The lamps had been dimmed to the soft warmth of candlelight, Shanghai outside somewhere, muffled behind curtains and doors. Daniel thought of his old room, after his father had read to him, sinking under the covers, safe. He looked around. No chinoiserie or display pieces. A Western room, comfortable. A chaise with an afghan and reading lamp. Cushions. An ottoman. Nathan sleeping, safe, where no one would think to look. Daniel felt his body relax. They'd found a place. For a while.

"Everything okay?"

"He's out," Sergei said, slumped in an easy chair.

"Markowski said a few hours. Get some sleep yourself."

"Duvey." A faint sound from the bed.

"I'm here," Daniel said, taking his hand. Not gripping this time, just resting his on Nathan's. "Sergei, too. You're going to be fine."

Nathan opened his eyes, a quick flutter to take in the room. "Where?"

"Somewhere safe. Don't worry. You should sleep. That's the best thing now."

"Irina?"

"We put more people at the Cat. I'm going now to check."

A faint smile. "Xi?"

"I'm meeting him tomorrow."

"Take Sergei with you."

"I will."

"Listen to what he has to say."

Daniel nodded. "No more now. Sergei will be here. There's an American lady who'll give you a shot. For the pain. Let her. You'll need it."

Nathan moved his fingers, dismissing this, as if he didn't want to be distracted. "The money you brought," he said, his voice barely audible. "On the ship. It's for you. In case you have to get away. Hard currency."

"I'm not going anywhere, stop worrying."

The fingers moved again. "It's yours."

"Okay. No more. I'll be back tomorrow. You're safe here. Get some sleep."

Nathan smiled, his eyes still closed, and tapped his finger on Daniel's hand. "You're the boss."

CHAPTER 7

Daniel walked a block past the car, then doubled back, a reflex, what he'd been trained to do. If anyone had spotted the car, they'd already be on him. Nothing would happen tonight, not with the meeting set. He felt a curious lightness, the way he'd felt on the *Raffaello* watching the land recede, a weight lifted, on the loose.

There was still some traffic on the Bund, even at this hour, but he managed to find a parking space on a side street behind. The lights were still on at the *Tribune*, the newsroom bright as day, the windows open to the muggy river air. A few reporters were hunched over typewriters, smoking, pounding out sheets of yellow copy paper for the Chinese boy on duty to run downstairs to typesetting.

"I thought you might turn up," Loomis said. "See how we're handling the shooting at the Gold Rush."

"It wasn't at the Gold Rush."

"So the police blotter says—down the street. But people I talked to say the shots were coming from the gate, which certainly puts it *at* the club in my book. Hell of a thing—opening night and people have to dodge bullets just to play a little blackjack. Discouraging."

"Is that what you're going to run? Can I see it?"

Loomis smiled. "Dear heart, we're not in the crime business, we're in the Merry-Go-Round business. Crime desk handles shootings and such. Old Harry." He nodded toward another part of the newsroom. "He usually runs what the police say. Not what you'd call inquisitive. But just in case—" He stopped, seeing Daniel's face. "Relax. I took care of it. Touching how you look after the Rush's interests. One would think you own the place."

Daniel said nothing.

"But then you do. Or will. Naturally you'd want to know. How about this? A shooting in the Avenue Haig. Chinese gangs. Something really should be done about the Badlands. Says the *Tribune*. Not that anything will be. The Gold Rush doesn't come into it. Above the fray, so to speak. All right?"

"Thank you."

"Not me. Thank old Harry. If he were any kind of reporter—but he isn't. A paycheck and a bottle and don't scare the horses. Anyway, we've got an interest to protect too. At the Merry-Go-Round. Want to see the layout for tomorrow?"

"It's done? I still have some items to do."

"We can run them later in the week. The story that keeps on going. The opening's the biggest thing we've had in months. Look." He moved aside so Daniel could see the layout. "Top this."

A full page, mostly pictures. Gus Whiting and his band. The exhibition dancers. Various people arriving. A layout for a Hollywood premiere. A woman with a pet monkey on her shoulder. No gambling, just the nightclub, Shanghai at play.

"And there's you," Loomis said, pointing. A photo of Daniel speaking to two guests. "The first of many, I'm sure. And who knew it first? The Merry-Go-Round. This is what happened at the Gold Rush last night. Not some Chinese hoodlums shooting up the street."

Franz's voice. No photographs. Ever.

"Take me out. Run another picture. Just the guests."

Loomis looked at him, surprised. "Not your best side? Why so shy?"

"It's supposed to be about the guests. Nobody's interested in me."

"They will be. You're going to be a somebody in our little fish-bowl. I predict."

"Selly—"

Loomis held up his hand. "All right, all right. I was just trying to help." He pointed to Daniel's face in the picture. "That's the Gold Rush you want people to see. Hair combed. Knows how to fill out a dinner jacket. Not your uncle, wonderful man though he must be." He cocked his head. "Somebody after you? Who, I wonder. Talk about interesting. Divorce lawyer with an alimony bill? Angry husband? Who?"

"You having fun with this?"

"All right, whatever makes you happy. Too bad, though. It dresses up the page. I think." He took a second. "Or maybe you don't want people taking potshots at you. That what happened tonight? Somebody try to take Nathan out?"

Daniel stared at him. "No. There was a gang shoot-out in the Avenue Haig. It's in the *Tribune*."

Loomis nodded. "He all right?"

"Fine."

"Then that's all that matters. Nobody remembers a shoot-out. Not these days. Anyway, it's buried. Bottom of the page. I don't know about the other papers, but the *Tribune*'s the only one your customers read." He looked up. "I took care of it."

"Why did you?"

"I told you, I have an interest to protect too."

Daniel glanced down to the page layout.

"Not the column. Or not only the column. You."

"Me? You do this for all your legmen?"

"I can always get a legman. You weren't even that good. But now you're—something else. I've had friends inside before, but never at the top. So I want to protect that."

"I thought your best sources were bartenders and maître d's."

"For who's out with who, yes. But there's information only management would know. They just don't know it's valuable."

"Like what?"

"Lots of things. Gambling debts, for instance. Sometimes people get in too deep. You'd know that, running the joint. But they wouldn't want anybody else to know. Especially the Chinese—their families get upset. The banks. You have a gambling problem, you get sent home. So it's valuable to know this."

"If they can't pay me, how can they pay you?"

"I don't know, but they do. Find the money somewhere."

"Loans that ruin them."

Loomis shrugged. "I can't be responsible for what people do. You misbehave, you pay eventually. It's the way of the world."

"Not mine."

"Daniel," he said. "It's Selly. You're in it."

Daniel said nothing, the room suddenly still.

"And you're going to be good at it. And I'm going to help. We're going to make the Gold Rush the smartest club in town. Smarter than Ciro's, the Cathay Tower, any of them. You don't want to be the face of it, fine, I'll keep you out of the papers. What friends do, look out for each other."

"And what do I do for you?"

"Give me an item from time to time. You pick."

"Who I want to ruin."

"It's better when they can afford it. Then everybody makes a little something." Loomis looked over. "You're going to be a powerful man. Get used to it."

"The king of Shanghai."

"Why not? You can do anything you want here. Except leave. No visas. So you have to make it work. That's why I'm betting on you. One reason anyway."

"You could, though. Leave. Why don't you? Why do you stay?"

"I like the exchange rate. I can buy anything here. Anything. Things I can't buy back home."

Daniel looked at him. How was it done? The twisting back alleys, the money changing hands, food for another day, the boy slipping through the door, a shadow.

"Anything," Loomis said again.

"Including me."

"Dear heart, I don't want to buy you. I want to help you. Make the Rush a hit. That's what you want, isn't it?"

———

There were two men on the street at the Black Cat, two more at the private entrance to the apartment, one on the stairs, and two more inside, all of them versions of Sergei, burly, smoking Russian cigarettes. Irina was at the table with a mug of tea, wrapped in a cardigan, chilled in the warm air. She looked up, a silent question.

"He's sleeping. He'll be all right. We'll move him when we get more men in place."

"You have half the White Russian army now," she said, motioning her head to the men by the door.

"He shouldn't be moved, anyway. Not yet."

"From where? That I can't go."

"It's better here. Just in case."

"Just in case," she said, a mumble. "You're sleeping here?"

"If that's okay."

"It's your room." She looked up. "How serious?"

"Serious. He was shot at close range. But the doctor says he'll make it."

"They always say that. What are they going to say? Here, have some tea. It'll keep you warm."

"I'm not cold."

"I know. Just me. I get like this. I start to shiver and then—" She looked up. "It's not the first time. I sit here and I know something's wrong. What if he doesn't come home? Lying there somewhere in the street. Not just late, feeling up some chorus girl. Not coming, period. I have all these thoughts and I start to shiver. It's going to happen sometime. So maybe this is the time." She stopped, looking straight at him. "Is this the life you want? Because this is what it's like."

Daniel looked away, not answering. Not a real question.

"Look what I found," she said, reaching for a snapshot on the table. "In his desk. It's you, yes?"

Daniel as a boy, at the zoo with Nathan and Eli. An outing, with ice cream. Who had taken the picture? Not his mother. Eli in his tight collar, but smiling, relaxed, his hand resting on Daniel's shoulder. Nathan the way Daniel remembered him, the glint in his eye, up to something.

"At first I didn't recognize you. You've changed."

Now greeting guests in a dinner jacket. A different photo.

"Look at Nathan," Daniel said. "So young. Look at his hair."

"That's what this life does to you."

"Well, life, anyway."

"An answer for everything," Irina said, but with a small smile, indulgent.

Daniel looked at her. "He'll be all right."

"One day he won't be. Then what?"

"Get him to stop then."

She got up from her chair. "And do what? Go fishing? This is what he does. But I'm the one who sits up waiting. Who gets cold." She placed her hand on the table. "You're meeting Xi?"

"We have to stop it. Before—"

"Pay the squeeze."

"To Xi? He isn't asking. He's a partner. It's not about that."

"Huh," she said, weary. "In Shanghai? It's always about that."

———

The meeting was held at Xi's house, a security precaution masked as a mark of favor. A traditional Chinese house in the Yangtzepoo district, blank wall facing the street, but a graceful courtyard inside, with seating platforms instead of chairs, Xi on a cushion, cross-legged, like a Confucian scholar holding an audience. Tea was served first, a formality. Daniel had expected a small army of bodyguards, but there were only servants in silk slippers, their presence so quiet they seemed no more than a rustling sound. After a nod to Sergei, standing near the wall, Xi turned his full attention to Daniel.

"Your uncle is well?" A social question.

"He sends his respects," Daniel said.

Xi looked up, not expecting this. "Is he at home?"

"He will be, when I can guarantee his safety."

"There was an attempt on his life. I'm told."

"Yes."

"And you've come—?"

"To make sure it doesn't happen again."

"So you've come to see me. You think I can guarantee that. There are no guarantees in this life."

"No. But there are promises."

Xi raised his head again.

"My uncle thinks you're a man of his word. He trusts you. He told me I should do the same."

"So you don't hold me responsible for this? They were my men."

"They worked for you. But they weren't necessarily following your directions."

Xi looked at him carefully. "An important distinction. I'm pleased that you make it."

"But they were following somebody's. They weren't acting on their own."

"I agree. So I have made inquiries."

"Inquiries?"

"Yes, so now we come to it," Xi said. "What's called brass tacks. Whoever attacked your uncle also attacked me. I was in charge of security. Those men worked for me. I paid them. But someone paid them more. Who? Of course this is something I have to know. No blame must come to me in this matter. That would affect my—standing? Is this the word?"

Daniel nodded.

"So I made inquiries. The men who were there are dead. But not you. So let me ask you. Was this a robbery? A kidnapping? Or an assassination?"

"Your man in the car—"

"Ai Wing."

"Ai Wing. Shot Nathan in the chest. Shot to kill. That was the start. The rest happened because he didn't want to leave witnesses. But our guns were already out. We shot back. Which they didn't expect. They thought it would be over in seconds. There was a getaway car waiting."

"So. And then what did they think? That they could hide, when I knew who they were? That they could run away from me? Of course sometimes it's a matter of intelligence. A foolish temptation. Greed. The guards, yes, I can imagine. Money is promised. But Ai Wing knew me. No money would have persuaded him to betray me. So, something else. Someone he feared more than me. I had to know— was he working for Wu? This wouldn't be the first time we had— different interests. In this matter we were supposed to be partners. But what does this mean to Wu? Maybe he's up to his old tricks. And the men are dead, they won't tell me. So I made inquiries."

"Where?"

"Someone close to Wu." He looked over at Sergei, still against the wall. "I will need your silence about this. Of course it was impossible to return him, once I had made the inquiries. If Wu knew—it would go back and forth. A war. So he had to disappear."

Daniel let this sink in. Franz said everyone talks. You think you won't but you will. He looked at Xi's hands, soft, folded in his lap. But someone else would have done the work, asked the questions.

"And?"

"It wasn't Wu. It was unfortunate, to have to take such measures, but we had to know about Wu."

"Are we sure? Maybe he was just saying what he thought you wanted to hear."

"No. People always tell the truth in the end. They think it will save them. End the pain." His voice calm, almost bland. "It wasn't Wu."

Daniel said nothing, his ears tingling, face muscles rigid, as if he were trying to control a tic. This is who we are now. In the corner, Sergei hadn't moved, impassive.

"So it wasn't Wu. It wasn't me." Patiently solving a math problem. "It wasn't Nathan. There are no other partners. No one profits from this. So what is the logic? It wasn't about the Rush. But it must have been. Opening night. A coincidence? No. The timing means something. Imagine if it had succeeded. What that would have meant for the Rush. A fiasco. Who would want that to happen? So I made more inquiries. Ai Wing was the key. Why would he do this? Not for money. Something else. A reliable man, not a troublemaker, not a gambler. But, it turns out, a father. The one thing in life we can't control—our children. His son, Ai Kao, takes a great interest in China's future. A public interest, when that is best kept quiet. So of course he was arrested and of course he's in Jessfield Road. Do you know what happens there?"

"It's the Gestapo. They torture people."

"And who would not want to save his son from that? Would you? Would you kill someone to save your son?"

"Yes," Daniel said, not hesitating.

"So. Who does he fear more than me?"

"You're saying the Japanese did it."

"The Kempeitai, yes. A message to send on opening night. No one is exempt from the squeeze. Your negotiation was too good. It made Nathan a figure of resistance. That couldn't be allowed."

Daniel felt his stomach turn. "Yamada," he said.

"I think so, yes. The Kempeitai could not do such a thing without his knowing."

"But we have a private deal with the Slipper."

"Which the Kempeitai may not know about. His name isn't on the documents, as I recall. Maybe this wasn't even his idea. Someone else at the Kempeitai. But once the plan begins he has to go along or expose himself. Or maybe it was his idea. It might appeal to his sense of—I don't know what, cleverness."

"He was at the club opening night," Daniel said. Gloating, Leah on his arm.

"The cat watching the mice play before he pounces. Or in this case, the other cat pounces. Ai Wing."

"So what do we do now?"

"Do? Nothing. We can't go to war against the Kempeitai. China is an occupied country. People in the Settlement don't want to believe this. They think the life here will go on forever. Lords and ladies. But the Chinese know. We've been invaded before. This will pass, too, but not before we live through it. So we do nothing. We wait. Until we see our chance. You give him his take from the Slipper. As if you suspect nothing. And now you pay the squeeze. What happened to Nathan made you realize he needs more protection. So you pay, but you save the club. No exceptions. And we wait for our chance."

"He tried to kill Nathan."

"But you don't suspect him. You think it was Wu, but you can't prove it. This will please Yamada. The Japanese want us at each other's throats. Weak. Only they will have power. That's the dream. And while he dreams it, we wait for our chance. Don't worry, we'll have it. And this time nothing will go wrong."

He uncrossed his legs and stood in one fluid motion.

"Do you want *me* to talk to Yamada? About the squeeze. Or someone else?"

"Oh, you, I think. You did so well last time." Smiling, his idea of a joke. "You'll know what to say. You don't have to give all the profits away. Just enough. And then there are no exceptions. It was a lesson we should have learned from Sid Engel. The Japanese are the war lords now. They want tribute. So we give it to them. Just enough. Daniel—may I call you Daniel? You are your uncle now. Yamada must think he's talking to Nathan. It puts him at a disadvantage. Talking to a man he tried to kill. An interesting conversation, no? One thing. Who shot Ai Wing? Sergei?"

"I did."

"Ah. Then your uncle owes you his life."

"Let's say we owe each other."

Xi looked at him, slightly puzzled by this, but not wanting to open it up. "A strong bond," he said. "Don't worry. We will have our chance. It's not difficult with the Japanese. They really believe they're a superior people. So they underestimate everyone. A nice card for you to play when the time comes." He nodded, the meeting over, opening his hand to lead Daniel out.

"What will happen to the son? In Jessfield Road."

"He is no longer there. He has disappeared. It frequently happens to people who outlive their usefulness there." He sighed. "Of course I'm sorry for Ai Wing. It would have broken his heart, this news. But he's dead. And I confess to you I'm never sorry to hear that a Communist has been dealt with. They are the only ones who won't do business with us, with anybody. They are not corrupt. Or not as corrupt as the others. So they will win. When, I don't know. But think what that will mean for us. For any of us." He shook his head. "Well. Give my respects to your uncle."

———

Daniel suggested the menswear floor of the Wing On department store.

"Why here?" Yamada said. "A new suit for the Gold Rush?"

"It's somewhere we could run into each other by accident."

"You have a liking for these things," Yamada said.

"What things."

"Meetings that aren't meetings. The secret world. An instinct. Or maybe training."

Daniel ignored this. "I have something for you." He picked a jacket off the rack. "Come. Try this on. See if it fits." He took the jacket and started toward the changing rooms, a row of cubicles with louvered doors. Yamada took off his jacket.

"May I help you?" An attendant, coming up to them.

"No, I can do it. Thank you," Yamada said.

"I'll hold it," Daniel said, taking Yamada's jacket, switching it for the new one.

"As you wish," the attendant said, disapproving. "It's a little tight. I can see from here." Watching Yamada put it on.

"Yes, you're right," Yamada said, taking it off and handing it to the attendant. When he moved away to return it to the rack, Daniel slipped two envelopes into Yamada's jacket, then helped him put it back on. A matter of seconds. Yamada faced the mirror, smoothing out the cloth over the pocket, then looked up to meet Daniel's eyes.

"What is it?" he said, speaking to the mirror.

"Your weekly take from the Slipper."

"There are two envelopes."

"And the squeeze from the Rush."

Yamada went still, staring into the mirror.

"Try this one," the attendant said, holding out a jacket.

Yamada turned, a willed politeness. "I hadn't realized the time," he said, glancing at his watch. "Another day."

"It would only take a minute."

"Another day." The quick flash of a sword cutting through skin. The attendant backed away.

"And you give this to me?" Yamada said, his mouth tight. "In public?"

169

"I figured you'll know where it's supposed to go."

"I thought you said—"

"I miscalculated. We need more protection than I thought."

Yamada waited a second. "Who agreed to this?"

Daniel opened his hand. "We did. Count it yourself. I think you'll be happy."

Yamada took out the envelope and riffled through the bills. "And what do you expect for this?"

"Some Chinese who don't like each other are playing shoot-'em-up and we're getting caught in the middle. I've noticed the Chinese are allergic to the Kempeitai, so if you put a few men around the place, they'll take their guns somewhere else."

"Do you think we are bodyguards for hire? Kempeitai? Patrol the grounds. Your police force?"

"Outside the gate, then. It wouldn't take much. Just so it's clear the Rush has your protection. I don't care where the Chinese shoot each other, as long as they don't do it at the Rush. It's bad for business."

"This is your concern?"

"And people get shot. I don't want to be one of them again."

Yamada glanced up, saying nothing.

"All you'd need is a man or two out front on Avenue Haig. They'd get the message. And you'll get the word out that we're paying the squeeze. You must have informers in the gangs. Let them put it around. Which is what you want people to know anyway: everyone pays, no exceptions."

"But how is that useful to us? There is no squeeze. It's not a Japanese custom," he said, his voice bland, talking simply to a child.

Daniel looked at Yamada's breast pocket. "I forgot."

"The Chinese, I can't say. Hands out everywhere. It's a way of life with them. But it's different for us." He paused. "I might, as a personal favor, have someone check your arrangements at the club. Outside on the street, as you say. Rumors I can't control. They take on a life of their own. But the Chinese may hear them. You understand?"

"Perfectly," Daniel said, still looking at the jacket.

"That shooting in Avenue Haig. I agree it was too close to the Rush. Of course you would feel alarmed. Your uncle—" His voice controlled, smooth, the way he would have pulled the trigger, a cobra strike, not like the hesitant Ai Wing. "Luckily he survived. He was armed?"

Not an idle question, wanting to know what had happened in the car.

"No. I was."

"You? You shot the man who is dead?"

Daniel nodded.

Yamada looked at him for a minute, thinking. "Then now you would be the target. If someone wanted to avenge him."

"But I'll have protection. The Chinese won't take on the Kempeitai."

"You know it was the Chinese?"

"I was there. Maybe my uncle got in their way. Maybe they meant to do it. It's a closed world, the gangs. I may never know. I just don't want it to happen again."

"No. A closed world, as you say. You hear things. What to believe? This— How should I say it? Change of heart. About the squeeze. It's not because you think we were involved, I hope. Those are not our methods. But maybe you've heard a rumor—" Staring Daniel down, a dare.

"People say things," Daniel said, staring back, feeling suddenly they were facing each other over a chessboard, his finger on a piece, afraid that when he lifted it he'd find it dusted with poison.

"But you don't believe it."

"Whoever said it doesn't know about the Slipper, our arrangement. Nobody does. Your name's not on it." He bent his head. "Just like the squeeze. It doesn't touch you. They don't know it's in your interest to keep me alive."

Yamada said nothing for a minute, as if he were translating.

"You are a great believer in arrangements," he said finally. "Honoring them."

"When they work out for everybody, yes."

"You know the saying, politics makes strange bedfellows? Sometimes I think Shanghai makes strange bedfellows too. Well." He glanced toward the elevator bank, getting ready to go.

"You're pressed for time," Daniel said, a quick nod toward the attendant. "You go first. These will take you to the Nanking Road entrance."

"I know the store," Yamada said calmly, probably the same way he ordered a kill. "Mister Lohr, you know sometimes arrangements change."

Daniel looked up.

"It's as you say, the squeeze doesn't touch me. Don't do this again. Someone will come to collect the envelope. Shall we say on Mondays? After the weekend?"

Daniel nodded.

"I wish your uncle a quick recovery," he said easily. "And you, I hope you'll be careful. Dangerous times and I rely on you."

"We rely on each other. To keep our arrangement quiet. We wouldn't want the Kempeitai to know we have private business." The trump card, taken from the bottom of the deck.

Yamada turned, his eyes dark and peering, as if he were seeing Daniel for the first time. "No." Sachsenhausen eyes. Not his father's, vacant, already somewhere else. The guard's, implacable, beyond bargaining. "Shall I give your regards to Miss Auerbach?" Something now from the bottom of his deck.

"She's well, I hope?"

"I think she's not happy in Shanghai. The climate. She complains of the damp. But all the Europeans do, until they get used to it."

"And her mother?"

"She doesn't notice. It's all the same to her. She should be somewhere where they can take care of her. But of course Leah won't hear of it."

Just her name, the familiarity, like a paper cut.

"She seemed so lively on the boat."

"Yes. How quickly things can change."

CHAPTER 8

By the time they finally moved Nathan—late at night, by service elevator and anonymous van—the Black Cat had become a fortress, Sergei's men everywhere. Still groggy from Markowski's painkillers, Nathan smiled throughout the move, as if he were watching a comedy behind his closed eyes, but by morning he was awake and fretful, refusing medication.

"No more dope. I've seen what that stuff does."

"It's not dope, it's medicine," Irina said.

"Same difference."

"Why shouldn't you be comfortable? Here, lie back. You almost died. You could take it a little easy."

"How about some light?" he said, sitting up. "Those curtains, it's like being back in the womb."

"How would you know? You have a memory that good?"

"I remember yours," he said, trying to grin.

Irina gave him an "oh brother" look. "I see you're back to your old self again."

But he wasn't. The bad boy back-and-forth was the same, the anecdotes from his bag of stories, the sharp eye on the club, but something had gone out of him, the glint dulled. He was afraid now, generally uneasy, reluctant to leave the house. Daniel shuttled between the Slipper and the Rush, but Nathan seemed content to stay at the Cat, indifferent to what was happening at the new club, the one that kept making the papers.

"It's aged him," Irina said. "He's like an old man now."

"He's recovering, that's all. Old man."

"You don't think so? Listen to him. You know how he's always talking about California? How he wants to go back there, if he could? So now it's about the climate. How nice it is. From him? Talking about the weather."

"Maybe he should go. A trip would do him good. Get away from here until things cool down."

"He can't. You know that."

"It's a long time ago."

"They hold a grudge. They're famous for that."

Daniel looked at her, skeptical.

"Listen. If he's right, they kill him. If they don't, they don't remember, he's not important enough to remember. All these years. So which is worse, you tell me. Let him be."

"He never comes to the Rush," Daniel said.

"He doesn't want to get in the way. He sees what you're doing. He's watching. Look how fast. You're just here and now—the boss. The others accept you. It's what he wanted. So why should he interfere? He's happy here. With the music. That's what he cares about. Now it's Nancy Dong. Nancy this, Nancy that. So let him enjoy himself."

"Jealous?"

Irina waved this off, not bothering to answer.

Nathan worked with Nancy Dong in the afternoons, before the club opened. Rehearsals that were really master classes, things

Nathan had picked up over the years. Nancy was thin and slight, barely out of her teens, but the voice was throaty, a real jazz voice, not the high trembling bird voices the Chinese liked.

"What she's got," Nathan said, "is natural swing. You can't teach that, it's just there. Listen to this. Sweetheart, you ready?"

Nancy stood next to the piano on the bare stage watching Nathan play, then came in right on the beat.

"'You had plenty money, 1922. You let other women make a fool of you . . .'"

Daniel sat back. "Why Don't You Do Right?" as it might be sung in some uptown club. Did she even know what the words meant? Would the audience here know? But Nathan was right—she had swing, her voice lilting with it.

"You see?" Nathan said later, Nancy gone to change. "She's got something. She knows it too. They always do. She wants to go to the States. It's a shame she doesn't fill out a dress, no tits at all, but you can't have everything. It's something different, a Chinese girl. I told her if she wants this, get rid of the name. Be Nancy Dawn, something like that. They don't like to do it, though. You remember the Polish girl we had in Berlin? No, that was when Rabbi Eli made me off-limits. Anyway, she was good. 'Them There Eyes.' But she's got a name. Irene Shemanski. I said in America it's a joke name. Change it. So what does she change it to? Irene Schmidt. Schmidt, that's what sounded good to her." He shook his head.

"When did you change yours?"

Nathan thought for a second. "On the boat. From Manila. They put us on a tender in the Yangtze and we're almost here and I thought, Who should I be? We pass the warehouses on the Pudong side and there's a sign, S. M. Green. So what's more English than that? And I liked the sound. So I'm Nathan Green, just like that.

You could do that here then, be somebody else." He stopped. "It's been good to me, Shanghai. Now, I don't know. It's changing."

"Business is still good."

"I see the figures. I'm also noticing everybody has a bodyguard. You go somewhere, you don't know what's going to happen. You know, you see a gun pointed at you, it does something to you. You could go, like that." He snapped his fingers.

"You're safe here."

"I know, I know. But when's the next time? Even Wu's having trouble, keeping his people in line. Wu. Used to be, you'd just hear the name and it's hands-off. Now it's grab it while you can. Time's running out. So maybe Shanghai's finished."

"It doesn't feel that way."

"No. Maybe just to me. But you read the papers, you begin to wonder."

Daniel looked at him. His new preoccupation, reading the newspapers, eerily like Eli, turning the pages for hours, looking for an explanation.

"How do you win a war if you don't fight? Nobody's fighting. Not since Poland. And here? Chiang wants to fight Mao, not the Japanese. So everybody waits. The British send the wives to Hong Kong, then nothing happens and the wives come back. The Americans send them to Manila. They come back. Why not? They're safe in the Settlement. Except they're not. It's like here," he said, opening his hand to the room. "You got one of Sergei's guys downstairs, you think it's safe. But what happens if the war spreads? The Japanese walk in—it would take them about an hour—and now all the wives are enemy aliens. What protects them then, the Municipal Police? Their passports? And we're worse, we don't have passports. German passports? All expired for Jews. No papers at all. That's what I wanted to talk to you about."

Daniel looked up, surprised, not expecting the rambling to lead to anything.

"I had a friend once. He said always have a packed suitcase. And as many passports as you can get. You never know. I never forgot that. A suitcase and a passport, ready to go. I don't know how long it's going to last here. You need to get ready, just in case. So I'll talk to Wu for you."

"About what?"

"He has someone can get passports. Real ones, not forgeries. Portugal."

"Why Portugal?"

"It's neutral. You get to Macau, down the coast, it's Portuguese territory. You're safe. Take a Portuguese boat, you're still safe. It's not the States, everybody wants the States, but American passports are too hard. Some technical thing, I don't know. They're no good to me anyway, so never mind. You'll be Portuguese, like me and Irina."

"You already have yours?"

"For a while now. You have to be ready. But, what? Now you're here, I could just leave you behind? Blood? So I'll talk to Wu. My present to you."

Daniel nodded a thank-you, trying to sort this out.

"What happens to the Rush? If you had to do this?"

"You're worried about the Rush? I'm talking about saving your ass."

"You already did that."

"Listen to me. There's a war. It's coming. And you're going to survive it. Even if I don't."

"What are you talking about?"

"Don't kid a kidder. Something knocks me down these days, it's not so easy to get up. But you—I watch you. You go from one frying pan to the next. It's hot, you jump. But you land. Maybe another frying pan but you jump from that. You keep going."

"So do you. Eli gave up. You didn't."

Nathan looked at him, then looked away, letting it go.

"So. Pick up some Portuguese. It might come in handy. You know what I'd do, your age? I'd go to Brazil. They speak Portuguese there. They used to *be* Portuguese. So you'll be welcome. I'll bet it's another place you could change names, start over. Nice beaches, too."

"You hate the sun. You never go out. You like it here."

"All right. But remember what I said. Always have a suitcase packed. You never know. Even here."

———

As it happened, Wang Ching-wei, the Japanese puppet, had been called away to a meeting, so he survived the bombing in Nanking. Twelve people were killed and half the building damaged, but the shock wave of panic went even further, all the way to Tokyo. Was Chiang finally rousing himself or had it been a lunatic act? When a second bomb went off, the lone bomber theory disappeared. Planned attacks, timed for effect. In occupied China, supposedly pacified. Troops were sent, a visual reassurance. Inevitably someone talked and the Communists were blamed, a few even rounded up and shot, but the uneasiness remained, Nanking living on its nerves.

Shanghai went on as usual, too preoccupied with its own violent outbreaks to take notice of what was happening in the capital. There had always been street crime, gangs fighting gangs, but now the violence seemed more brazen, desperate, as if even the gangs knew they were living on borrowed time. The air felt heavy with it, waiting for a storm, the sky filled with lightning. Only Nathan seemed to sense this, though, with the clarity that comes from step-ping back. Everyone else was busy. Wu moved more opium than ever. The Gold Rush was beginning to live up to its name. Going to the Badlands with an armed bodyguard became ordinary, even part of its appeal, the glamour of '20s Chicago, with speakeasies and tommy guns. The social pages of the *Tribune*, thanks to Loomis, still brimmed over with club gossip but the front page was increasingly grim. A factory manager held for ransom in Pudong. A car pulled over and robbed in broad daylight. A gunfight right in front of the Sincere department store, shoppers ducking for cover. Alarming, part of the heavy prestorm air, then simply the way things were.

The more Daniel learned about Nathan's business, the more it felt like the city around him. What might have been dismay-ing became what was. Nathan led him in stages through the maze of what was accepted: lines he wouldn't cross, lines that could be stretched, lines he couldn't see. It was uncannily like Franz. Things you wouldn't do became things everybody did. What was.

"Irina handles the girls. You don't want to get involved. It's al-ways something with them. But it's steady money. Rent. We don't have anyone on the street. There's no money in it. Go down to Soochow Creek, you can get your dick sucked for a cigarette. But in the houses you can do all right. If you know what they want."

"Which is?"

"Young. Too young. I won't go near that. Kids, for chrissake. I don't do boys, either. Your pal Loomis. Think what it's like for them. But what they really like is European. The Chinese love the Russian girls, it's some kind of dream for them, and Irina knows where to get them. You know, they're stuck here, the Whites, and somebody's got to support the family. Sometimes the boyfriend gets a job—bouncer at a club, maybe, the muscle—but mostly it's Olga on her back. Or have I told you this already? Sometimes you forget. Anyway, Irina takes care of it. But the real money's going to be at the Rush now. The only thing better than gambling is opium and we can't touch that. That's all Wu. I did some work for him when I first got here and I can tell you, if anything's off, he doesn't ask for an explanation. You're gone."

Daniel enjoyed these sessions, the unexpected nuances, Nathan guiding him through the shoals of his life to where the current was. He knew, in the part of him that was still outside, that he was being drawn in deeper, was crossing his own line of what he wouldn't do, until there would be no way out. But that was three a.m. thinking. The rest of the time he was sinking into something warm, Nathan enfolding him, everything moving fast now. The first rule was to survive. So he kept jumping—Nathan had this right, at least—from one frying pan to the next, trying not to get burned, not thinking about it, just jumping, from the Cat to the Slipper to the Rush, a hundred details, days in perpetual motion.

It must have been why he missed Leah's calls. The houseboy at Kiangse Road told her to try the Slipper, but he'd already gone to the Gold Rush, so it was hours before he got the message.

"I thought you weren't going to call back," she said.

"What is it? Something wrong?"

"My mother died."

"Oh," he said. "I'm sorry." Genuinely surprised.

"I thought you should know."

"Will there be a funeral?"

"I don't know. It depends." A short pause, switching voices. "Do you know what I was thinking? How much she liked—you know, that bar where we ran into you? With the girl singer?"

Daniel said nothing, puzzling this out. The Horse and Hounds. Her mother had never been there. Something off. Code. "Oh, yes," he said finally.

"I thought, the next time you go there, raise a glass to her, yes? She'd like that."

Telling him to go. He imagined her twisting the cord, playing innocent with the phone, as if her listener could see her too.

"All right, I will. I'm sorry about—"

"Yes. The drink. It's superstitious, I know. But she would like it so much."

"As soon as I can. Thank you for letting me know."

"She always liked you. She said you were a good dancer."

"What happened? Was she sick?"

"An accident. I'll tell you about it when I see you." The bright voice again, more code.

"Okay. I'll let you go. This must be difficult for you. I'll talk to you soon."

He called down for the car. Sergei insisted he have someone with him all the time now and it was easier to use one of the drivers than argue. When they got to the Cathay, he would fade into the background, there but not seen.

Leah was sitting at a corner table, smoking.

"So you understood what I meant."

"Let's hope they didn't. Who's 'they,' by the way?"

"He has the phone tapped. You hear a click sometimes. That's what they do, isn't it? I don't think he has me followed. Not that I would know. Ming, the houseboy, probably reports. So far that's been enough. I'm a very good girl."

"If anybody did follow, we both just had the same idea."

"Pure coincidence," she said wryly. "I wasn't sure you'd come."

Daniel shrugged an "of course."

"I've been feeling so sad all day. I can't talk to Ming. Your name came up in the lottery."

"That isn't going to help," he said, pointing to the drink.

"No. But what is? Time? Time heals all wounds. I wonder."

"Where's the colonel?"

"Tokyo. Being promoted or something. Don't worry, he won't show up."

"I'm not worried."

"No? I do." She rimmed the glass with her finger but didn't pick it up. "You know she used to serve him tea? When he came. Tea cakes, china, cloth napkins, all of it. She'd ask questions. Polite. The weather. Like Am Modenapark. Someone expected for tea. Then he'd take me into the other room. And she'd pretend she didn't see that." Leah looked away. "At least we won't have to go through that anymore."

"Tell me what happened. You said an accident?"

Leah took a breath. "You know she wanders? I try to have someone with her all the time but sometimes Ming— Anyway, she thinks we're back in Hongkew and she goes looking for Chusan Road. You know, Little Vienna, with all the shops. But really she's on Avenue Foch and then on the block with all the Russians, so the signs are in Cyrillic and she gets confused—no idea where she is, even the alphabet is foreign. It must have been terrible for her. I used to tell her, if you get lost, wait in a shop until someone comes—at least she's off the street. But this time— I don't know what she was seeing, what she was walking to. Some mirage. People said she walked into the street without even looking. And the truck couldn't stop in time."

"A truck?"

"One of those delivery vans they have here. We don't know who because he didn't stop. Hit her and kept going—what kind of person doesn't stop? And later, when I went there, I was so crazy I thought, what if he arranged it? He was always saying I should put her away somewhere. What if it's not an accident?"

"Yamada? You really think—"

"No, it was the craziness. She wasn't important enough for him to take the trouble. She served him tea. It was just—" She put a finger to her temple. "Craziness. But imagine even thinking that. Thinking he could do it. What does it tell you?"

"What?"

"That he could. Not this time. Some other time. That he's capable of doing that."

"Has he ever threatened you? Ever—"

"No, no. It's not about that. It's just—that I could think it." She put out her cigarette. "It was an accident. He was in Tokyo. It was just—how crazy I was." She looked down, her eyes filling. "I wish you had known her. Not the way she was at the end. Before. So elegant. Gloves, always. Well, of course, my father made them. But always dressed. A lady."

"She was still that. Even at the end."

Leah nodded. "She said it was a matter of character." A quick smile. "And posture. Posture was important." She looked away, not facing him. "She was certainly right about me. My character. Imagine what went through her head, when I went into the other room. My god." Real tears now, a small dam finally breaking.

"Shh," he said, using a finger to wipe her cheek. "Don't."

"How else could she think? She never understood it. Herr Blauner. What the Nazis were like. She never understood why we came here, why we couldn't have our things. What you have to do sometimes. It was easier for her that way." She took out a handkerchief, drying her face, calmer. "But maybe she did understand. Maybe she knew what she was doing. When she saw the truck." Her eyes looking away, across the room, as if she were watching it happen.

"Don't think that."

She turned back, his voice like a tap on her shoulder. "No? You're right. If I think that—then it's all I'd think about, another thing to blame myself for."

"You don't have anything—"

"Yes. My character. Think how disappointing it must have been for her. Every time I went into the other room."

The bar, dim and quiet, now began to buzz as the musicians took their seats for the next set.

"Let's go. Get some air."

"I should fix my face."

"It's fine just the way it is."

"Thank you—for this. Not very pleasant for you. Listening to this."

"You called. Did you think I wouldn't come?"

"No. I thought you would. That's something else I thought about today. Something like this happens and the first thing I do is call you. Not even thinking about it. The first thing I do. So what does that mean?"

They went out the Nanking Road entrance and turned left to the Bund, the air moist, making halos around the streetlamps.

"It's going to rain," she said. "It's always going to rain here. You can tell because your hair frizzes up. Is that car following us? See how slow—"

"It's my driver. Somebody usually goes with me now."

"A guard? Like a gangster? The colonel said you were a gangster, so he's right?"

"You talk about me?"

"No, but he's—I don't know, interested in you."

"Does he know? About us."

"No. Well, how would I know? I used to think, you sleep with a man, you know him. But I don't know him."

"But you know me."

She turned to him, about to speak, when the rain started, not drops but sheets of it, the heavy air like a balloon someone had just punctured. They darted into the nearest doorway, a bank with an arched overhang between columns. The Bund, always busy, now exploded with activity, rickshaws and carts like birds startled into flight, people huddled under roofs on the loading piers, the smell of mud, always there, the air saturated with it.

"The car's over there."

"Give it a few minutes," she said. "It never lasts very long. Anyway, I'm glad. It'll make the river go faster."

"What?"

"I put my mother there. The ashes. I sent her back home. She hated it here. I couldn't leave her here. Forever. So."

"I thought you said there was a funeral."

"That was for the phone. So they wouldn't know what I was doing. Who would come? Frau Mitzel?"

Daniel glanced at the other people taking shelter in the doorway. Chinese waiting it out, watching the rain, Daniel and Leah just part of the noise around them, people talking.

"You just—put them in the river?"

"I got Ming to help. At first I thought Soochow Creek, you know, by Garden Bridge. The public garden is right on the river, easy. But the water is so filthy there. I thought, she'll just sink into the sludge and never leave Shanghai. I needed to get her out to sea. So Ming hired a boat to take us on the river, where the current is, and we scattered the ashes there. She'll float to the Yangtze and after that, who knows? Wherever the ocean carries her. Maybe back to Europe. But not here. Look, it's getting worse." A sudden gust sprayed the street, people moving closer to the bank doors.

"Here, put this around you," Daniel said, draping his jacket over her shoulders.

"I thought it would feel funny. You know, putting your mother into the river like that. But it wasn't her, just a box of ashes. It's just the thought of it, floating home." She pulled the jacket tighter. "So now it's just me. I used to think it was all for her, everything I did. To take care of her. That's what I told myself anyway. And now who do I do it for?"

"Leave him."

She shook her head. "Not yet. I can't. I don't have enough."

"I have money. You won't have to sell your clothes."

She smiled. "Oh, that. How long ago was that." She looked up. "What money? Gangster money?"

"You can wash it if it's not clean enough."

"I can't. Maybe I'm a little bit of a coward about him. You don't know what he's like. If we did that, he'd– I don't know. It's not that he wants me so much. He just wants to prove he can have me. But that's now. He'll get tired of me and then it's his decision, he cuts me loose. Nobody gets hurt."

"Do you really believe that?"

"I don't know. I don't have a lot of choices. Let him get tired of me."

"He won't."

Another spray from the street, pushing people tighter against the doors, Daniel's face now almost touching hers, her breath warm.

"Leah–"

She pulled back. "My mother's dead and I'm doing this? What kind of person does that? It's what she said, I'd go with anybody."

"I'm not anybody."

She looked up at him, her eyes darting, lost for a minute.

"I know," she said, her voice resigned. "I know that. I called you. Who else would I call?"

———

Markowski came to check on Nathan, a late visit arranged by Sergei.

"I'm still not a hundred percent," Nathan said.

"At your age no one's a hundred percent. It takes longer to heal. Be patient. You're doing fine."

"I'm all right?"

"If you take care of yourself. Lay off the tap dancing."

"A comedian. They must love you at the heim."

Later, alone with Daniel, Markowski was more concerned.

"I thought he'd be further along. Has he been complaining? Chest pains?"

"No. But he doesn't. Irina says it's aged him."

"Well, that happens. Just keep an eye on him. I'll send somebody next week to look."

"Not you?"

"I'm going to disappear for a while. They're rounding up Communists. I don't want to get caught in that net."

"Who's rounding them up?"

"Officially, the Nanking government, but if Selden Loomis supports it, you know it has to be coming from Tokyo. Don't you read your own newspaper? They're blaming the Communists for the bombings. Which for all I know maybe they did, but I doubt it. It's not the way they usually work here."

"I don't want to hear this."

"That's right. You're retired. But the rest of us have to lie low for a while."

"From the police?"

189

"No, the Municipal Council doesn't take orders from Tokyo. Yet. But the Kempeitai do. It's their kind of operation, picking people off. No more slaughter of the lambs, like in the bad old days, when Chiang took out thousands. There aren't enough of us left for that kind of attack now anyway. So the smart thing to do is target us one by one and say somebody else did it. The gangs, usually. Then Loomis writes it up and people say crime is out of control. Politics doesn't come into it. Except here it always does. The Japanese don't want the Chinese to unite against them. And so far Chiang's making it easy for them—he'd rather fight Mao—but they don't want the Communists throwing bombs either. They can barely control the territory they occupy. So a few targeted assassinations can send the right message. And it's the business the Kempeitai are in—either hire somebody or do it yourself. Just work down the list."

"And you're on it?"

"I don't know. But I can't get any of the heime involved. Technically, they'd be sheltering me, so I can't be there. I have to go away for a while, at least until this pogrom burns itself out."

"Where?"

"Hong Kong would be safe, but no Jews allowed without papers. Like everywhere else. So I'm stuck here. Find a sewer somewhere and be a sewer rat."

"I thought you had places all over. When Nathan—"

"Just one. And that's off-limits. I can't put her in that position. Don't worry, I'm not asking you, either."

"I owe you a favor."

"And I'll collect on it. Someday. This isn't big enough."

"They have a list? You know that? If someone had access—"

"It's an expression." He looked over at Daniel. "Franz had a list. That's what we were training for. It didn't have to be written down."

"We weren't assassins."

"What word would you use? We were being trained to kill people. Don't tell yourself fairy tales about what we were doing. We were going to kill people."

"Nazis."

Markowski looked at him, surprised. "That's right. Nazis. We were going to kill them, go down a list."

"It wasn't like that."

"I always wondered, maybe that's why you stopped."

"I stopped because everyone else disappeared."

"You didn't try to find them. You . . . left."

"So did you."

Markowski nodded. "I thought about it, too, what we were doing. What that would do to us. I used to think, how do we kill them without becoming them?"

Daniel was silent for a minute. Eli's question, over and over. "And what answer did you come up with?"

"No answer. There isn't one. But that doesn't mean you stop." He glanced up. "Me, anyway."

"This isn't Germany."

"No. As far away as you can get. And I'm still playing duck and cover. So maybe you're right—to leave."

"But you don't think so."

"What does it matter what I think? Anyway, do we ever get out? You pick a side, it stays with you. Well, I'd better go. I'll send someone next week to have a look at him."

"How do I get in touch with you? If he needs—"

"You don't. I've left the hospital. One of the comrades knows a place in Chapei, so I'm going native. No phone, nothing. No Kempeitai, either, let's hope."

"Wait," Daniel said, holding up his hand, thinking. "Do they have photographs? The Kempeitai."

"No pictures. Franz's rule."

"So they won't know you by sight? Someone would have to identify you?"

"Turn me in? Yes."

"The hospital, the heim," Daniel said. "Who else knows you?"

"The group, but they wouldn't—"

"The hospital was quiet about Nathan. And all the heime—they stick to themselves. The last thing they'd do is go to the police. Any police."

"Yes, but you have to assume the worst."

"I remember. But the odds are—" He stopped, turning to Markowski. "Do you play blackjack?"

"What?"

"If you can count to twenty-one you can play. Practice sliding the cards out of the shoe and you'll look like a professional. We're the same size—my black tie should fit. No one would think to look. A blackjack dealer in a casino. No customers from the heime. No one's going to recognize you."

"Where?"

"At the Gold Rush. Which happens to be under the protection of the Kempeitai—something you don't know and don't repeat. There are some staff rooms over the garage. Not the Cathay, but you'd be tucked away out of sight. With the Kempeitai keeping you safe. The only one who'll recognize you is Sergei and you're a god to him since you helped Nathan. No politics with him, by the way. He's a White, he'd slit your throat if he knew. No politics with anybody. No meetings, nothing like that. I don't suspect anything. I just thought you were someone from a heim. Whoever heard of a Red croupier?"

Markowski looked at him, a thin smile. "Welcome back."

Daniel shook his head. "This is for you. Not the Comintern

or whatever they're calling themselves these days. I'm out of all that."

"Not if you're hiding me. Look, there's someone—just see him, hear him out."

Daniel held up his hand. "No politics. I mean it. You want the room or not? That's the deal."

"And what are you getting?"

"Me? A doctor in the house. You won't have to send somebody. You'll be here."

CHAPTER 9

Nathan went back to the Gold Rush a few days later.

"I have to show my face, see everything's okay. People think you're weak, they take advantage. Anyway, I want to hear Gus. We're paying him enough. You know he used to play with Teddy Wilson, I tell you that?"

The sky had threatened rain earlier but it cleared by evening, one of those days when everything goes right, even the weather. It was opening night again, without the flashbulbs, a long line of cars pulling around the circular driveway, women in gowns being helped out of the back seats. Inside, the rooms gleamed with fresh polish, as if the maids had just finished, the hum of conversation bouncing off the shiny surfaces, and underneath the click of roulette wheels and playing chips being raked and glasses tinkling with ice. In the nightclub, Gus Whiting was already on, a few new players added to the original five for a bigger crowd. Nathan looked around, taking it all in, smiling. At the Cat, he was always looking for the tiniest flaw to correct, the spill that needed wiping up, but here he just gave in to the spectacle of it all, the details somebody else's problem. He put his hand on Daniel's shoulder.

"I told you, you could do it."

"It mostly does it by itself."

"Like hell." A smile, beaming. Then he was swallowed up by well-wishers, part morbid curiosity, part homage for old times' sake.

Daniel made one of his walk-throughs, club to gaming rooms to private floor, Sergei's men positioned where they should be, caryatids holding up the walls, bulges in their pockets. Markowski working the blackjack shoe, hair slicked back, someone else. Waiters balancing trays. Coins dropping into slots, the sound of money.

The Cincinnati Five were on their break when Xi arrived, so the noise in the driveway sounded like a small army, the lead car flanked with guards on the running boards, a politician's car in a parade.

"Did you know about this?" Daniel asked Nathan.

"The element of surprise," Nathan said blandly. "He's careful, Xi."

He went down the stairs to greet him. Guards in the other cars got out, slamming doors, and fanned out over the grounds. Even for the Badlands it was a showy entrance, almost a paramilitary exercise, and people near the door turned to watch. Who? A Chinese businessman in a suit with a carnation in his lapel. They turned back.

"My old friend," Xi said, a formal bow. "You're looking well."

"You mean I'm not dead."

Xi smiled. "Fortunately. I'm sorry to bring so many with me," he said, turning to indicate his men. "But this part of town now. Shall we go inside?"

"Would you like to see the place?"

"Later, perhaps. A private interview? In the office?" Xi stopped and pulled his head back to take in the building. "You've come up in the world. Ah, Mister Lohr," he said, seeing Daniel. "The peacemaker."

"I hope so. Any trouble?"

"Brush fires only. Meanwhile, my friend Green is here, looking well. Shall we go in?" He opened his hand in a follow-me signal, as if he were the host.

"Did you know anything about this?" Daniel said to Sergei. "Make sure his men are okay. Comp them a drink if they want."

"They're not going to drink on duty."

"Is that what they are, on duty?"

"It's a very big gesture, his coming here. It shows how safe the Rush is."

"If you bring your own protection," Daniel said, looking at the cars. "And don't tell the reception committee you're coming. Christ, and now look. Loomis. Do you think he followed them here?"

"The scent maybe. His big nose," Sergei said, pleased with his joke.

Loomis was handing over the car keys to the attendant.

"Well, well, well. Quite a powwow. And not a word from you. One would think you were disloyal," he said to Daniel.

"It's a surprise visit."

"What one wouldn't give to hear what they're saying."

"Well, we won't, so don't work yourself up. Looks to me like a get well visit and congratulations on the club."

"Xi doesn't congratulate. Hmm. A peace conference?"

"Nobody's at war."

"In the Badlands. Well, you're probably right—nobody's going to tell us anything. But Xi and Nathan together? Just think if somebody threw a bomb now. You'd solve the crime problem out here in one bang."

"That's not funny."

"All right, all right. Where's the phone? I need to get Jerry out here with a camera."

"No pictures."

"Says who?"

"Me. I'm the manager."

"Oh, really—"

"I mean it, Selly. You put a camera on them and you don't come to the Rush again. No newspapers."

"Well, that speaks volumes for your story sense. Xi and Nathan meet and you don't think that's news?"

"I don't care. It's private."

"The *Tribune* would pay. I'd pay."

"You didn't say that. And I didn't hear it. That's how we're going to stay friends."

"Well, listen to you all of the sudden."

Daniel said nothing for a minute, a standoff, then looked away. "Go have a drink at the bar. On the house."

"And here they come. Well, that was short. Sweet? Hard to tell."

Xi and Nathan waited at the front of the steps for the car to be brought around.

"Mister Xi, Selden Loomis. The *Tribune*."

Xi half turned, a look of contempt. "I've seen your name."

"Well, thank you."

"No compliment was intended. A guest of China who seeks favor with the Japanese." He spat on the ground.

Loomis reeled back, not expecting this, then kept going. "Well, you have to go where the news is. I didn't realize you were a patriot. That wouldn't be the usual description."

Xi stared at him. Nathan took a step forward to intervene, but Xi held up his hand.

"What do you want?"

"What do I always want? News. I'm a newsman."

"That wouldn't be the usual description."

Loomis almost smiled at this, pleased. What he wanted, Xi engaged.

"What do you think of the Rush, for instance. Not a very long visit."

Xi didn't reply.

"I mean, would you say it brings a new level of– What? Elegance? To the Badlands?"

"I might say that. But I wouldn't say it to you. And if you say I did, I'll have your fingers broken. The ones you type with. One at a time." His voice even, stone-faced. "Ah, the car. Good night, Nathan. Very impressive," he said, glancing back at the club. "Shame about the pests." His eyes back on Loomis.

No one said anything, watching him get in, door held open by one of his guards. He looked back to Loomis. "One at a time," he said, then gave the signal for the driver to start.

"Putz," Nathan said to Loomis. "You ought to be careful with that mouth of yours."

"Or?"

Nathan just looked at him, then turned, dismissive, and walked away.

"Well. Quite a crowd you're running with these days."

"Selly, you gave me a job when I needed one, so I owe you. But you can't talk to him like that. Not here. They're in business together."

"So kiss the ring. And that's who we kowtow to now? In the New China."

"The old one, too, as far as I can tell. And I don't want to hear about either of them. The Rush makes money, and politics stays at the *Tribune*. Now do you want that drink or not?"

"Never say no to anything on the house. First rule of

journalism." His voice lighter, then serious again. "You think we're out of the world here. Island Shanghai. But we're not. There's a broom coming and it's going to clean the place out, all the Xis. You don't want to be with him when that happens."

"I'm not with him now. I'm not with anybody."

"But you will be. You'll have to be. People will insist."

Daniel looked at him. "In the new order."

Loomis heard the sarcasm and smiled. "If you like. Not the German model. The Japanese are too subtle for that. But the point is, there will be order. Not—this mess."

"You think you'll like that better?"

"Oh, I know. Not madly me, is it, all the spit and polish? The samurais. But they're winning. That's what matters."

"In Nanking they used people for bayonet practice. Buried them alive."

For a minute Loomis said nothing. "I believe there were excesses on both sides."

"Christ, Selly."

"Well, I won't quarrel. Not when there's a drink waiting. Oh, look. Island Shanghai in all its glory," he said, nodding to the Packard sweeping around the driveway. "The carriage trade in the Badlands. Who would have thought? I told you we'd put the place on the map. Florence, what a wonderful surprise." He took her hand as she got out of the car.

"Selly, I should be cross with you. You said you'd write up the Chamber Music Society and not a word."

"Florence. Not the sort of music our readers—"

"Well, you can make it up to me. We're launching a new literary review, half Chinese, half English, and you're going to mention it."

He put a hand on his chest. "At your service."

"I think you know everyone here." She introduced the rest of the car. "And before you ask, Albert's in Nanking and he asked Eddie to be my escort. We're all happy as clams."

"I'm glad to hear it."

"I'll bet," Florence said, enjoying this. "Daniel, how nice to see you again. It seems ages. And look at all this. Well, who's for roulette?"

Nathan had come up to them, looking slightly puzzled, Florence's face like something in a sickroom dream. He took her hand and kissed it, a courtier. "Dear lady," he said, "welcome." Polite, not suggesting anything more.

"Well, I must say, there's nothing like Old World manners. Gets me every time. Vienna?" Nathan someone she didn't know.

"Berlin," Nathan said.

"Ah. Alas, not now. The manners, I mean. Selly, are you playing roulette or just snooping?"

"Snooping," he said, smiling.

"Well, not over my shoulder. You'll bring me bad luck. Come on, gang," she said, a ringleader in a satin evening dress. "Let's win some money."

Nathan said nothing until they had all gone. "It was her apartment. Why?"

"She's a friend. I needed to hide you somewhere."

"What kind of friend?"

"Nothing like that. We met on the boat. She had the room, that's all."

"For a dying man."

"You weren't dying."

"I might have been." He looked up at Daniel, about to say more, than let it go. "She knows Loomis."

"Everybody does. He's a gossip columnist, that's his business."

"Insulting Xi."

"Not anymore. I talked to him. Don't worry." He paused. "He's done a lot for the Rush. Publicity. We can't just throw him out. Not when we're doing business like this."

"Money isn't everything."

A line so unexpected that the surprise must have registered in Daniel's face.

"All right, all right," Nathan said, an end to it.

"What did Xi want?" Daniel said, shifting.

"You don't want to know."

Another surprised look.

"Sometimes something needs to be done. Xi, he doesn't like surprises. For anybody. So he tells you what to expect. No surprise."

Daniel saw them at the desk in the office, coolly nodding their heads, okaying a hit. Just like that.

"I should know too. There's no such thing as being halfway in," he said quietly.

Nathan nodded. "But not yet. This isn't what I want for you."

"Everything that comes with it, you mean."

"That's right. What comes with it. I don't know. It's something to think about. It gives me a headache, thinking about all this."

"You want to go home? I can get the car—"

"No, I'll go listen to Gus for a while. You notice the sound here isn't as good as the Cat? A room this size, you're always going to have that kind of trouble." He turned to Daniel. "We'll talk. The place is going great. This is what I want for you. Not the other business. You know, you're young, you don't think about things. Nothing's going to happen to you. Now I'm worried about everything. Afraid of my own shadow. You see the gun pointed at you, it's there all the time. That's not what you want."

———

Daniel caught up with Florence as she came out of the ladies' room.

"Is this a good idea?" he said. "I thought—"

"Couldn't be helped. A little blackjack and I'm gone. There was no other way to get a message to him."

"You're not even supposed to know he's here. But you do." A question.

"It's safe. I've been careful."

"Nathan recognized you."

She shrugged. "He's better?"

Daniel nodded. "Did I ever thank you properly?"

She brushed this aside. "Karl asks, you don't question it. That's how it works. He has great hopes for you."

"He's going to be disappointed."

"He says you're a natural."

"Natural what?"

She avoided this. "Anyway, it was quite a thing, hiding a gangster. I had no idea until Karl told me. Something new every day. And now you. The last thing I would have imagined—running a casino. What a funny world it's getting to be." She looked over at him. "You heard about Clara Auerbach? A terrible business. Who walks into traffic like that? When I think how she was on the boat. Well, I'd better go play some blackjack so I can get out of your hair. I can see I make you nervous."

"Nervous for you, that's all."

She put her hand on his arm. "Well, don't be. I'm careful."

"Can I ask you something? Why are you doing this?"

"Given my position in society?" she said, an ironic fluty voice.

"For a start."

"Things won't change until we change them. Chou En-lai said

that once. I never forgot it." She looked at him. "It's not much, you know. Lend out a room and carry a few messages. But it's something. Where's the blackjack?"

"Upstairs."

"Give me five minutes and then I'll round up my posse and head on out," she said, an American drawl.

Daniel watched her go up the double staircase, slowed by the tight skirt. A woman with a secret life. But whose wasn't? He thought of Nathan, suddenly afraid of shadows, behind the office door with Xi. No surprises. Nodding his head. Something to take care of. It might have been anything, an increase in squeeze, a favor. But it wasn't. Not what I want for you.

"There she is," Loomis said. "I've been looking all over. Those stairs. It's one thing coming down. Show off your dress. But up? Must be the old pioneer stock. Or a mountain goat somewhere."

"Was it really? Pioneer stock?" Daniel said, suddenly anxious to keep Loomis there, give Florence time. Just a message.

"Must have been. She's from the West somewhere. They were all pioneers there, weren't they?"

"I didn't know."

"Oh, they sent her east and polished her up. But you can still hear it sometimes, the wide open spaces. Me, I'm an elevator man. Let's see who gets there first," he said, turning toward the elevator door.

"How about letting her lose a little money first? For the good of the Rush. Come on, I'll buy you a drink." Away from Karl.

"Another one? You'll put yourself out of business." But moving away with Daniel, Florence already half-forgotten.

By the time Daniel got upstairs, Florence had moved on from Markowski's blackjack table to the roulette wheel, flanked again by the party from the car, a small pile of chips in front of her, evidently having a good night. He caught Markowski's eye, a silent exchange, Markowski looking apologetic, then slipping back into character, dealing cards. Message presumably delivered, but at what risk? What if Florence were being followed? Leading someone right into the Gold Rush, to Karl's table.

Daniel circled the room, meeting Markowski's eye again. This time, a small shrug. What could I do? Then Florence, looking at Daniel over the wheel, a quick nod. Everything okay. The click of the white ball rimming the wheel, finding its slot. He looked around. The room was busy without being crowded, people focused on the tables, nobody passing messages. Where did they usually meet? In Berlin, never the same place twice, the rules. And still caught.

The shot was a sharp crack, the second so fast it sounded like a ricochet. A half second of stopped time, then screams, the sound of people running, Florence pitching forward, face onto the table, then her body sliding down to the floor, crumpling. Everyone moving at once, the gun shooting again, this time into the ceiling, the blur of the gunman racing to the fire stairs, heading down to the back of the club, Sergei's men, startled, now coming off their spots against the wall, not sure who to chase, women still screaming, some ducking under the tables, some racing for the stairs. Another shot, one of the guards, firing after the gunman, doors slamming. Markowski ran over from the blackjack table and knelt down next to Florence, leaning over her, feeling for a pulse in her throat.

"Call an ambulance. Quick." Authoritative, a doctor's voice, so that Daniel glanced over, alarmed. But what did the cover matter now? "She's still alive."

Daniel knelt down, joining him. Somewhere the bang of a door, more shots, but here there was only a body, eyes wide with terror. People were still heading for the stairs, fleeing the building.

"Can you hear me?" Markowski said.

Florence managed a faint nod. "I can't feel my legs."

"An ambulance is coming."

"You're all right?" she said.

"Yes."

"So just me. They don't know. About you."

"Don't try to talk."

"No. Careful." She started to smile. "They said it wouldn't be dangerous. You'd better get away, before they–" She looked up at him. "They'll see you're a doctor."

"Shh. It doesn't matter. Can you hold my hand?" he said, taking hers.

"I can't feel anything. My back."

A siren now, pushing through the crowd out front.

She looked at Daniel. "Sorry. I thought it was safe."

"We'll get you to the hospital," he said, what people said, an echo of that night with Nathan.

"Oh god, what will Albert say? Imagine how surprised he'll be."

Her escort, who'd been at the next table, now joined them, kneeling next to her. "Honeybunch, you're going to be fine. I can hear the ambulance."

But she was looking at Daniel. "Things won't change until we change them."

"That's right," he said, a murmur, like patting a child.

"Oh–" she said, as if she suddenly remembered something, then gasped in surprise, a sharp intake of breath, her eyes still.

Daniel took her other hand, grasping it, as if he were pulling her back, out of the water, but there was no response. He looked at her face, eyes open but not moving. Someone who saw a thousand years in a bowl.

"She's gone," he said to the escort.

"Oh my god."

"Call the police." Giving him something to do, out of the way. He turned to Markowski. "Make yourself scarce," he said quietly.

Markowski hesitated.

"You're not a doctor."

Markowski nodded, then slid away, missing Loomis by a minute.

"Jesus Christ, they shot Florence? Who would shoot Florence?"

"Nobody. It was an accident. They were shooting someone else."

"Who?"

Daniel shrugged. "Chinese. They get the guy?"

Loomis knelt down. "I don't know. There was shooting out back. Jesus, Florence. It's like she's looking at us."

Daniel reached over and closed her eyes, Loomis moving back, squeamish.

"How do you want me to play this? I can't not cover it. I mean, Florence Burke."

"Cover it the way it was. A gang fight, and she got caught in the middle. No one else hurt." Daniel looked up. "A freak accident."

"How do you know?"

"I was here."

"I mean, who would want to shoot Florence?"

"No one." The cover good to the end. Her death just an accident. He stared down at her face, utterly still, and an anger swept through him, his cheeks hot with it, the way he used to feel in the beginning, before the fear took over. It wasn't much—offer a room, take a message—but it was something. What Daniel used to think. Who does nothing? And for a moment, the last few months, the group rounded up, the boat, Nathan's world, all of it seemed to have happened to somebody else, not him. The anger, kneeling over this dead frivolous woman, was who he was. Things won't change until we change them.

"This isn't going to make the Rush look good."

"Things happen. Especially out here."

"Be another story if, say, Albert had done it. Jealous husband. You know."

Daniel looked at him, trying to stop the distaste from reaching his face. This is who we are now. But it wasn't. Don't let him see.

"It was an accident, Selly," he said, his voice steady. "No one else was hurt. Will you stay until the ambulance gets here? I'd better go calm things down."

Daniel looked down again. As the skin drained, gray now, you could see the thin film of makeup, no longer cosmetic, paint on a corpse. People had stopped running, the panic replaced with an eerie stillness. All the gaming tables had stopped.

"Let them through, please." Nathan, in charge, clearing a path for the ambulance attendants with the stretcher. He glanced at Daniel. "You see who did it?"

Daniel shook his head.

"The police will want a description."

"He got away? How did he get past Yamada's men?" Daniel said, lowering his voice.

"They were in front. Avenue Haig."

"Jesus Christ. He got *away*? With all the men we—"

"He knew the layout."

Daniel looked at him. "So do a lot of people. What do we do now? Close down for the night?"

Nathan made a calming gesture with his hand. "Give it a few

minutes." The attendants were moving Florence onto a stretcher, her face now covered with a sheet. "This table's a crime scene, but the others are all right. After they take her."

"You think people want to play? After this?"

"Give it a few minutes. I'll walk around, show them we're back to normal."

"Somebody has to call Albert." A voice from behind, sounding vague. The escort.

"I'll call," said Loomis. "Nanking, yes? Where is he staying?" Almost eager, wanting the first response.

"No, I'll do it," the escort said. "He'll want to hear it from me. God, what do you say? One minute she's—"

"The police," Loomis said, recognizing a man in a suit followed by some uniforms. "That was quick."

"They patrol the Badlands now," Daniel said.

"And look how effective," Loomis said. "George, how are you?"

"I've had better nights," the cop said, an East London accent. "I'll want to talk to your people," he said to Nathan. "Anybody near her when it happened."

"I'll clear out a room down the hall. We don't want to scare the customers."

"Right in the back," the cop said. "Sounds like he didn't want to miss. Shoot a woman in the back—"

"There's a theory she just got in the way," Loomis said. "He was trying to get someone else."

"Whose theory?"

Loomis shrugged.

"Shoot somebody in the back, you have to believe he meant to do it. Well, let's find out. You have that room you mentioned? Let's start with who was at the tables with her."

209

"Daniel, you want to get Charlie?" Nathan said. "The croupier," he said to the cop. "He'll know who the others were."

"She a regular?"

"No, first time," Nathan said, his eyes following the stretcher out. "A hell of a thing. First time and—"

"Any objection if we start the other tables back up?" Daniel said. Keep Markowski busy, out of it.

"And her not even cold," the cop said.

"People will leave."

"And we don't want that to happen."

Daniel ignored this. He nodded toward the customers, standing around, not sure what to do. "They didn't shoot her."

The cop was quiet for a second, staring at Daniel. "You people," he said finally.

Daniel looked up, for a second back in Germany, another rush of heat to his cheeks. Don't respond. "You can use one of these," he said, leading the way to the back rooms. Past the service stairs, where the gunman had gone. To the back where Yamada's men were. Except they weren't, not tonight. "Can I get you anything?"

The cop didn't answer, turning instead to one of the uniforms. "Bring them one at a time. Check anybody who tries to leave. And talk to the men outside. Chances are nobody got a good look. If they were that close, they would have shot him. But you never know."

"He was Chinese," Daniel said. "We know that much."

"Well, that'll make it easy, won't it?"

Daniel drifted back to the tables. A few people had begun to play again. No music yet, just the click of the roulette ball and the soft slap of cards. He looked at the stairs where they'd carried out the stretcher. The escort would be on the phone now telling her husband—what? Your wife's been in an accident. Not the truth.

Which he probably wouldn't believe anyway. A banker. What was his name? Albert. Maybe standing at the phone, stunned, unable to take this in, his life changed in a second. And he'd never know why. But the others would, the group. How many? Who was the next name on the list? Or did it end with her?

He went over to the blackjack table.

"It's quiet," Markowski said. "Should I stay?"

"As long as you're here, nobody sees you. It's where you're supposed to be."

"I mean after. Do you want me to leave the club?"

Daniel shook his head. "I want you to see your friend. Tell him I'll meet with him."

CHAPTER 10

The Ohel Moshe Synagogue on Ward Road was too small for the expected crowd so Florence's memorial service was held in a theater, closed for the afternoon, on Avenue Joffre. For a while it was thought that Albert, a Christian, would want a church, but he seemed indifferent to the plans, too shaken to do more than nod a vague agreement to anything Florence's friends proposed. Now he sat in the front row looking lost, waiting for Florence to tell him what to do. Daniel had imagined a fleshy man in a somber banker's suit, someone you'd see at the Long Bar in the Shanghai Club, but he was natty, pocket handkerchief in peaks, lively eyes in an otherwise dull face. Had he found her amusing? Exasperating? What had brought them together? The mystery of people.

To Daniel's surprise, Nathan had insisted on coming.

"You'll just be reminding people that it happened at the Rush."

"Somebody does something for you, you need to show respect. Maybe she saved my life."

"Nobody knows about that. That's between you and her, so it goes with her. Understood?"

"If you say so. There's a reason?"

"Yes."

"Which is?" Then, seeing Daniel's face, "More secrets."

"For your own good."

"And now you're deciding that." He let it drop. "Anyway, you wouldn't want to miss this. It's better than a show."

Daniel looked around. The seats were filling up with what seemed to be all of Shanghai. Sid Engel's funeral had been a small, tribal affair, scaled down, like a B picture. But Florence seemed to have touched the entire city, from rich Kadoories to the volunteers at the heime to the string quartet that played in the lobby as everyone filed in. A Chinese poet in a long traditional robe read in Chinese and English. The rabbi praised Florence's charitable work for the refugees. The Fine Arts Association. The Chamber Music Society, which Loomis refused to cover. A back row of household staff, acquired over the years and kept on. Someone from the Sassoon office, Sir Victor being away. The usual Settlement people, Jardine executives and card-playing wives. Her mah-jongg group. But not Markowski, still hiding at the Rush, not whoever had sent her with a message, not anybody from her secret life, now closed and put away for good. In the large vaulted theater, no one had any idea who Florence really was. Unless Ivan was there, the friend Markowski had sent to meet Daniel. "Don't worry, he'll find you." But he'd be outside, a chance meeting in public, the way they used to do it in Berlin. The restrooms at Anhalter Station, the S-bahn platform at Alexanderplatz. No one noticed anything at stations, hurrying for trains. Unless they were looking. Daniel glanced around the theater, back in that life again, checking behind, over his shoulder.

A Chinese girl was singing, presumably some traditional mourning song, her high childlike voice quivering with sadness. "Jesus," Nathan said under his breath and Daniel thought of Nancy Dong singing "Why Don't You Do Right?" Neither singer truly authentic, the dirge made melodic for Westerners. They might have been at one of Florence's evenings, the cultures lapping against each other but not quite mingling, uneasy together. Under the scratchy singsong voice, you could hear the rustling of programs, the audience polite but restive. But how could it be otherwise? What none of the speeches mentioned was how Florence had died. Not a sudden heart attack, not a lingering illness. Shot in the back playing roulette. The chamber music, the ceramics were just veneer, part of what Island Shanghai used to insulate itself. But today the violence was all around them, the real city.

The next speaker, the founder of the Ikebana Society, had fond memories of the first trip they'd made to Japan. First trip. Florence, Daniel thought, had done a lot of traveling. Germany "for the music." Japan to prune saplings into miniature landscapes. What else? It's not much, she had said, lend out a room. But had there been more? On the *Raffaello* he'd had the impression that Florence never stopped talking, but now he realized he knew nothing about her. Ivan, if he knew, would say that he didn't. How this was played. He looked around again. Someone Russian. Down front, Loomis was taking notes. Maybe writing his column, the funeral like a club opening. Who was here. What they were wearing. Albert's grief. A quote from one of the Kadoories.

"What's she talking about?" Nathan whispered. "Those dwarf trees? Christ."

"Shh."

"And now look who's here. He's got some nerve. The guy got away. So what are we paying him for?"

Daniel followed his gaze. Yamada with Leah on his arm, late, finding seats about a third of the way down. Had they been part of the crowd earlier or just slipped into the back row, they might not have stood out, but now it seemed that all eyes were on them, a distraction from the Ikebana woman's tired eulogy. Heads turned. He was wearing his uniform, just the sight of it a kind of provocation. Daniel thought of him on the *Raffaello*, pushing a boundary, waiting for a response. Now people twisted in their seats, then quickly turned back, as if they had been caught doing something wrong. The woman onstage, slightly flustered, raised her voice, but the attention of the room had shifted, the dial turned, the rest of her talk fading out.

Daniel stared at Yamada. Why had he come? A killing he'd ordered, or at least knew about, just as he'd ordered Nathan's. Daring someone to accuse him? Or just a show of power? This is what it means. I can do these things. Kill people. Take Leah into the other room, while Clara Auerbach washes the cups. Next to him, Leah had lowered her head, not meeting anyone's eye, taking her seat. A quick glance toward Daniel, then a flush, the same look she'd had selling her coat, embarrassed and defiant. Don't look at me.

"We should cut off the squeeze," Nathan said.

"And then what? Look what happened the last time." Daniel nodded to Nathan's chest. "Look what happened to Sid Engel."

Nathan said nothing for a minute. "It's not the same town, is it?" He looked over toward Yamada. "They don't own it. They think they do, but they don't. The Chinese own it."

"Xi said to wait for the right time."

"Xi likes to wait. He can afford to." Another look to Yamada. "Why did he come?"

"He knew her. On the boat."

"He should have done a better job protecting her then. His men. They're out back, except when they need to be. Funny, no?"

Yamada put his hand on the back of Leah's neck, straightening her collar. Mine. Another nick at Daniel's skin. Clara washing up.

"And there's another thing," Nathan said, still whispering. "How is it an accident if they aim right at you? They're after *you*. So what did she do? Like an angel with the charity work and someone still wants her dead. So, why?"

"I don't know," Daniel said, the lie easy, her secret safe.

There was a reception afterward in the lobby–flutes of champagne and passed canapes and the Shanghai dumplings Florence always offered at her parties. Albert, still in a daze, shook hands and accepted condolences, but the center of attention, as it had been inside the theater, was Yamada, bowing politely, making small talk, seemingly unaware that he was the only Japanese in the room. Daniel watched as people stepped around him, a social choreography, careful not to offend. He thought of the table on the *Raffaello*, the awkward good manners.

"I'm going," Nathan said. "If I stay, I'll have to talk to him and what the hell do you say? Nice job? I still say we cut the squeeze. You coming?"

A quick glance around the room. Where was Ivan? Maybe passing one of the trays.

"No, not yet. You take the car. I'll get a taxi." He took a breath. "Somebody has to talk to him. We're in business."

"If that's what you want to call it." Nathan looked up. "Just don't turn your back."

Daniel made a circle around the room. A word with Albert, whom he'd never met. A small group listening to the Chinese poet. No Ivan. Finally there was Yamada, standing with Leah, unavoidable.

"A sad occasion," Yamada said.

"I'm surprised you came."

"I have fond memories of our trip."

"No, I meant given the screwup at the Rush. With the so-called security arrangements."

Yamada blinked. "Do you think this is the right time for such a discussion?"

"Pick another one, then."

Yamada moved his head back, surprised. A glance to Leah. "I will call you. Or perhaps you're interested in a new suit?" Almost a wink, pleasant.

"I leave that to you. But we should talk."

"Florence," Leah said, not really listening to them, missing any undertone. "Of all people. I didn't know she went to—places like that."

"Like what?"

"I just meant—"

"I know. It was her first time, if that makes you feel any better."

"I didn't—"

"It's not Blood Alley. We like to think anyway."

"Your uncle, you mean," Yamada said. "He was here earlier." Not missing anything.

"He had to leave. He sends his respects."

"Do they know who did it?" Leah said.

"No. Shanghai's a dangerous place." A look to Yamada. "Hard to control."

"And only the Settlement police to keep order. We're hoping to put more Japanese on the Municipal Council. That should help."

"Do you really need to do that? What diff—"

"It's the Japanese way, to follow the legal procedures. There are now more Japanese than British in the Settlement, but whose voice is heard? Only the British lion. Of course, one doesn't want to antagonize a lion. We're asking for two seats only. A small change."

Daniel looked at him, the face as bland as his words, reasonable, a councilman but still ordering hits. Taking Nathan out. And Daniel, just for being there. No witnesses. Wait for your time.

"Well, let's hope it has an effect," Daniel said. "We can't have this again. It would ruin the club, another incident. It can't happen again," he said slowly, stopping on each word, Yamada nodding.

"Let's hope not," Yamada said, solemn, as if he were promising something. But of course it would happen again. The deal was already made. Words meaningless. Daniel would pay and Yamada would do what he wanted. More bodies, more squeeze, a death spiral with no way out.

A shout in Japanese, one of Yamada's aides rushing up to them, saluting, a message that couldn't wait. A question from Yamada, almost a bark. More Japanese.

"I'm sorry," Yamada said. "I'm wanted at headquarters." Pleased with himself, so that for one improbable moment Daniel thought they might have caught Ivan, all the fish now in Yamada's net.

"Trouble?" Daniel said.

"As you say, it's a dangerous place, Shanghai. You'll excuse me?" He turned to Leah. "Hiro's sending a car to take you home."

"I can drop her," Daniel said.

"The car's already on its way," Yamada said, an end to it. "A few minutes only. You'll be all right?" he said to Leah, a question to a child.

"Of course," Leah said, embarrassed.

"If you would look after her until the car gets here," Yamada said to Daniel.

Daniel nodded. An absurd request on busy Avenue Joffre, the afternoon light streaming through the trees. Another declaration of ownership. Daniel turned slightly, expecting Yamada to embrace her, a husband's good-bye, but he simply bowed politely to them and hurried to his car.

"Don't," Leah said, as they watched him go.

"All right. How are you?"

"I can't stop thinking about Florence. It doesn't seem real, somehow. Shot. People don't get shot."

Daniel said nothing.

"Not people I know anyway." She looked back to the theater. "But here we are. What happened?"

"I don't know. A mistake, maybe. It would have to be."

"What kind of mistake? You must have some idea—it's your place. You act as if this happens all the time."

"At the Gold Rush? No. But the Badlands can be rough. Gangs." He looked at her. "Maybe the colonel will clean things up when he's on the Municipal Council."

"It's not funny."

"I'm not laughing. I liked Florence. I wish it hadn't happened. But things—happen."

"Just part of the business."

He looked at her. "That business, yes. My uncle was shot, did you know that?"

"What? No. How would I know that?"

"I thought maybe one of your cozy chats with the colonel."

She shook her head. "But he's all right?"

"He survived. He's lucky." Daniel paused. "You're right, that's the business he's in. And now me. I know what it is. I don't pretend it's something else. But I can't walk away from it. We don't always get to do what we want to do."

She looked away. "No," she said quietly. Then, "Do something?"

"For you?"

"No, for you. If you start to enjoy it. Walk away then. As long as you don't enjoy it, there's something to hold on to."

"We're talking about me now."

Leah looked at him. "Who else? Look, my chariot, right on time."

A Buick with the window rolled down, the driver signaling
to her.

"He looks after you."

"Yes," she said, then turned to him, holding up a wait finger
to the driver. "He hates me. All of us. He thinks—I don't know.
Remember how it was in Vienna? You'd think why do they hate
me so much? Why me? But it isn't you. It's some idea of you. So
the hate—nothing satisfies it. You know what this was today? This
spectacle, showing me off? Making sure everyone saw, everyone
knows. So I'm marked. Not like going to a nightclub. Who sees
you? Other people who go to nightclubs." She looked up. "You
know what I mean. But here—it's everybody. Everybody respectable. So who would take me now? He wanted to ruin it for me. Any
chance. Who would marry me now? The Japanese whore?"

"I'll marry you," he said, a stopped second with no sound, a
coin tossed in the air, held up by nothing, weightless, just before
it falls.

"Will you?" she said, her own coin, suspended, nothing around
it, some trick, then a rush of bus exhaust and the click of rickshaw
wheels, back to earth, her voice pretending nothing had happened.
She looked away. "Wonderful. Every door in town would be open
to us."

His arm began to reach for her.

"No. Smile, so the driver thinks we're just talking."

"I have money. You don't have to—"

"Do you think I would take money from you? Then what
would I have?" She looked up, her face soft. "Sometimes I think I
made you up. So I'd have a story. When I'm a *gnädige Frau*. See the
smile on her face? Some secret, from years ago. A boy on a boat.
She never talks about it, but something must have happened. You
can tell. You'd never think at first—" She stopped, hearing her voice

drift. "Anyway, money, yes. Maybe someday I'll need a loan. A loan. So thank you. But what I need now you don't have."

"What's that?"

"A way out of here. Legally. Somewhere to go. When I put my mother's ashes in the river, I thought, not me, I'm not going to die here. I'm going to get out. So how? Marry somebody from Jardine's, one of the banks. Become British, anything." She glanced toward the car. "Now he's ruined that for me. No one would go near me—no one like that. So now what? Maybe find some sailor off a boat. An American, maybe. They're not choosy."

"Leah—"

"I know. But it's the truth. How many choices do I have? Anyway—" She started for the car, then stopped, turning halfway. "One thing? I want you to know. I don't enjoy it. I'm still—all right."

Daniel looked at her for a moment, not saying anything, then nodded. Another stopped second, no noise in the street, then she broke away and got into the car, Daniel watching, the traffic on Avenue Joffre surrounding it like water. The things we tell ourselves.

A minute later, a taxi pulled up.

"Ivan," the driver said, leaning across to the passenger window.

Daniel shook his head, an automatic reaction.

"No, I take you Ivan." Jerking his head back, a "get in" gesture.

Daniel looked around, people still milling in front of the theater. But what could be more natural than getting into a taxi? What he was going to do anyway.

They headed north out of the French Concession, threading their way up to Nanking Road, joining the traffic where it became Bubbling Well Road. The racetrack.

"The tower. Wait," the driver said, stopping where the road curved around the bottom of the track.

Daniel took out some money.

"No, already paid. Go wait."

Daniel looked at him. What kind of cabbie refused a fare? A member of the local group? He got out and started for the Race Club's tall brick tower, a Shanghai landmark, as familiar as the Cathay. The usual lines at the betting windows, collecting chits, people packed in near the racecourse, pushing toward the rail to get a glimpse. Loudspeakers and the constant buzz of Chinese, noisy, an easy crowd to get lost in. A man near the club entrance folded a newspaper and came over to him.

"Daniel? Ivan. Right on time," he said, looking at his watch. "Sorry for the cloak-and-dagger. Any trouble getting here?" Not especially Russian looking, any European, thinning hair combed back, a suit off the rack, an office worker out for a flutter.

"No, not that I could see."

"Well, you'd know. They say you develop an instinct. Shall we go?"

"Go?"

"I thought we'd have a drink at the Park. You pretty much have the bar to yourself when the horses are running." He opened his hand to lead Daniel to the hotel. "The story, if it comes to that, is that I'm looking for Karl and thought you might have some idea where he is. So a quick drink, no more."

"The story. Who'd be asking?"

"The Kempeitai or their Chinese bullyboys at Jessfield Road. It's a tricky time." He lowered his voice. "We can't be sure there isn't a leak. The last time they went on the warpath like this, we found out they were getting—well, never mind. Old news. But it's safer to have a story. Even for one drink."

"Why take the risk then? Why not just go through Karl?"

Ivan smiled a little. "I wanted to get a look at you. See for myself."

"See what?"

"How we can use you."

"I said I'd meet. I didn't say I'd do anything."

"But you have. Just by coming." He looked over. "Why did you?"

"I want to know what happened."

"You were there."

"How, then. There are two ways it could have happened. She was followed and she came to the Rush, so they killed her there. Or they knew where she was going and set it up to happen there. There's a difference. Aside from anything else, it might mean they know about Karl."

"But they didn't shoot him. So unlikely."

"Likely isn't very much. I'm hiding him. I owe him more than that."

"We think he's safe where he is. If they knew, they would have killed him, too. But why should they suspect? It was perfectly natural for her to go there. A night on the town. There was nothing to see."

"Until they shot her. At my club. You know who did it?"

"Specifically? No. Ultimately, yes. The Kempeitai. Two other Communists were killed that night. Just picked off, like her. That sends a loud message. You'd have to be deaf not to get it. Here we are," he said, nodding to the hotel doorman. "Shanghai's finest. Or was. Until Sir Victor built his."

As he predicted, there were only a few people in the bar. Daniel ordered a plain tonic.

"Keeping your wits about you?" Ivan said.

"It's early, that's all."

"Karl said you were careful."

"If I were careful, I wouldn't be here."

Ivan smiled. "True enough. I should have started by saying it's a pleasure to meet you. Finally. I thought you were dead. After they rolled up Franz's group—well, we just assumed. But now, of course, think what an advantage that gives us."

"How so?"

"You don't exist. By any name. Franz's gone. You never joined the Party, so there's no record of you in Moscow. Or Berlin. Or here, for that matter. If we do have a leak, he can't betray you because you don't exist."

"Unless the leak is you."

Ivan looked at him. "Unless. But you see the advantage. Karl will be your contact—the only one who knows. Otherwise, you're a ghost."

"If this is a recruitment pitch, save it. I'm not in this anymore."

"No one ever leaves," Ivan said softly.

"Well, now you've met the one."

"I knew Franz. He saved you."

Daniel nodded. "So did my uncle. I owe a lot of people. But I don't owe the Comintern. When they came after the group, where were you? Helping Stalin make his deal with Hitler? So much for the international dream. Is that what you sold Florence? Did she know the risk she was taking, or did nobody mention that?"

"She knew. And even if she didn't—" He stopped as the waiter put two glasses on the table.

"And even if she didn't, so what? She could be useful. Like me."

Ivan looked at him. "That's right. What do you think this is? History takes a long time—you need to keep looking ahead. Stalin signs a pact with the devil. So he buys us a little time."

"Ask the Poles if that's how they see it." Daniel looked away. "You used to be about something. Now you're about Russia. I don't care about Russia. Everything we did—Franz, all of us—was about Germany. That's all done now. It didn't work. Now we're just trying to survive. No world order. No better days ahead. You told Florence she'd be part of history, and she's dead."

"But she will be part of it," Ivan said, his voice still low and steady. "Up north they're living in caves, waiting for the battle. Which they'll win."

"I don't care."

"Yes, you do. It's the same battle. Hitler has Stalin in a bear hug, but that won't last. He'll attack. You don't care about Russia? You will when they're fighting the Nazis. And what would cripple Russia when the fight comes? A second front. Another Japanese war, but this time while she needs all her resources in Europe. The Japanese are already in Manchuria. How easy it would be to cross into—" He paused for a second, letting Daniel finish the thought. "Except for one thing. They're tied down in China. Overstretched. They won the war, but not the occupation. All these ambitions and here they are, trying to keep China under some kind of control. But bombs go off in Nanking, an ammunition dump goes up in Harbin. Pinpricks? Maybe, but it keeps them where we want them. Out of Russia. So, yes, I want people who can be useful to us."

"And do what? Use the Gold Rush as a safe house?"

"We have other safe houses. Florence was useful because she was so unlikely. So are you. A Red casino owner? Almost a contradiction in terms. No one would suspect."

"Suspect what?"

Ivan looked up. "We need you to use your special skills. Your special access. Do what you were trained to do. Fight Nazis."

"Here? What, blow up the German consulate?"

"No," Ivan said, staring at him, slowing things down. "We want you to take out Yamada."

"Take him out," Daniel said.

"Yes. Kill him."

For a second Daniel didn't react, just looked back at Ivan, who reached over now and picked up his glass. Two men having a drink, what anyone would see. A quick look to the bar, nobody listening.

"Kill him," Daniel repeated.

"He's running it, their little war against the Communists. Picking us off. Then trying to blame the Chinese. They think it'll weaken Mao. It won't—what's a few, more or less, when you've got an army? But it makes trouble for us here, in Shanghai. People get nervous. They don't want to take chances. Work with us. So we need it to stop. And it all goes through him. Take him out and you solve the problem. At least temporarily. They'll get someone else, but it'll take time and meanwhile we have a little breathing room."

"Breathing room," Daniel said, another echo.

"That's right. But so far we haven't been able to do it. Get to him. With all his men. We know his movements, his schedule, when he takes a piss, but we can't get near him. Unless you want to make it a suicide mission and what's the point of that? Then you're doing his work for him. But now you show up. One of Franz's men but nobody knows it. Not on anybody's list. And a friend of Yamada's. You have business with him."

"How do you—?"

"We know things. We have to. Otherwise, we'd be dead." He took another sip. "But the point is, you have access."

"Special access," Daniel said, the earlier phrase.

Ivan nodded. "You can meet with him. Just the two of you. And then—" He stopped for a second. "I don't care how you do it. How you set it up. Nobody's asking you to take one for the cause.

In fact, it's better if nobody knows you did it. Then everyone did it and they get spooked." He looked over at him. "Afraid of ghosts."

Daniel said nothing for a minute, waiting.

"You pick when," Ivan said. "But the sooner, the better. We don't want another Florence. And you don't want any more trouble at the Gold Rush."

"How did they know about her?"

Ivan shrugged. "We don't know. But the important thing now is to cut the head off the snake before he can strike again. I'm assuming you have a gun? In your line of work. If not, I can—"

"Do you really think I'm going to do this?"

Ivan raised his head. "Yes, I do. It's important. And nobody else—one of us, I mean—has this kind of access. You have to do it."

"I don't have to do anything."

"He killed Florence. Who's next? Karl?"

"I can't help that."

"But you can. That's what I'm telling you. Think of it as a field exercise. The kind you and Franz used to plan. This time for real."

Daniel looked at him, the smooth face, calmly proposing murder. "I won't do it."

"Yes, you will."

Daniel raised his eyes, a question.

"I'd rather appeal to your better instincts. But there are other ways."

"Such as?"

"I'd rather not stoop to that. There are plenty of good reasons to get rid of him. Isn't that enough?"

"Such as?" Daniel said again.

Ivan put down his glass. "We need to get this done. We can't afford to have any scruples about it. He wouldn't."

"Well, that's the difference between us."

"Then let me make this easy for you. We've been worried about a leak. But that can work two ways. We could set up our own. And leak information about you. Who his business partner really is. He'd have to kill you. Does that make it easier? If you don't kill him, he'll kill you."

———

Nathan rarely left the Black Cat now, so the visit to the Rush took Daniel by surprise. It was late afternoon, the club like an empty theater before opening, the cleaning staff still vacuuming, the gardeners edging the lawns.

"Anything wrong?" he said.

"Why should anything be wrong? I own the place. Can't I look? Maybe you're stealing from me."

"Very funny. So what's the occasion?"

"I have something for you." Nathan moved them toward Daniel's office, Sergei following. "There's only one door," he said to Sergei. "Even Houdini couldn't get out. So park yourself there and take a load off." He turned to Daniel. "My shadow."

"You want anything? Water?"

Nathan shook his head. "In a minute I'm gone. Just wanted to give you this," he said, taking something out of his pocket as he closed the door.

A passport, gold seal stamped on its stiff cover.

"Who's Joao da Silva?"

"Look at the picture."

"Me," Daniel said.

Nathan nodded. "The real thing. It takes a while to arrange the paperwork. Birth certificate, whatever they might check. Wu's got a man in Lisbon. The booklet's real. The stamps. You carry that, you're Da Silva, nobody's going to question it. You're in the files. The way things are going, it's something you want to have, just in case. And this." He took out another packet. The money Daniel had brought in on the *Raffaello*. "It was always for you. Emergency money. If you need hard currency. You never know."

"What is all this? Are you asking me to go?"

"What? No, no. Stay forever as far as I'm concerned. But you don't need a crystal ball to see what's going to happen here. It's just a matter of time. This way, you can get out in a hurry. That's usually what happens, you need to get out in a hurry. So."

"What about you?"

"Me? Where else would I go? I'll be all right. They close it down, the clubs, I'm still all right. Who's going to worry about me? An old man. I don't make trouble for the Japanese. I pay them. Not like poor Sid. The *dummkopf*. So I'm here."

"You could go to California."

"No, you close a door, that's it." He paused. "You know what I would like, though? To visit. See if Jeanine's still there. I mention her to you? She wanted to be in the movies."

"Maybe she is."

"No, I'd know. I keep up. She'd be in the magazines. She probably met somebody. We had a place in Encino. The other side of the hills. A view, even."

"I can't take this," Daniel said, holding out the money.

"Why? It's yours. All of it," Nathan said, gesturing to take in the club. "But if you have to leave, at least you'll have the cash. Hard currency. Now put it somewhere safe. And do something for me."

"What?"

"Tell me what's going on. I see my doctor dealing cards and I think I'm seeing things. And you're not saying anything. Then a woman hides me and she gets gunned down at the roulette table. And you're still not saying anything. So say something now."

"The doctor—Karl—needed a place to lie low and he'd helped us, so—"

"We helped him. Fine. He's not bad, by the way. Good hands. But who's he lying low from?"

"The Japanese."

"Why?"

Daniel looked away, hesitant.

"Don't make me ask twice. Why?"

"He's a Communist. They're hunting them. Killing them."

"At the roulette table."

"Sometimes."

"Jesus. Both?" He looked at Daniel. "Are you—?"

"No. I knew Karl in Berlin, that's all."

"And you took me to him."

"And he fixed you up. I didn't ask his politics."

"But you knew."

"What did it matter? He didn't ask yours."

"And the other night—why just her?"

"We assume the Japanese don't know about Karl."

"Yet."

"That's why I haven't said anything. I don't want you to be part of this."

Nathan dismissed this. "I've been part of worse. Not knowing never protects you. Not from them."

"I'll move him if you want. It'd be safer."

"Oh, safer. No, we owe him." He shook his head. "A Communist. At the Rush. Christ. The ones I knew, you could never do business with them. They're like the Orthodox, they have an idea. And you'd better have the same one." He looked up at Daniel.

"You know, they win and it's the end of all this. Your inheritance. The Japanese, they just want to be paid, but the Communists want to shut us down."

"Good to have a few favors to call in, then."

"Even better to have an escape hatch," Nathan said, nodding toward the currency.

"Well, let's hope not for a while, anyway. I like Shanghai. I'm getting used to it."

"You mean you don't smell the shit anymore. People come here, it's the first thing they notice. It smells like shit. You know they collect it at night, to use in the fields. Imagine, growing vegetables in shit. I suppose we're no better, with the manure, but still. But after a while you don't smell it. Maybe Soochow Creek, places like that, where you can't get away from it, but otherwise— There's a lot of things like that, you stop noticing. All right, so now it's the Japanese and the Communists, something new to worry about. But there's still the old things too. You get used to them, like the shit, but they're still there."

Daniel looked at him, taking this in. "Meaning?"

"I'm hearing things about the gangs. Xi and Wu. We're supposed to have a truce, but don't hang around Great Western Road late at night. Unless you've got your own gang. So keep your eyes open. They start up again, you'll have another war to run away from, not just the Japanese."

"Xi's a partner."

"So is Wu. I'm just saying, keep Senhor da Silva handy. Meanwhile," he said, the tone of a business meeting, "what are you going to do about Yamada?"

Daniel looked up, alarmed. "What?"

"The squeeze."

"Oh, the squeeze. We pay it. You take it away now—"

"You start something. I know. Hell of a thing, though, providing protection that isn't there."

"It's worse than that. He ordered the hit. At the Rush. Florence. He was providing protection against himself. Which is why it wasn't so good."

"And what do we do about it?"

"Nothing. We wait." Daniel got up, moving away from Nathan's look. "And hope somebody does it for us."

"One more stunt at the Rush and I'll do it myself," Nathan said.

"You?" Daniel took a breath. "You know, I asked you once but you never said–did you ever kill somebody?"

"Why?"

"Just curious. How it felt."

Nathan thought for a minute. "At the time, it didn't feel like anything. But after, you think about it. How the bullet doesn't stop. It just keeps going. You know, you take somebody out of the game it affects the whole game. So maybe he had a wife and now what's her life? And so on. Some old father gets the news. You did all that. You think about it." He looked over. "I don't know why you're asking, but I'll tell you this. It's better to get somebody else to do it."

CHAPTER 11

It took several days to plan it, detail by detail, no surprises. The tricky part would be getting away. Nathan's killers had had a car waiting, Florence's had the conveniently absent Kempeitai, but Yamada moved in a fortress of guards—you could get to him, but not away from them. Daniel watched, making mental notes, following at a distance. How an animal hunted, stalking, waiting for an opening, then the lunge to the neck.

Ivan gave him a copy of Yamada's schedule, remarkably detailed, passed at another meeting at the racetrack, two men in a sea of hats.

"You must have somebody inside to get this," Daniel said.

Ivan shrugged. "It became available."

"Fixed times for calls to Tokyo," Daniel said, glancing through it. "They keep him on a short leash."

"You'll notice he's never alone."

Daniel ignored this. "Same driver?"

"No, different ones. Depending."

"Okay, thanks for this. Now we disappear. No more meetings.

Here," Daniel said, handing Ivan a betting stub, "maybe you'll get lucky."

"That's not the way we work."

"You want this done, those are the rules. No meetings, no risk of being seen together."

"How are you going to do it?"

"You'll know when it's done. This way, nobody tips him off. If there's a leak."

"We can help."

"If I need you, I'll send a smoke signal through Karl. Just give me a little time."

"To do what?"

"Get him alone."

———

One day, putting things into place, Daniel tried to imagine how his day would look to somebody following him. A hopscotch of random errands or pieces of a puzzle falling into place? The shipping office on the Bund, making inquiries. There were fewer boats since the new restrictions, even Shanghai finally closing its doors. Check several dates. Outside, there was a sudden rainstorm, so that when he slipped into the *Tribune* offices next door it was just a familiar shelter, not the point of the trip. Frank O'Brien, sleeves rolled up, was in the photo lab, where he always was.

"Don't tell me you're coming back," he said.

"I'm not that crazy."

"Says you. You're all wet."

"It's raining. Been out yet?"

"They keep me busy. So what is it this time? Or have you just come to chat?"

"The Gold Rush opening night. Is there a file?"

"And then some. Cameras all over the place. What are you looking for? Here." He took a thick folder out of a file drawer.

"Pictures of the guests."

"They're all there. Look for yourself. I have to check on the prints," he said, nodding toward a door with a red light. "Don't steal anything while I'm gone."

"Scout's honor."

Frank grinned. "You never were."

There was a stack of prints, everybody smiling. Tables watching the floor show. Women holding their skirts as they climbed out of cars. Nathan beaming, his night. Leah and Yamada. Daniel looked at it carefully, using his hands to frame it, see if it would work.

"Find something?"

"You have a negative of this? Could you crop the face? Just her, on her own."

"Sure. What size? Single column?"

"Not for the paper. Personal. Wallet size. I want to give it to somebody."

"So he can keep her near and dear?"

"Something like that."

"What happened to the Jap? Or is he the lucky guy?" Then, before Daniel could answer, "Give me a minute. We're not supposed to do this, you know."

"Anybody asks, say it's for the Merry-Go-Round."

"Nobody asks. Nobody comes here. They think the pictures happen by themselves."

"Thanks, Frank."

"It's not you with the wallet, is it? Going all sappy."

"Never."

By the time the picture was ready the rain had stopped and the sky was growing dusky. Selly Loomis was just coming out of the newsroom.

"Well, well. I thought you'd given all this up for a life of crime."

"I got caught in the rain. So I came in to dry off."

"But not in my office, I notice. Never mind. I was just going to start my round. Come. Be like old times."

"I have a dinner," Daniel said, glancing at his watch.

"I'll get you back in time. They give me a car and driver now. Impressed? I have to say, the one thing about China, you get spoiled. With the servants. What were you doing in the lab?"

"Just saying hello. Where to, tonight?"

"Well, your uncle has a singer he wants me to hear. I may or may not. But that's later. Now? The usual. Tower Room at the Cathay. Horse and Hounds for a quick one. Ciro's. You could practically do this blindfolded. But it gives us a chance to talk. I still can't figure it out."

"What?"

"Florence. Who'd want to kill her?"

"Maybe nobody did."

"Oh, I know, we're supposed to think it was an accident. She just got in the way. But we both know that's not true. Right in the middle of the back. That's an aim, not a stray bullet."

"Maybe the wrong back."

"Not with me, please, okay? I said it's a mystery, I wrote it that way, but I'd like to know. So why?" He kept pressing as they walked along the Bund. "Why do people get killed? Passion. Hard to believe when you look at Albert. Still. But unlikely, wouldn't you say? Money. But he had all the money. That's why she married him, I always assumed. Gambling debts? I would have heard—*you* would have heard. Drugs? Florence? Someone with a grudge? What else?

What else is there? And all these would mean someone she knows. And the man was Chinese."

"I thought he was never identified, not really. The police couldn't do a sketch."

"Because all anyone said was that he was Chinese. That's typical. No one even noticed him until the gun went off. And then—he's gone. He was lucky. That could have gone wrong. But the gangs don't care. There's always someone else to do the job. If this goes wrong, try again."

"You think one of the Chinese gangs ordered Florence killed? But why?"

"I know. Back to square one. Maybe somebody who hated foreigners. You hear about that sometimes. But then he'd go after a man, don't you think? Albert, even. Some banker. A lord and master. Not some woman who gives tea parties. There's a story here, though. There has to be. Could be a valuable piece of information."

"Or asking for trouble."

"I was thinking, maybe it's political."

Daniel looked up. "Political?"

"She knew Chiang and Madame Chiang, when they lived here. Who knows what skeletons are in those closets. So maybe she knew something she could use with the Americans. They live off the Americans. They wouldn't want—"

"Selly."

"I know. But it's a thought. Chiang was very cozy with the gangs. They helped him, he helped them. You have any idea how much opium money there is?"

"Let me get this straight. Florence knew Chiang. Years ago. Now she's blackmailing him—we don't know why—and he gets one of his old gang friends to shut her up. Is that it? Roughly?"

"I admit . . ." Loomis started, then let it fade. "But it has to be the gangs. It's the way they do things."

They were at the Cathay door. Daniel turned to him. "My advice? Leave it alone."

"You're just trying to protect the Rush."

"From what?"

Loomis shrugged. "People talk. Why there? And there's Nathan, friends with them. Xi, Wu, they're not exactly choirboys. So maybe Nathan had something to do with it." He stopped. "Maybe you."

"But they're not hearing this from you."

Loomis looked up, stopped by Daniel's tone, and Daniel saw that something had shifted, a new wariness. "No."

"It's not something Xi or Wu should hear," he said, his voice steady, a verbal stare. "They might . . . misinterpret."

"That's right," Loomis said, more than uncomfortable now, anxious. Daniel one of them.

"We don't know what happened to Florence."

"No," Loomis said, and in a rush Daniel saw that he could do it, plan it and get away with it, everyone looking somewhere else.

"Then I'd leave it alone."

It was still early but a few of the tables in the Tower Room were already filled. Some visiting Brits from Hong Kong up to see the bright lights. Two couples in dinner jackets and evening dresses having a quiet drink before they set out for the evening, maybe even on their way to the Rush to play roulette. A double-breasted suit and a peroxide blonde, both staring out the window to the Whangpoo, already bored. A small combo was playing but it was too early for dancing, the gleaming waxed floor still without a scratch.

Loomis checked in with the bartender for column items, then

nursed his drink, talking about anything but Florence. Changes at the *Tribune*. The peroxide blonde, whom he'd seen before, not a professional, but close. The parade the Japanese were planning.

"What's the occasion?" Daniel asked.

"Something about the *Izumo*, the battleship they keep in the Whangpoo. Some anniversary. But really I think it's just to have a parade. Show they're here. Who's boss now."

"But you don't see them celebrating," Daniel said, nodding toward the waxed floor.

"Watch the parade. How they look. The uniforms. Who's really in charge." His voice admiring, and for a second Daniel saw him young, a boy with toy soldiers, millions of boys playing soldiers.

Downstairs the girl who wanted to be Billie Holiday was singing in the Horse and Hounds. An after-work crowd, nobody for the Merry-Go-Round. A few girls in high-necked qipaos with slit skirts. Daniel made a silent toast to Clara, now out to sea.

Traffic was worse than usual on Bubbling Well Road, the rain having disrupted the racing schedule, and Loomis decided to skip the Canidrome and go straight to Ciro's. Sir Victor was expected later. But there was a young Kadoorie for Loomis to talk to while Daniel sipped his drink and watched the dancers. A nice sprinkling of Chinese in evening clothes, no Japanese. He thought of them marching down the Bund, a victory parade without a victory. Unless they thought they'd already won. A girl danced by, her satin dress catching the light. When he had first come here he thought he had walked into a movie, the lamps on the tables, the flicker of cigarette lighters, the overall sheen of the place. The same people were on the floor tonight, the same tight skirts, but now he saw them as figures in some tired *danse macabre*, already in the past, faded pictures in albums, already dead.

Then, finally, a Japanese, being led to a table away from the dance floor, discreet. Yamada in a suit, not a uniform. A woman in a silver dress, his hand on the small of her back, with him. Not Leah. For a second Daniel just stared, too surprised to think, then felt a flush across his face, oddly embarrassed. Something he wasn't meant to see? Then why go to Ciro's? Unless he did it with all of them. All along Daniel had imagined Yamada obsessed with Leah, the unattainable, something almost quixotic in the attempt to possess her, the birdcage he'd created a prison for both of them. Now he saw she was just another girl, someone else to guide by the small of her back. Worse. Someone he could cheat on, toss away. He'll get tired of me, Leah had said, who saw what Daniel hadn't, that she was nothing to Yamada, his Thursday afternoon. For how much longer? The one time he would be alone.

"Quite a ladies' man," Loomis said, catching Daniel's look.

"Are you going to say hello?"

"While he's looking down her dress? Have a little sense. Anyway, you don't talk to the Kempeitai until they talk to you."

"The gang's all here, too, I see," Daniel said, taking in the guard by the exit door, the Japanese at the other end of the bar, scanning the room. "Hell of a way to live. Wherever you go—"

"That's since the trouble in Nanking. Better safe than sorry."

"Well, safe. Better not to go out at all. If you're that worried. Somebody could take a shot at him right now."

"Somebody could," Loomis said. "But he'd never get out of the room alive."

"No," Daniel said, looking around. The man at the bar, the exit door, presumably somebody outside. Impossible to shoot and run, unless the guards melted away, leaving Yamada open, like Florence.

He looked at Yamada, who had seen him and made a faint nod. Daniel nodded back, the end of the exchange, but he kept looking for a minute longer, as if he were lining up Yamada in a gunsight, head in the crosshairs. What it must be like at the end, nothing personal to it, just getting the sights in place before you pulled the trigger, the head at the other end unaware, grazing, until it heard the click.

———

Xi's house had been a memory of old China, the courtyard like a scene on a silk scroll, but Wu's was up-to-date, a high-rise apartment not far from Florence's building in Frenchtown, the big living room gaudy with lucky red and swirling gilt. No formalities, no tea, just a photograph and a date.

"No sooner?" Daniel said.

Wu looked down at the picture. "She's a traveling companion?"

"No, it's for her. I'm not going anywhere. We're not—"

"But also Portuguese. Like yours."

"I didn't know you had others. She doesn't have to be Portuguese. Whatever you can do."

"Well, as it happens, Portuguese would be the easiest. So, not as your wife?"

"No. Her name—whatever it is."

"We'll find one," Wu said, a thin smile. "She wants to leave Shanghai?"

"She's afraid of the Japanese."

Wu tilted his head, a question mark.

"If there's a war. With the West. What will they do with the foreign nationals?"

"Something you might consider too."

"I can't leave Shanghai. Nathan's here. The business. How much do I owe you?"

"There is no charge for partners. The Gold Rush is doing well," Wu said, dipping his head to Daniel.

"But it must be worth—"

"Yes, I know. How do you put a price on something like this? A new life. So, my gift to you. Or to Senhora—whoever she will be. But you can make me a promise."

Daniel looked up.

"Nobody buys these to put them on a shelf. They're bought to be used. So when the time comes, when you use yours, I want you to sell me your share of the Gold Rush. The other clubs, too."

"They're not mine to sell."

"They will be. Don't worry, I'll give you a good price. Better than anything Xi would offer. If he offered anything. With Xi, it's a matter of taking. But I'll buy them from you."

"And Nathan?"

"Of course this assumes he goes with you. Or—is already gone. He's in poor health, I'm told. Not surprising after that—"

"He's okay. He'll outlive us all."

"I hope that will be the case. I'm just guessing that if you leave— Senhor da Silva—he will want to go with you. I make the offer to both of you. But I want your word that you won't offer the business to Xi."

"Why not? Out of curiosity—"

"It would give him an advantage. I've spent half a lifetime making sure he doesn't get an advantage. We check each other. He makes one move, I make another. That way, we keep some kind of peace. So it's possible to do business. Your uncle understands this. That's why he brought us both into the Gold Rush. But if Xi were to have an edge—"

"You don't trust him?"

"And that's why I'm alive. Never turn your back on Xi. So, do I have a promise?"

Daniel nodded. "And what if the Japanese close it down?"

"It's a risk, I agree, but what business doesn't have risk? And I think I know the Japanese a little. They are fond of squeeze. Look at how things are now. Anyway, I will have this for you in a few days," he said, holding up the photograph. "A real passport, stamped, birth certificate in the files. We're agreed?"

"I can't thank you enough."

"The look on Xi's face," Wu said, mischievous. "That will be thanks enough."

———

Ivan pressed for another meeting so Daniel agreed to a walk in Chusan Road, Little Vienna, browsing through the stalls of second-hand clothes. He wondered for a second what had happened to the Persian wool coat—still warming Frau Mitzel, or had she grown tired of it? A hundred years ago.

"This isn't a good idea," Daniel said. "Somebody could—"

"Let's be quick then. Any news? The days are passing by."

"You want it done right? I'd like to come out of this alive."

"What's the problem?"

"More guards. Since Nanking. Depends how you want this done. You could hire somebody to do a drive-by."

"Gang style?" He shook his head. "I want them to know it's us."

"All right."

"Can't you just set up a meeting with him? Some business?"

"Not without his friends. Don't worry. I'll get it done." Daniel held up a jacket, shopping, then put it back on the barrow. "And then we're done." He turned to Ivan. "Just so we understand each other. I'm finished. I know what this is like. You'll have another one for me. Then another. It won't stop. I'm not an assassin. Karl can stay at the Rush if he needs to, but I'm done."

"Just like that."

"And don't bother to threaten me again. Leak to Yamada? He'll be dead."

"But the next one won't be."

"Is that what you want to do? Throw your own people away?"

"We need to get this done," Ivan said slowly.

"And I'm doing it. But I'm not doing the next one. People get a taste for it and then they can't stop."

"But Yamada—"

"Is a special case. I agree. And I have special access. He tried to kill my uncle. He ordered the hit. And me. Both of us. But so did you, come to think of it. Say you'd throw me to the Kempeitai if I didn't—"

"I was just making the case, that's all. To show you how important this was to us."

"I heard you. But it's a funny thing. You put a gun in a man's hand and you never know where he's going to point it. Right now it's aimed at Yamada. But if there's a leak, I'll know it's you—nobody else knows, we've been careful about that. So I'd have to point it at you." Daniel looked at Ivan. "I'd have to kill you. My last hit. Unless Yamada's the last. You pick."

"You wouldn't."

"No? That's some chance to take. Now, we understand each other? I'm not going to be an assassin for the Party. I don't believe in your bright, shining future. Not anymore. I think you're another gang, that's all. And I'm already working for two of them."

Ivan looked away, not sure how to respond. "Just get it done," he said finally.

Daniel nodded. "And since we're here, where everyone and his mother can see us, let's do a little business. You making any plans for this Japanese parade?"

"What kind of plans?"

"I don't know. A bomb. A sniper. Something disruptive."

"You're doing it then? You want a diversion?"

"I didn't say that. Just thinking about the general atmosphere. What's in the air. You want a political hit, not some gambling fight out in the Badlands. Making trouble at the parade would start people thinking along those lines, no?"

"I don't know if we have the resources for something like that. Throw a bomb at Yamada."

"I didn't say at him. Kempeitai don't march in parades. They're supposed to be secret. And the way things are these days, he's probably not even going to watch it. Too exposed. Just something to make everyone nervous."

"The Municipal Police will be all over that parade. It would be suicide, doing something like that."

Daniel shrugged. "Find somebody expendable." He looked over at him. "The way you do."

There were always two other people in the car—the driver and somebody who'd go in with him, wherever they were. Sometimes there were more, Yamada flanked by men on both sides, a show of force. By now Daniel knew the routine, the arrival in Hongkew, the staff meeting, the daily visit to Jessfield Road, where Wang Ching-wei's people had set up their own Prinz-Albrecht-Strasse. What happened to a puppet government once the invaders withdrew? A blood bath of retribution. So they held on, a viselike grip. Yamada rarely stayed long, maybe the basement tortures upsetting to over-hear. An errand downtown usually required two guards, the private meetings at department stores a thing of the past. Only at Leah's flat did he go in alone, the driver waiting patiently in the street, smoking, looking up from time to time, the drawn blinds like some erotic tease. One man, no one at the back. Sometimes the driver strolled behind for a quick check, but never for longer than a min-ute or two. One man out front, but armed.

Sergei had given up trying to shadow Daniel and rarely left Na-than, so Daniel tracked Yamada alone, careful to stay well behind, which meant he sometimes lost him. But after a while, the routine became so familiar that he could anticipate where the car would be. It was the pattern that mattered, where Yamada might be on any given day. Only Thursdays were tricky. He couldn't park in the street near Yamada's waiting car and couldn't risk having the driver spot him if he drove past more than once. In the end, the far corner worked, with an angled rearview mirror. All the details he needed: the driver smoking, bored, the houseboy sent away on errands, Yamada evidently too modest to have someone listening in the other room. Except for Clara Auerbach, her presence a dif-ferent pleasure.

Unlike Ivan, however, Xi advised patience.

"There is no rush," he said.

"No, it's time. We don't want to miss our chance. There's a rumor he may be recalled to Tokyo."

"You have heard this? Your sources are better than mine. Who told you this?"

"He did," Daniel said. "He mentioned it one night at the Rush." Something that couldn't be checked, except with Yamada himself. "Maybe wishful thinking—he sees this as a promotion—but you never know. Anyway, I'm ready."

"You have a plan? What are you going to do?"

"I can't–not even for you. You understand?"

"You are perhaps too careful. I could help."

"Yes. I need two men."

"Two? To take on the Kempeitai?"

"To take on one man. Two. Good shots. With instructions to follow me."

"Young Daniel."

"I'll call the day we do it and I'll tell you how and if you don't like it, don't send them. And that's that. But nothing before, no leaks. And you'll have them ready to move right away. All right?"

Xi smiled. "Your uncle was like this. Eager."

"He almost died. Your men did. And Yamada's still walking around. It's time."

———

Nathan had the first heart attack that weekend. He had made an afternoon visit to the Rush to look at the books. He had been closeted in the office, away from the public areas, shuffling papers and then, a small cry of surprise, grabbed his chest and slumped over the desk. Sergei ran across the room, shouting for help, calling for Karl, for the car, doors slamming, the frenzy of a fire drill. The closest hospital, no need to hide this time, no one pointing guns, yet Daniel felt the same helpless panic, the same squeal of tires on the road, Nathan with his eyes closed, slipping away.

By the time Irina arrived, he had stabilized, drifting in and out. She stood for a long minute looking down at the bed.

"So he'll live. Is that what they're saying?"

"For now," Karl said. "You want the truth? It's not good. The shooting weakened him."

"So they get him in the end," Irina said, still looking down. "And what do we do?"

"Keep him quiet. The body repairs itself if you let it."

"Keep him quiet," she repeated, a wry shrug. "And what else?"

Karl didn't answer.

A faint stirring in the bed, Nathan touching her hand. "I'm not dead yet," he whispered, trying to make a smile, eyes still closed.

Irina covered his hand with hers. "No," she said, then looked away, trying to control her face.

"Duvey," Nathan said.

"I'm here," Daniel said, taking his other hand, and this time Nathan did smile, then drifted off.

They stayed like that for a while, Daniel's hand trapped by Nathan's, Irina moving over to the window to smoke, the room now cloying with the smell of disinfectant and Russian tobacco. When Nathan finally spoke again, he still seemed half-asleep, talking to the ceiling, not turning to meet Daniel's eyes.

"When you were little, you were just like him. Serious. Like him. Eli's boy. You know what's going to happen now? You remember Sid Engel? Probably not. He told me once there's this hill in Bombay. Sid used to get around a lot—Bombay, Batavia, all those places. He'd sign on as a ship's mate and just go places. You could do that then. Of course, this is before Esther. Then it's here, the Slipper. Anyway, there's this hill there. For corpses. The Zoroastrians, I think it is, put the dead bodies on these platforms in the open air. Like drying racks. And the birds peck at them. Vultures. Until it's just bones. Picked clean. That's what it's going to be like now. They're going to try to pick me clean. You too. I can't let them do that. Eli's boy. He'd never forgive me. All I wanted was for him—what? To think I was okay, I guess. And you know it was him gave me the money. To get out of Berlin. So maybe he did.

When you see him, I want you to tell him I did this for you. Sent you away, before they could get you. You tell him that, okay?"

Daniel looked over at Irina.

"You're busy," she said, answering his expression. "You don't notice things."

"How long?" he said quietly, as if Nathan weren't there.

"Since the shooting. At first, he'd repeat things, forget he said it. Now it's worse. His head—goes somewhere else."

Daniel looked back at Nathan. He'd need somebody all the time now. He thought of Clara Auerbach, walking into traffic. His uncle's hand still gripped his.

"I want you to get away, before they start."

"Who?"

"Xi. Wu. They'll both start picking now. Maybe somebody else. You put the body out there, the birds come. Use the passport."

"Nobody's picking. I'm here."

Nathan shook his head. "You don't know them. Once you're lying there, they can't help themselves. Like the birds. They'll pick it clean. The Rush, the Black Cat. Then they'll go after each other. I've seen it. You don't want to get caught in that."

"I won't. Get some rest now."

But Nathan's other hand started fingering the sheet, restless.

"It's finished here anyway. It's time. It was good in the beginning. Anything goes, you know? Be Nathan Green, whoever you want. The Chinese didn't give a damn. Anyway, what did they have to say about it? About anything. But it's their place, you know? The Japanese take over, it's not going to be just changing flags. They'll round us up, the foreigners, put us in camps. Irina will get me out in time, she's got a good nose for things like that. When. But I don't want you to wait, take any chances. Eli, he'd be—you know what he's like."

"We'll go together."

"With me like this. No. You have the hard currency, right? That's what you're going to need now. Until they sort things out, who's in charge. In my desk at the Black Cat, there's a power of attorney. That's you, if you have to do anything legal. With the clubs. While there's still time. The will, too. Which says it's all yours. But you know what? Who's going to honor it? Wartime, people just take. And who gives it back after? And then we might be talking Chinese courts. You have the paper, but I don't think it's going to mean much. But hard currency? You can start over with that. What did I have when I came here? Not even that. So you're ahead. Irina and Sergei, you don't have to worry about, that's all taken care of. If I don't make it, she'll probably want to go back to Harbin and there's plenty for that."

"Shh. Don't talk so much. Nobody's going anywhere."

"You? Your age, the world's your oyster. I remember."

Daniel looked at him. Hopping off a tramp steamer to try his luck. Before all the doors started closing.

It went on like that, Nathan in and out, a period of drowsy quiet followed by talk, fast, slightly breathless, as if he were afraid someone would cut him off. Eli was alive. The brothels in Thibet Road were filled with sailors playing the slots and getting the clap. Stay away. Gus Whiting had played with Teddy Wilson. How long was he going to be in here?

"A few days maybe," Daniel said, vague enough to mean anything.

"Don't forget the squeeze gets paid on Monday."

"I won't."

Then quiet, so still that Daniel looked over, alarmed, but Nathan's chest was moving, breathing.

Irina went to get cigarettes.

"And some chai for Sergei. He never thinks to get anything for himself."

"He's outside?" Daniel asked.

"Where else?" She looked at Nathan, peaceful now. "Pay no attention, this business with your father. He's alive in his mind, that's all."

"I didn't know it meant so much to him. What else? That I haven't noticed. Does he imagine things?"

"Not so much imagine. Suspicious. Careful about everything. The opposite of the way—well, we all get older."

"He's going to need somebody around."

"He has somebody. Right now she needs cigarettes. Stay with him until I get back, okay?"

Daniel nodded. How it was going to be now, working in shifts.

"She go?" Nathan said, one eye open.

"Yes."

"Come close, so I don't have to shout. It's important."

"What?"

"You have to know this. So you can watch yourself. I got it from Liu. You know him? No, he's from before. Never mind. He's with Xi now. I did him a favor or two, so he thinks he owes me. He's going out to Chungking, join the army, so he wanted me to know. In case. He couldn't say before. If Xi found out. But he thinks he'll try it again, so he wanted me to know."

"What?"

"The night I was shot. It was Xi. His men."

"His men, but not his orders."

"Who told you that?"

Daniel thought for a second, a kind of chill running through him. "He did."

Nathan nodded. "I should have seen it. It's what he always does, blame the Japanese. But I wasn't thinking straight."

"You said to trust him."

"I was wrong. So this is how I pay for it," he said, touching the bed, the heart attack part of some punishment. Daniel looked at him again, uneasy. Eli was alive and Xi was trying to kill him. "If I hadn't been shot, this wouldn't have happened. You don't think so?" he said, reading Daniel's face. "It's my body, who knows better?"

"No one," Daniel said, placating, everything rational.

"So now we have to be careful. He'll try again. Everybody's looking at the Japanese, not him, so he thinks he has a clear shot. But he doesn't know we know." Almost whispering now, conspiratorial.

"But why?"

"And then there were two. Partners. Who knows, maybe he thinks he can take out Wu Tsai, too, then it's just one. I should have seen it, it's how he does things. I got sloppy. But once you know, it all falls into place. Why would the Japanese do it? They didn't have to kill me to get squeeze. And you, if it had worked. Both of us in the car. Which would have left who—Irina?—at the Rush. A woman. It would have been up for grabs. Xi grabbing it."

"Nathan—"

"Xi's men would never go against him, take orders from anybody else. That would be a death warrant. It had to be him."

"Nathan," Daniel said patiently, "they had Ai Wing's son in Jessfield Road. The Japanese. He'd have to do anything they said."

Nathan looked at him for a second, his eyes clouding over, confused. "I don't know. You think Liu lied to me? Why would he lie to me?"

"Maybe he just thinks he knows. The only people who really know—Ai Wing and the other guy—are dead."

"And they're not talking," Nathan finished. "But what if it's true? Then what? They'll come after me." Real alarm in his voice now.

"You've got Sergei's people around you all the time. You're protected."

Nathan brushed his hand against the sheet, waving this away. "Nobody's protected. Not if somebody really wants to get you."

Daniel said nothing. What he thought, after all, about Yamada.

"They'll come," Nathan said, his voice weaker, quavering. "I don't want to be gunned down like an animal."

"You won't be."

"That's what they do. When you've had it. Somebody gets through. I've seen it. It's the nature of it. For years you think, well, that's the way things are. And then it happens to you." He grabbed Daniel's hand. "I don't want you to see it, see me like that. Promise me you'll go—"

"When you're better. I promise."

"When I'm better," Nathan said, confused again, trying to work this out. "I'll tell you one thing. It won't be Xi himself." He raised his free hand in the air. "Clean hands. It's the ones around him you've got to watch out for."

"I will."

"You will," Nathan said to himself, closing his eyes. "Already like somebody in this life. You know you have to decide who you're going to be. Me. Eli. Maybe neither. Nobody's one thing or another. You do things . . ." His voice faded. Daniel sat still, watching him breathe, seeing him young, free, full of fun. Now waiting for someone with a gun, not sure who. "You should go to America," Nathan said suddenly, his eyes still closed. "Look up Jeanine. Let me know what happened to her. She probably met somebody. Encino. Did I tell you about that? A view. But I got greedy. Sometimes you don't know when you have enough. You do something and you have to start running. But you're smarter than that. Like Eli."

"He's still talking?" Irina said, walking in. "What, the old days again?"

"Family stories."

"They always look better from here. Years later."

After Nathan drifted off again, Daniel asked, "How long has he been confusing things?"

Irina shrugged. "It's not so bad. You know, half the time he's right. And half—"

"He thinks people are after him. Make sure Sergei shows himself so Nathan knows he's there."

"You know, if someone really wants to get you, Sergei isn't going to make a difference."

Daniel looked at her. What Nathan had said. But was he right? "You okay here for a while? I want to make some phone calls."

"Where would I go? My life is here." She shrugged, embarrassed. "For better or for worse."

Selly was at his desk and the *Tribune* operator put the call right through.

"I need a favor," Daniel said. "Do you have anybody inside at Jessfield Road?"

"Dear heart, not exactly Merry-Go-Round territory."

"I thought your reach went further. Someone with access to the files. Never mind about what goes on there. Just the record-keeping."

Selly waited a moment. "What do you need? And are you going to tell me why?"

"Someday. Around the time the Rush opened—I can't be more specific than that—they had a kid in custody. Ai Kao. He died."

"That sometimes happens. Not always what you think."

"I don't care why. I want to know when. And when they notified the next of kin."

"Usually right away."

"When, exactly. Could you find out? I need it as soon as—"

"Where are you? I'll call back."

Daniel gave him the number. "Thanks, Selly. I owe you."

"You keep saying that and never paying."

It took half an hour, remarkably fast, which meant Selly's source had easy access. Daniel wondered who it could be and what Selly did to be trusted there. But right now what mattered was the information. Daniel jotted down a few notes.

"So he died of heart failure. A seventeen-year-old."

"It's possible," Selly said.

"And his parents were notified on the eighth."

Two days before the Rush opening. So Ai Wing already knew his son was dead, would have no reason to do anything for the Japanese, hadn't been blackmailed. As Xi had said. Why hadn't Daniel checked? But why not believe Xi, the trusted partner? Nathan had, now lying in his hospital bed, troubled, waiting for someone to appear in the door.

———

Xi was in his floor-length Chinese robe again, slippers visible when he walked.

"Are you telling me I'm going to be used as bait?" Almost amused.

"Let's say, an incentive. To have the meeting."

"I don't go to meetings. Other people do that."

"You're meeting with me."

"You're a partner."

"So is Yamada. In a way. When I sell my share to you, you'll be the controlling partner. Naturally he wants to meet you."

"To renegotiate the squeeze."

"He might try, but just say no. I think he wants to formalize things. He's got a lot of pride. He doesn't like to think of himself as a corrupt cop taking envelopes. In his mind, he's a partner. So he wants an understanding. I'll be gone. He'll be dealing with you."

"In secret."

"It has to be. A Kempeitai on the take? It's not like here. It would mean his job."

"Just him."

"And one man outside."

"He doesn't have more?"

"Nor there. It's an apartment he keeps for his girlfriend. Strictly private. Except for the driver outside watching the front door."

"Always?"

"Like clockwork."

"How do you know?"

"I've been following him."

Xi looked up, interested. "But I have two? You asked for two men."

"Also in the street."

"And you?"

"Sergei. Also downstairs."

"A crowded street."

"It won't be. Just our men. Everybody else will be at the parade, so nobody's snooping around. Every Thursday, same time, same place. The driver will think he's up with his girl but this time he's meeting his new partner. Nobody knows. Just us."

"Sergei. One man. You're comfortable with this?"

"You want more, bring an army, I don't care. As long as they're outside. You bring them in, it'll spook him. He's careful. Just us in the room."

Xi nodded, thinking about this. "That means that one of us will have to–"

"Yes."

"Are you prepared to do that? You? Not one of your men?"

"Since opening night at the Rush. When he tried to kill me. Don't worry. I won't have any problems doing it. You told me we had to wait for the right time. This is it. I've planned it all out. All you have to do is show up."

"The bait," Xi said.

———

There was only a piano player tonight at the Horse and Hounds. Astaire songs, light, pitched to tourists. "They All Laughed."

"Lucia Braga," Leah said, running a finger along the side of the passport, some rare object. "I think I like it better than the one I have. Lucia."

"I think it's said Lu-cia, the *c* like *th*."

"God, I can't even say my own name. How do you expect–"

"You'll be fine. It's who you are."

"How do they do it? Use a dead person?"

"I didn't ask. All I know is that if they check on you–birth certificate or identity papers–you'll be in the file. You exist on paper. They're guaranteed."

She smiled. "Guaranteed. Honor among thieves. Well, that's me now too." She looked up at him. "I don't know what to say. Why are you doing this?"

"It's what you wanted–a way out of Shanghai. This will get

you to Macau. Portuguese territory. From there, to Lisbon. After that, anywhere you can get a visa, which will be a lot easier for a Portuguese than an Austrian Jew. Unless you stay in Lisbon. They say it's nice."

"But this must have cost—"

"It's a gift. That reminds me." He pulled out an envelope, one of the hard currency packets. "Some walking-around money. You'll need it, until you land on your feet."

"So much," she said, then looked up. "I can't take money from you."

"A loan, then. Leave a message with your address at the poste restante. Even better, leave it at the best hotel. Is there a Ritz in Lisbon? Whatever the best is. They won't lose it. The post office might."

"So you're not coming," she said. "Joao da Silva."

"Pronounced John. I can't. Not yet. Nathan's dying. Later. Leave an address."

"You don't want me to wait here for you?"

"I don't know when I can leave. And there's not a lot of time. Anyway, you'll like it there," he said, shifting tone, cheerful. "You can go to Sintra. On the coast. I read about it. Where all the exiled kings go. They sit on the hotel porch and rock and watch the ladies go by. Maybe one of them— And the next thing you know, Queen Lucia."

"No. Or royal mistress, either. How do you say whore in Portuguese?"

"That's a word you'll never have to know."

"No?" she said, flustered, looking away. "I don't understand. Why are you doing this?"

"I want to be a hero. I want to save your life."

"Oh," she said, her face softening.

"You know why," he said, his eyes steady. "There's a ticket in with the money. The tender out to the ship leaves from French-town pier. Get there early for customs. You don't want to miss it."

She stared at him, taking this in, all laid out.

"You said before, there's not a lot of time. Why not? What do you mean?"

"Nothing in particular. Everybody knows we're living on borrowed time here. If the Japanese occupy the city, it won't be so easy, to get out. For anybody."

"No, something else. I can tell. Remember the way my mother used to say you're up to something? Berliners are like that. Always up to something. So what are you up to? Saving my life."

He hesitated, taking a sip of his drink, her eyes still, watching him. "You know I hear things. At the Rush. Around. There's trouble between the gangs. It's getting worse. And I think they're going to take it out on Yamada. They hate the Kempeitai. It's a symbol—you know all this. I think they're going to go after him, make an example. You don't want to be anywhere near him. You need to get away. Which you want to do, anyway. Now."

"You know this?"

"I hear things. I don't want you to wait around to see if they're true. Get out now. The ticket's for tomorrow. Just go. Leave him a letter."

"A letter."

"He'll never let you go. If he knows, he'll stop you. And he can. He has that power."

"But if it's true, somebody should warn him."

"He already knows. He travels around with a small army for protection."

"I can't just leave—"

"Yes, you can. The ship's tomorrow. You'll be safe."

261

"I have to—"

"No. I'll do it. I'll meet with him, warn him. I don't know what good it will do, but at least he's warned. You won't have anything on your conscience. He comes tomorrow, right?"

"How do you know that?"

"You told me. Every Thursday. I'll tell him. But you'll be gone. Promise me. If he knows, you'll never get out of Shanghai. All this will be for nothing," he said, looking toward the passport. "You know it's true. You know what he's like."

"Not always," she said, talking to herself.

"He's Kempeitai. Don't forget that."

"No." She looked up. "And you want to do this at the flat? Why not just—?"

"He has to know you're really gone. Otherwise, he'll start looking for you. Probably at the Rush. I don't want that."

"No, something else, I think. You want to see his face. Who won. Like boys."

Daniel looked away. "All right, yes. I want to see his face. He won't be expecting this. Just his Thursday. How does he get in, by the way? If you're not there."

"I'm always there. But there's a key under the mat. He likes to let himself in. It's his flat. Everything there, my clothes even. He bought them. So is it stealing to take them?"

"No."

"Maybe he wants to keep them for the next one."

"Leah—"

"So. Pack a bag and go. Why didn't you tell me earlier?"

"I didn't have the ticket. And I didn't want you sitting around, worrying."

"Or talking to him."

"Or talking to him. You never have to see him again."

"What if he follows? After you tell him?"

"I'm not going to tell him you took a boat. It probably won't occur to him. You don't have a passport. Anyway, by that time you'll be gone."

"So, it's my last night in Shanghai." She looked around at the dimly lit bar, the piano player, the candles against the dark wood paneling. "At the Cathay Hotel. Maybe if there had been more nights here—" She stopped, then looked up at him. "What if I don't see you again? It's the last time?"

"The Ritz, Lisbon. I really will check."

"And what if it's not up to you? Something happens?"

"Then let's have another drink. Enjoy our last night. In Shanghai."

She clasped his hand. The same look, that night on the boat, standing at his cabin door. "What if it is? The last. Not here, not in the bar." A tighter squeeze, hurrying now. "We could get a room."

He felt himself get hard, as if she had grabbed him there. "Yes?"

"Yes, I want to."

"You don't have to—"

"No, I want to. One night. The way it used to be."

Another look into her eyes, something leaping inside him, urgent. "I'll be right back."

"On the river," she said. "My last night in Shanghai."

The desk clerk knew him from the Merry-Go-Round days.

"You're supposed to have luggage. House rules."

"It's coming later, by taxi."

The clerk lifted an eyebrow as he handed Daniel the key. "Need a bellboy?"

"No, I can find it."

"Sweet dreams."

And it felt dreamlike, not quite real, blurry, like the Lalique sconces in the lobby. In the elevator, they stood looking straight ahead, the white-gloved operator watching them in the polished brass. At the door, he kissed her, fumbling with the key at the same time, and just inside pushed her against the door, the way it had happened on the *Raffaello*, feeling the length of her, excited.

They undressed each other, dropping clothes on the floor, and she broke away once to push back the curtains, so that they were open to the city below, the lights on the Bund, the river moving in a shimmer, Pudong across, dark, dotted with the glow of cooking fires. Not above the clouds, but above everything else, naked now with no one to see them, her skin catching the light from the window. His face at her neck.

"Leah."

"Shh, shh." Her hand on the side of his face, then both of them kissing, moving toward the bed, falling onto it, every piece of skin touching, feeling her breast, his mouth on it, then taking him in her hand, kissing again, mouths open, smearing. His hand below, opening, her body moving with it, rubbing against it, her breath coming faster. There was enough light to see and they looked at each other as he entered her, both present, there, that moment. Then moving, finding a rhythm, then going past it, racing, until she was there, the sound of her in his ear, both of them noisy with pleasure, high up in the air with no one to see, as if they had been making love in the sky.

He stayed there for a minute, still hard, feeling her around him, then slowly came out, falling on his back. She lay next to him, quiet now, catching her breath.

"It's different with you," she said, looking at the ceiling, patches of shadow. "From the first."

"When you came to my cabin," he said lazily.

"Like a crazy woman. I don't know what was in my head. I

thought it was my last chance. I don't know for what. Before the end, I guess." She slid out of bed and walked over to the window, naked in the light from outside. "Look, you can see Hongkew pier. Where we got off. And they loaded us on trucks for the heim. Standing there in the back, like cattle. I thought, it's the end. I should have been grateful. Somebody providing shelter, even there, at least you're not on the streets. But all I could think was it's the end of everything. And now look, a room at the Cathay. So it wasn't the end."

"You told me you were going to survive. Remember? And you did."

"Yes," she said, looking out the window. "I did."

She walked over to the pile of clothes and began dressing, slipping into her panties.

"What are you doing? Come to bed."

"I can't. If I sleep out, Ming will report it and then I won't be able to vanish." She waved her hands. "Into thin air. That's what you want, isn't it? Poof, just disappear. To do that, everything has to be normal. Another day, that's all. Not the last one."

Daniel sat up. "Ming. He waits up for you?"

"I'm not out much. On my own, I mean. He makes sure I'm all right and then he goes—I don't know where, the old Chinese city, I think—and then he's back first thing. Quiet, like a cat."

Daniel nodded. But not on Thursday, his afternoon off. "A little longer," he said.

"No, then I would stay. In my wonderful Cathay room." She leaned over and kissed his forehead. "You should leave too. Shanghai. It's dangerous, what you do. How do you know what gangs say? You must be doing something with them to hear that."

"I'll be all right."

"You say that, but how can you know?" She finished dressing, smoothing her skirt, then put a hand to the side of his face. "You were my bad boy. But you're not a bad man, not yet. So leave. I'm afraid—"

"You? You aren't afraid of anything."

"You think so? No, the opposite. A coward. I just want to be safe. Even if that meant—" She stopped for a minute. "But now that's over. Thank you."

"Just leave an address at the Ritz."

She smiled a little. "So, no thank you. No good-byes, either. Well, good-bye to Leah Auerbach. However you say that in Portuguese."

"You have your ticket?"

"Here. Don't worry."

"The money—put it in the purser's safe. You never know who might be on board."

Now she did smile. "No, you never know."

———

Afterward, he sat up for a while smoking. He should get dressed, too, sleep at home, everything normal. Ming usually left around noon. The tender to the ship ran like a ferry, all day, and she'd be early, plenty of time to get Sergei's men in place. He started going over things again, a mental checklist, but his mind kept drifting, the smell of her perfume still in the sheets. He got up and walked over to the window, Shanghai at his feet. The Garden Bridge, Broadway Mansions, the pier where they'd landed and she'd been loaded on a truck. Nathan welcoming him like a son, Yamada observing, interested. Yamada everywhere, except on Thursday afternoons, his head filled with the same perfume.

CHAPTER 12

Ming left first, walking his bicycle out of the vestibule, then climbing on at the curb, pedaling away, like all the Chinese, to some unknown life. Daniel saw the streets in his head, the now familiar diagram. They were only a block in from the avenue, but already quiet, away from the buses and horns, a street of trees and small apartment buildings, trim and prosperous, why people liked Frenchtown. How did Yamada afford it? It struck Daniel suddenly that squeeze was paying for it, the Gold Rush subsidizing his Thursdays. The back of the building faced a Chinese neighborhood of courtyards and alleys that hadn't been leveled yet to put up Western buildings. Daniel had spent an afternoon walking through the maze, the only way to know the exits, the most direct routes out. If he needed them. But everything should happen on this side, in the street. Yamada's driver would wait out front, because he always did. Xi would want his men at the front door, maybe even inside, within earshot. Sergei with them, where everyone could see him.

A taxi pulled up, idling for a minute, and there she was, coming out of the building, only a small bag, no heavy luggage. Going. Not even looking around, the street just as it always was. Most of the neighbors had already left for work. Only a few cars. The street wasn't a cul-de-sac, but it wasn't commercial, either, so just occasional residential traffic. Earlier there had been a gardener next door clipping the shrubberies and Daniel wondered if he could be one of Xi's men, scouting, but after a while he'd finished and gone away and the street went back to sleep. What did she do here all day? Go shopping? Drink tea with Clara, talk about Vienna? And now even that gone. When he thought of her, she was always in motion, a motor ticking over, the way she'd been on the pier in Trieste. But this was how she lived, a quiet you could hide in. I just want to be safe. Now the taxi was pulling past him, not noticing anything. A parked car. He watched it turn at the corner.

A glance at the time. Sergei should be bringing his men through the alleys to the back door and up the service stairs, quietly, single file, like Indians in the woods. Only four floors, the elevator not worth the risk, and no building higher, so the roof commanded all the sight lines. A waist-high parapet, the men invisible to the street below. Assigned places, covering the perimeter of the building. Xi would lie and bring more men, as he always did. Now the waiting. No smoking. Slop buckets, if someone needed to pee. Details mattered.

They had set a time for Xi but he would probably ignore it, wary of any setup, and pick his own. So Daniel would have to be even earlier, in control of the meeting. Sergei came out of the front door and walked to the car.

"Any trouble?" Daniel said.

"Quiet as a tomb. There's a radio going somewhere, but otherwise no one home."

"The roof?"

"All set."

"They know what to do?"

"They know. You don't want to be down here if they start shooting. Fish in a bowl."

"Okay. I'll stash the car. You be doorman."

"I was one once, did you know that?"

Daniel took in Sergei's burly frame, rough face. "I'm not surprised."

"All the Whites. The men were doormen. Bouncers. The women—well, that was the work we could get."

"I'll go up the back way. Keep an ear out."

"It's quiet," Sergei said, looking around. "You listen hard, you can hear the insects."

Daniel drove to the avenue and turned right, then another right to a street parallel to Leah's on the other side of the Chinese buildings. Where no one would see it, waiting. He locked the car and made his way through the alleys to the back door. No one, the custodian gone till evening, when his shift began. Up the stairs, the distant sound of the radio Sergei had mentioned. A maid ironing, maybe, or just somebody who'd left it on. No neighbors in the hallway. The back door to the apartment was locked, but the key to the front was where she'd said it would be, under the mat. The stillness of an empty apartment, the faint click of a wall clock. He stood, looking around, Yamada's gilded cage, a place he'd imagined a hundred times, just an ordinary apartment. Tidy, no dishes in the sink, a clean ashtray on the drying rack, a neatly hung tea towel. Nothing personal, not even a knickknack, some memory of Vienna. But that would have been seized before they left.

The bedrooms were side by side off the main room, so that even if you retreated to yours, you could hear the other. Clara washing teacups, running the water. He opened the door to one, softly, feeling like a burglar. A modest room, neat as a pin, Clara's, to judge by the clothes in the closet. Not much bigger than a maid's room.

Again, nothing personal and then, jarringly, a frame with a missing photograph, the blank backing oddly sinister. Probably a family picture Leah wanted to take. Herr Auerbach at the glove factory. Leah in the Prater. Clara herself, a wedding picture? But why not take the frame, too? He lifted it. Not heavy. He imagined Yamada sliding the picture out of the frame, erasing somebody.

Leah's door was open. He stood for a minute looking at the bed, not sure what to feel. No point in imagining anything, not now. That was over. Nothing personal here, either, but a few signs of life, a tracing of powder on the bureau, a drawer not quite shut, things Ming hadn't got around to or had happened after he left. He opened the drawer. Underwear, left behind. Clothes in the closet. He thought of the small bag, the no-strings freedom it suggested. But something else. No suitcase for Ming to notice, nothing out of the ordinary. And more. Keep your clothes. Maybe they'll fit the next one. No note, not here, not propped up on the kitchen table. Just gone.

He went back into the living room and started checking the vantage from each window. The back was a blind spot, except to the men on the roof, but otherwise it was an open view to the street, no place for surprises. Cars could be seen at either end. He touched the gun in his pocket. Now there was just the wait.

He was still standing by the window, looking at the street, when the phone rang, loud and jangly, as if an alarm had gone off. He stared at it, frozen. Who called here? Did Ming write down the number? When madame returns. Yamada checking up? Or saying he couldn't make it today? But maybe Leah calling, to say good-bye. He looked down at his watch. She'd be on the boat. Who else? And it kept ringing, insistent. Maybe some kind of test. But he wasn't there, no one was there. Don't pick it up. Nobody's here. Then it stopped, the clanging now fading, everything quiet again.

But not the drowsy quiet of the street before. Now the air was jumpy, the insects awake.

Xi arrived first, as Daniel had expected. The car pulled up in front. Two men, one from either side, then Xi, in a Western suit, standing by the car and looking around, lifting his head, a dog sniffing the air. The driver pulled the car up a little and parked. Sergei came down to meet them, a quiet pantomime, bowing heads, an almost ceremonial politeness. An exchange, presumably asking if Daniel were here yet, then all of them entering the building, the whir of the elevator, the sliding gate door, footsteps in the hall. Daniel there, waiting.

"You don't mind if they look around?" Xi said, nodding to his men, already in the apartment.

Daniel made a be-my-guest gesture. The search was done in a minute, nothing to see.

"All right, wait downstairs. We don't want an audience. Do we?" Xi said, looking at Daniel. "Or a gang at the door, either," he said to the men as they were leaving. "When he gets here, make yourselves scarce. But don't go far."

"There's a storage room," Daniel said. "Off the hall."

Xi shook his head. "The stair landing. They're out of sight, but they can hear."

"What if he takes the stairs? He might recognize Sergei."

"They can go up higher. There's another floor over this one, yes? No closets, somewhere they can move fast." Organizing things. His meeting.

Daniel nodded, a glance to Sergei as the men melted away, following Xi's orders.

"Not much of a place. It's his?"

"He keeps a girl here."

"And that's why he comes alone?"

"And the driver."

"Where is she?"

"Away for the day."

"Without telling him? He won't like that."

"He'll be dead."

Xi looked at him, but said nothing, walking over to the window instead.

"How is Nathan?"

"Not good."

"I'm sorry," Xi said. "What is it?"

"His heart. Don't worry, he can still sign the papers. For his share. Or I can."

A slight dip of his chin. "It was a personal concern. I hope he recovers."

"He's pleased it's you, taking over. The money's been good. And now, with Yamada gone, the squeeze gone–"

"You may be hasty about that. Let's see who the new man is, what kind of Kempeitai. A man you're paying is often more reliable. Worth the expense." Xi paused. "You have a gun?"

"Yes."

"And me," he said, patting his pocket. "Kempeitai are always armed. So all three of us. We should say this right away, then everybody knows. No surprises, sudden movements." He nodded to the hall. "And no one gets out. This keeps everybody safe."

"You worry."

"I'm careful." Xi looked out the window again. "Get rid of the gun afterward. The police can match bullets."

"The SMP? They can't even move traffic. They're not going to bother. And the French are worse."

"Still. The Kempeitai will take an interest. Who did it?"

"Anybody who's spent any time in Jessfield Road. Maybe his girlfriend, something you want to cover up, not investigate."

"Yamada. A crime of passion? They would think this?"

"The Merry-Go-Round might suggest it."

"Ah," Xi said, looking at Daniel, weighing this. A sudden movement out front. "Someone's coming."

Daniel looked down at his watch. "Right on time."

The car pulled in front of the building, the driver hopping out to open the door. Yamada stepped out, glancing around, then leaned back into the car, extending his arm. The legs came into view first, then the rest of her. She looked up, her face a kind of signal. *Run.* Yamada took her by the upper arm, a prisoner's hold.

"I thought you said she was away," Xi said.

"She was."

"This makes a complication. A witness."

Daniel looked at him, then back out the window. Not dragging her, but holding her as she walked. "She's not happy," he said.

"She's a witness," Xi said again. "We'd have no choice. Do we wait for another time?"

"We can't just leave. Let's see what he has to say. The point was to meet you. We can still do that."

"The men—"

"Are here if you need them. He's only got the driver and he's still in the car."

The whir of the elevator, not taking the stairs. Had Sergei seen them? Xi stared at him, both of them waiting, watching the door as it opened.

They had switched positions, Yamada now behind her, Leah leading. In a second, Daniel saw why, Yamada holding a gun at her back, her eyes frightened.

"Daniel," Yamada said. "I would ask what you are doing here, but I can guess. Have you made yourself at home? My home."

"Leave her alone. Let her go."

273

"I will, but right now she's useful. And you are Xi. I know your photographs. We have several at the office. So many interests."

"Including yours," Daniel said. "He's taking over my uncle's share of the Rush, so he's now the majority partner. We're here to renegotiate the squeeze." A glance to Xi. "Somewhere private. No prying eyes. Not even Kempeitai. I didn't think you'd mind."

For a second, Yamada was at a loss, the reasonable tone at odds with the feeling in the room.

"Somewhere I would be alone. But as you see, I'm not."

"Let her go. She has nothing to do with this."

"I agree with you. But now you've put her here. You were going to surprise me, now I surprise you. You know Ming has a sharp eye, well trained. So she comes home last night, out, but not drinking alone, he thinks. Then she goes through her clothes, picking this and that, not much, just a little. So where is she going? And today he follows and then alerts me. Me, not my colleagues. As you say, private business. She says you're going to explain it to me. At the flat. You know I'm going to be there. But what if it's more? It would be useful to have some insurance at such a meeting. Not more men, more Kempeitai, talking. A protective shield. You see where my gun is? Any more surprises and I can shoot. So, what do you want?"

"Let her go. You can't stop her leaving."

"I don't want to stop her. She can still make the boat. There's another tender. If you don't waste time. So go. She's finished in Shanghai now anyway. You want to 'cut in'? Take her. After we finish our business here. Now, I assume you both have guns. Put them on the floor, please. Both of you. If one of them went off accidentally, I might think it was meant for me and shoot her. If it is meant for me, I could shoot her and still have time to shoot back. So either way— You see how useful she is to me. Her last favor."

Pushing the gun closer to Leah's back, making her wince, her eyes still wide with fear.

"Do you want to hear our proposal?" Xi said. "It means more for you."

"On the floor, please. Then we talk."

Xi slowly took out his gun, looking from Daniel to Yamada, and bent down, finally dropping it to the floor. A muffled sound on the carpet, something the men on the landing wouldn't hear. Leah gasped, a little cry at the back of her throat.

"Now you, my old friend," Yamada said. "Who wants to meet me alone. To kill me maybe. Why?"

"No one would need a reason for killing you," Daniel said, taking out his gun, fingering the safety. "But you shouldn't have gone after Nathan. Ordered the hit."

A sudden cloud of confusion in Yamada's face. "But I didn't."

"I know," Daniel said, beginning to bend down, and then, a half second, so fast the eye couldn't take it in, pivoted, swinging around in a blur, and fired at Xi, a direct hit to the chest, blood spurting, his mouth forming a circle of surprise, then pitching forward, his body crashing to the floor. A second when no one moved, then Daniel swiveled back, aiming at Yamada now. A reflex response, to block the shot, Yamada pushing Leah at Daniel, the impact knocking Daniel's hand, the bullet he fired going wide. Then Yamada jumped forward, a chop to Daniel's neck, then the gun hand again, some Kempeitai training, knocking him over, both on the floor, rolling over, Yamada on top, pinning him down, the gun angled now to Daniel's head. He grunted, trying to throw Yamada off, squirming away from the gun, but not moving far enough, waiting for the shot. The roar, when it came, was deafening, an explosion in his ear, but it was Yamada's head splitting open, Yamada falling flat on him, Leah standing over them with a gun, looking stunned, her eyes growing wider and wider, not noticing when Daniel wiggled out from under and took the gun from her.

"Why?" she said dully, in a kind of trance, looking down at Yamada, blood pooling now around his head.

"They had to kill each other. It has to look that way," Daniel said, then, seeing this wasn't what she was asking, nodded toward Xi. "He tried to kill us. Nathan. And me. Him, not Yamada." Raising his hand, feeling Yamada's blood on his face.

But she didn't hear this, either, just kept staring, her body rigid. "He killed my mother. Killed her. No, I did. We both did."

The air, empty as a vacuum, suddenly crackled with sound, two shots fired somewhere close, Sergei following the plan. And now at the door, pushing through, taking in the bodies on the floor. Daniel looked at him, a question, and he answered with a quick nod, Xi's men taken out.

"Come on," he said, swatting the air to urge them out, then grabbing the tea towel from the sink and tossing it to Daniel. "Your face," he said.

Daniel wiped the gun with the clean towel, then blotted his face. So much blood. Another swipe. He stuffed it into his pocket, something to lose in the alleys, then glanced out the window. Yamada's driver had leaped out of the car and now stood in front of the building. The shots could mean anything. Four shots, no five, Daniel's second into some wall. The driver twisted left to right, go in, stay, who was alive? Someone with a bullet for him? And then he saw them coming, Xi's hidden men, running down the street, fanning out, trying to find cover as they moved.

"Now," Sergei said, shouting, and Daniel started for the door, pulling Leah, body still limp with shock, retreating into itself. They used the back stairs, Sergei separating for a minute to climb up the final flight to the roof, giving the order. When they reached the ground floor, it began, a barrage of rapid shots, the men on the roof firing down into the street, Xi's extra men shooting back, but at vague targets, dropping, the street a battle zone, men crumpled on the pavement, a gang war. Daniel was pushing through the back door when he heard the clump of shoes on the stairs, Sergei's men fleeing the roof, none of Xi's men left to fire back. The plan was for them to spread out in the back alleys, eventually to safe houses, before Xi's gang could respond, not yet knowing what had happened, the gang broken, Xi himself gone. Daniel was running ahead through the now empty alleys, Leah's hand in his, Sergei herding them and keeping an eye on the men behind. In the distance, finally, a siren, someone having reported the shooting, maybe the radio player, anybody on the quiet street, now at war.

The car was where Daniel had parked it. They climbed into the back seat, Leah looking straight ahead.

"He had a child," she said. "A son, I think."

And there it was, the bullet that didn't stop. It kept on going, through the body, into all the lives that surrounded it, tearing through one after another, so that you never killed just one person. The bullet didn't stop.

Sergei started the car and drove down to the avenue, looking in the mirror.

"Anyone?" he said to Daniel.

Daniel turned. "No. I don't think any of the others made it into the building. The roof worked."

"So," Sergei said.

"They'll think I did it," Leah said to the air, another train of thought.

"Who?"

"The police. I live there. They'll think I did it. Well, I did. Didn't I?" Her voice vague.

Daniel looked at her. "No one saw anything. It's okay."

"Okay," she said flatly. Another idea. "I paid a boy to call you. To warn you. But he didn't."

"I didn't pick up."

"But it didn't matter anyway. You were waiting." She looked up. "To kill him?"

Daniel said nothing.

"Everyone knows. That he keeps me. The driver knows me."

"He's dead."

"Oh," she said, still trying to grasp what happened. "All of them. All?"

"Yes."

She looked out the window. "What if my father knew? What would I say to him?"

Daniel took her by the arm. "It's all right. We'll get you to the boat and you'll be gone. Nobody saw anything. It's all right."

She nodded, then looked away. "But so many."

"There's something going on," Sergei said. "Up ahead."

Daniel looked up, alarmed. Not just heavy traffic, people walking toward the Bund, a crowd of them. Now the sound of whistles, drums.

"A parade," Sergei said, glancing at his watch.

"The Japanese," Daniel said. "Can we get across?" The French-town pier on the water, the tender waiting.

"Not here. We have to go around. They usually come down the Bund, then out the Edward VII. We can head down toward Nantao, then back up the river side."

"We have enough time?"

"We can't go on foot. You'd have to walk through the Japanese army."

"Okay, but hurry." Another glance at his watch.

"They're blocking the intersection. The traffic police." A group of Annamites in uniform, recruited by the French.

"Can we back up? Make a wider circle?"

"They'll open it when this group passes. They stagger it that way. Maybe a minute. We pull out here, it looks funny, somebody notices. There they are, the Rising Sun. Christ, you could see yourself in those boots. Spit and polish, huh?"

Dress uniforms, starched collars, legs stepping high, then clomping down on the pavement, a loud rhythmic thud, like pistons in some relentless machine. Eyes right, rifles on their shoulders, Chinese spectators staring blankly, but the troops smug, chests out, pleased with themselves, what was about to be theirs. Not an ordinary military parade, a demonstration and a warning. It will all be ours. And Daniel saw, in a flash, the shiny boots kicking, then stomping down, that the catastrophe in Europe was spreading, some of it already here, and the rest following, all of it—the internment camps, the tortures, the electrodes on genitals, the bloody fingernails, the orphans, the ruined lives, all of it spreading, the world determined to have a bloodletting, all of it clear and inescapable in the eyes of the Japanese soldiers, the sullen faces watching them pass. How could you not do something to stop it? Even if there were no way to stop it? How could you not? I'm not an assassin. What happened won't stop the horror coming. To kill Yamada was one thing—first you have to survive—but the catastrophe would keep spreading whether you killed or not. Florence's voice: *You do what you can.* How could you not? Even if it was only offering a room. To help another assassin, even the well-meaning helper complicit, everybody. He watched the boots, trapped in one of Eli's self-debates. How could you not? Would it matter? What if all of it matters? None of it?

"Here we go," Sergei said, putting the car in gear, the

Annamites waving the traffic forward. "Now what?" Their hands suddenly held up, whistles.

Farther back in the parade a fight had broken out, Settlement police hitting people with their batons, a scrum of confusion, people on the sidewalk rushing in to help, fight back, others running away, people beginning to swarm, a crowd with a life of its own, sucking people under, trampling down anything in its way. Screams, people breaking away now, running in every direction, the Japanese troops still in formation, watching, their order and swagger now a pose, toy soldiers.

"Jesus Christ," Sergei said. "What the hell—"

"Get out of here," Daniel said. "Before somebody starts shooting."

"Oh god," Leah said.

"They're going up the Bund," Sergei said. "That way." Pointing north. "Look, we're starting to move." Cars had begun to cross the intersection.

"Wait," Daniel said, rolling down his window.

Not everybody had headed toward the Settlement. A few stragglers had broken away from the crowd, running, some being chased, dodging people in the street, a few just getting out, blood on their heads, looking behind them for police with truncheons.

"Ivan!" Daniel yelled. "Here."

Ivan turned, following Daniel's voice, then spotted the car. A look behind, then back to Daniel, frantic.

Less than a second to decide. "Get in."

"We can't stop," Leah said.

"Quick," Daniel said. "And keep down. Here." He handed him a handkerchief to wipe his head.

Ivan jumped into the seat next to Sergei and slid down.

"What happened?"

Ivan turned slightly to face Daniel in back as the car lurched forward. "No bombs. Somebody yelled something at the soldiers—not very nice—and the SMP were all over him. They must have had orders, keep things bright and shiny. There were newsreels. Show how happy we all are to have the Imperial forces protecting us. Not people calling them shit. But I don't think it'll make the cut. So." He looked at Daniel, serious. "And you. Is it done?"

"Yes."

"Is what done?" Leah said.

"Problems?"

"No problems. It's done. Xi did it, so you can't take credit, but it's done."

"Xi?"

"A disagreement about squeeze. That's the only politics Shanghai cares about."

Leah looked again, edging herself away, an unconscious reaction.

Outside a police van was speeding past. The tender was still at the pier, the last passengers passing through customs. Daniel thought of Trieste, the inspector fondling her silk.

"Where's your bag?"

"On the launch. They send them separately. I was through the line when he showed up."

"So just your passport."

"And my ticket," she said, patting her clutch purse.

"They're stopping cars," Sergei said. "Up ahead. Looking for something."

"I'll get out," Ivan said. Once they see my head—"

"No, it's the French, not the Settlement police. It's not about the parade."

"They're looking for me," Leah said.

Ivan turned to her, but said nothing.

"Keep calm," Daniel said. "They don't know you. They're looking for a name, a description maybe. And that would fit a lot of people. Leah isn't on the boat. They're looking for someone else. You understand?"

She nodded, eyes still anxious, darting.

"It's safer if I go," Ivan said.

"Not for you. We'll take you to the Rush. Bunk in with Karl for a while."

"Yes?" Ivan said, asking something else.

Daniel nodded. "You do what you can. I can do this." He looked again at the pier. "Drop us here. You ready?" he said to Leah. "They'll ask for your passport, that's all. It's who you are."

They got out of the back seat, heading toward the pier, seconds away from being swallowed up by the crowd.

"Stop." A policeman at the car, bending down to look inside, then up again at Leah and Daniel. "Your papers."

Leah stood still, unable to move.

"What's the trouble?" Daniel said pleasantly.

"And yours," the policeman said, but still looking at Leah.

"I'm just seeing her off. Show him your passport, darling."

Leah took out her passport and handed it to the policeman. He flipped it open to the picture, looking at it, then at her, then back to the picture. A moment, not breathing. Then he handed the passport back and waved them forward, saying something in Portuguese. Another moment without air. What? Something she'd be expected to know. But the gestures, the familiarity of it, said "have a good trip." She mumbled "*Gracias*," an all-purpose answer, hoping it was the same in Portuguese. The policeman now turned to the car, another wave, keep the line moving.

"We'll wait for you up ahead," Sergei said, pulling away.

Daniel took her by the elbow as they waded into the crowd, people saying good-bye, showing tickets at the barrier.

"I'm shaking," Leah said. "How am I going to do this?"

"You just did." He turned to her, taking her by the shoulders. "It'll get easier. I have to say good-bye here. Passengers only." He nodded to the barrier, the people headed to the gangway. "So. Another ship."

"I was nervous then, too," she said, looking at the crowd, the same memory. "What if we missed it? How would we get out? Running. All that luggage. Then you—" She stopped. "What happened before— At the flat. What I did."

"Somebody else did. You have to think that way."

"But nobody else did. I did it. Me." She took a breath. "They don't show you what it's like. In the films. Someone shoots and someone falls down. They don't show you the blood. The pieces of—"

"Don't."

"On the carpet," she said, finishing.

"He had a gun to my head. You had to do it."

"Yes," she said, looking away, uneasy. "I had to. And now what?"

"You're Lucia now. How many chances do we get, to start over? Maybe this is the last one."

"We thought the *Raffaello* was that. Our last chance."

"It was." He touched her cheek. "So now, one more."

A bell rang on the ship. She looked up, hurrying. "What happened to Leah? When the police ask."

"People disappear in the East. People like us, I mean. Nobody's keeping track. You go to Manila, or someplace, and you just disappear." He brushed back the hair over her ear. "But you won't."

"What if you don't come?"

"I'll come."

She looked down. "I don't know if I can do it."

He tilted her head up. "I'll help you. With the luggage. The Ritz, Lisbon."

"Or poste restante. I remember."

"Or whatever the best hotel is. The best."

She nodded, then moved her arms up around his neck, pulling his face next to hers. "So good-bye," she said. "In case anybody's looking." Hugging him, a real good-bye, then turning away, handing over her ticket at the barrier. At the gangplank, she looked back over her shoulder and smiled at him. "The Ritz," she said, her voice bright, casual, a bird out of its cage, pretending its wing wasn't broken, that it really could fly.

———

The second heart attack was worse than the first, clutching at his chest, nurses running, and Daniel thought this time Nathan would slip into unconsciousness, then away, but he hung on, grimacing, wanting to talk. They were all in their usual places, Sergei standing guard at the door, Irina smoking at the window, Daniel by the bed, a hospital quiet, waiting.

"Sergei said you did the whole thing," Nathan said, running his tongue across his dry lips. "Anybody get away?"

"No, we don't think so," Daniel said, giving him some water.

"No, huh? So Xi wasn't expecting it. Now what?"

"The Japanese go after the gangs, the gangs fight each other. We walk away."

"Why do they fight each other?"

"Because I'm selling Wu our share. Xi's people think Wu wanted Xi's piece, too, so he could have it all. Which is the way it will work out, once the fighting stops." He looked down at Nathan. "It was time to sell. I didn't tell you because—"

Nathan raised his hand. "It was your call."

"It was time. Xi tried to kill you once. Why not try again? So. But just the Rush. Not the Black Cat. You keep that. The music. And there's a nice cut for Irina and Sergei."

"They're already taken care of."

"Now they'll be more taken care of. And we don't have to fight the Japanese. Anybody wants to keep the Rush open, he's going to need an army. Like Wu."

"You get hard currency? Not Chinese money."

Daniel smiled to himself. "No, not Chinese."

"They used to pay with anything here. Anything foreign. Mexican silver dollars. With silver in it, so you know it was worth something. Not just backed by silver. Silver in it. Sid used to carry them around in a bag." He paused. "What about you?"

"I don't know. Let's get you better first."

"I'm not getting better. It's time to go. You, I mean. The Japanese are going to ruin the place. And after? What if it's Mao? So go now." He looked up. "We didn't have enough time. People always say that, they didn't have enough time. So what's enough? It doesn't matter, they just want. I thought it would be safe for you here. At least no Nazis. But where's safe? Not here, not anymore. You should have come sooner, seen it then. But . . ." He drifted for a second. "Should have. Could have. What the hell. What is. You have to look out for yourself. Stay one step ahead. One step. That's what I did. They think I'm in Manila, I'm already here. One step ahead."

After a while Daniel realized Nathan wasn't talking to him, just talking, giving dictation to some invisible steno.

"You know he didn't want me to see you. Said I was a bad

influence. Maybe he's right, I don't know. But he was the one gave me the money. When I had to get out of Berlin. So he must have—"

"He did."

"I know," Nathan said, a faint smile. "I know. He was the way he was, but still— We used to have fun when we were kids. Hard to picture now. But we did. And I was the one who'd get us in trouble. I didn't mean anything by it, but it would happen. He'd blame me, but I didn't mean anything by it. But he's the one got me out." He reached over and touched Daniel's hand. "Wu ask you to stay? At the Rush?"

"I said no."

"Good. He just wants to keep an eye on you. They don't trust anybody. It's too rough out there now, the Badlands. You didn't come all this way to get shot. Anyway, it's time. One step ahead. That's why I gave you the passport. Go anywhere. So you're always one step ahead of them."

"Who?"

"Everybody. Whoever they are. Listen to me on this. One step ahead."

And then he was quiet. Daniel could hear his breathing, shallow but regular, then patchy, eyes closed, maybe having a dream, his hand twitching a little on Daniel's. He was like this for a few minutes and then there was a ragged gulp of air, a last breath, and suddenly his hand felt lighter, as if life were something tangible, with weight, and now it was gone.

———

The funeral was smaller than Sid Engel's had been, Nathan's community dwindling, the gamblers and bad hats and people who changed their names on the pier. The new arrivals, in the heime, had come for shelter, to wait out the storm and then move on. Shared meals and Hebrew classes and sports teams for the children, Nathan's Shanghai so far from them it barely seemed to exist. Irina had arranged everything, the cremation, the stone in the mausoleum. Nathan Green. A name taken from a factory sign in Pudong.

Wu had brought men with him, standing close, the street wars now a permanent fact of life.

"I never thought Nathan would sell," he said to Daniel, a private huddle after the service.

"We made a deal."

"And he went along with it?"

"He was dying. It was the right thing to do."

"For a passport."

"And something in the bank," Daniel said.

"Take my advice, move it around a little. The Bank of China—you never know what's going to happen."

Daniel nodded, having already moved it.

"Nathan said they used Mexican silver dollars in the old days. They'd carry them around in a bag."

"Times were different," Wu said, polite, not really interested. He looked up. "Change your mind about the Rush?"

"Work for you?"

"I'd cut you in. There's still a lot of cash to pick up there."

"Not if the Japanese squeeze you too hard."

"Let me worry about that."

Daniel looked up at him. On and on, Wu up now, Xi's men sorting themselves out. A drive-by on Avenue Haig. Nine lives, how many of his already gone? Stay useful.

"It's not going to make me very popular with Xi's people."

"Let me worry about that too."

Look tempted. "Let's talk about it. Not here." He moved his hand to take in the other mourners.

"My place. Later."

"I can't leave Irina, not today. Tomorrow. Six okay? Sergei drives." He raised his voice, public. "Thanks for coming." Taking Wu's hand. "It would have meant a lot to Nathan." Then lower again. "We don't want people talking."

Wu dipped his head. "I'm sorry for your loss," he said, moving away. "Tomorrow."

More condolences, more handshaking. People he didn't know. Gus Whiting. Finally, Selly.

"Well, that was cozy. You and the King of Shanghai."

"Is that what he is now?"

"Until the next one comes along. Not poor old Xi. So trusting. I'll bet Wu's hiding her."

"Who?"

"*La belle dame sans merci.* Who lures unsuspecting men to their doom. It was her place, after all. Somebody must be hiding her and who came out on top?"

"Why hide her?"

"He'd owe her that much. If the Japanese find her—" Loomis let the thought finish itself. "So she must be lying very low." He looked up. "You knew her, too, I seem to recall. Maybe you—"

"We met on the boat. And Yamada. He had a thing for her. Right from the start."

"More fool he. Right into the spider's web."

"She isn't like that."

"No? What is she like?"

"A well-brought-up girl. A lady."

Loomis smiled. "Oh, my heart, I do miss you. Your take on things. Come back to the Merry-Go-Round, why not? They say your uncle sold the business to Wu, so that puts you out of a job. I would think."

"Maybe I'll stay at the Rush."

"Is that what the little chat was about? You don't want to do that. The Chinese stick to themselves. You'd be a poor relation. Not to mention people keep getting killed there. No, come back to the paper. People like you. You're easy to talk to. I'd give you Ciro's."

"Selly."

"Plus aren't you the least bit interested in what happened to the girlfriend? Knowing her too. I could use the help. You know she left her clothes—"

"No, I didn't know. How do you?"

"The police report. The French very kindly—"

"That must have cost you."

Loomis smiled. "You see? You understand how things work. That's what I need. What does it tell you, that she left her clothes?"

"That she's running scared. Or somebody snatched her."

"Either way, a story, no?"

"You sure you want to go after this? Your Japanese friends won't be happy. Married Kempeitai with a mistress."

"Not all of it has to be reported."

Daniel looked at him. "Just setting him up. Why did she, by the way?"

"Well, that's the story. Maybe somebody paid her."

Daniel shook his head. "She's not like that."

Loomis ignored this. "Or forced her. Or a lot of things. You know Yamada was a special target for the Communists. Be interesting if—"

Daniel's head spinning, tangle within tangle. "Or she could be dead."

"She could be. Let's find out. Look, I know this isn't the time. You've got people to— My god, Nassim Kadoorie. What's he doing here?"

"He was a customer. At the Cat. He likes jazz."

"The people you know." He put his hand on Daniel's arm. "Come and have a drink tomorrow. We'll swap notes. I can tell you're curious. There's something here, you can feel it. We'll do the rounds and I'll tell you what I know so far." What Selly always knew, the bad behavior, the half-truths. But maybe there were only half-truths.

"All right," Daniel said. Draw the tangle tighter. "Six? The Horse and Hounds?"

"Six. Now I'd better go say hello to Nassim. I'm sorry about Nathan. It really is the end of old Shanghai, isn't it?" The obit already in his head.

———

The next morning Daniel ran errands, what looked like ordinary stops at the bank, the post office. One step ahead meant you needed to be careful, but even as he checked behind him, he knew it would work. Be where you were expected to be, until you weren't. No complicated timing, a simple day. And as he got nearer the time, he saw everything clearly, an odd light-headedness he had first felt in Nathan's hospital room when he realized that all the Lohrs were gone, that he was floating free, like a hot air balloon rising as the last mooring rope was thrown off. He wasn't Eli's anymore, or Nathan's, either, and now not even himself, somebody called Da Silva, sailing today, about to vanish. He saw that both Wu and Selly, then everybody, would think that he was dead, another victim of the gang wars he'd helped set in motion. He saw that Selly, lazy and distracted, would never write about Leah, that she would vanish, too, as if neither of them had ever been here.

Even one step ahead required some luck. Maybe someone on the tender would recognize him. But no one did. No one followed the taxi, noticed the suitcase. Customs made a cursory search, his passport was stamped. As he stood on deck facing the Bund, he felt the freedom of being invisible, the way Nathan must have felt when he came up the river from the other direction and seen the same waterfront for the first time, the rickshaws and honking cars and coolies with baskets hanging from their shoulders. Who should I be? What name? Where do I start? He had felt this before, on the boat at Trieste, pulling away from the pier, from Europe, safe. But nowhere was safe.

When the tender started down the Whangpoo, making the bend after Garden Bridge, heading to the Yangtze, he imagined seeing it all as she had seen it, just a few days before. The curving sweep of buildings, China's dream of the West, then the factories and kilns and warehouses, houseboats and muddy inlets. When they transferred to the ship, there was nothing left of Shanghai to see, just the brown water turning blue and he knew, what he hadn't admitted before, that there would be no message at the Ritz, nothing at poste restante, that he had frightened her, it had all frightened her, and she would vanish into the safety of anonymity. He thought of her at the door of his cabin, the boldness of it. But they had been different people then. The time here had done something to them that couldn't be undone, or they had done it to themselves.

Start over. Nathan had. And made a mess of his life, Eli would have said. But now they were both dead and what did it matter, the old argument? Live a good life, Eli again. But first you had to survive. He saw the Japanese parade. How could you not act? Do what you can. Another address. 24 Rua Carelo. Memorize it, Karl had said. Franz's training. The boat began to pick up speed. He imagined Selly looking at his watch, Wu worrying. He had done it, disappeared. Think what an advantage, Karl had said. He'd survived and he'd survive what was coming. And maybe there would be a message from her after all, how they were together stronger than her fear, even stronger than the pull of memory of what she'd lost. It's different with you. Her eyes shiny in the half-light. But even as his spirits rose, higher, unmoored, he knew that she had already disappeared, too. He looked at the blue water again, what she would have seen, the last thing she saw before her ship fell off the map.

About the Author

Joseph Kanon is the Edgar Award–winning author of *Los Alamos* and nine other novels: *The Prodigal Spy*, *Alibi*, *Stardust*, *Istanbul Passage*, *Leaving Berlin*, *Defectors*, *The Accomplice*, *The Berlin Exchange*, and *The Good German*, which was made into a major motion picture starring George Clooney and Cate Blanchett. Other awards include the Hammett Award of the International Association of Crime Writers and the Human Writes Award of the Anne Frank Foundation. He lives in New York City.

SHANGHAI 1939

BADLANDS

INTERNATIONAL
SETTLEMENT

BUBBLING WELL ROAD

GREAT WESTERN ROAD

AVENUE FOCH

AVENUE HAIG

AVENUE JOFFRE

FRENCH
CONCESSION

0 Miles   0.5   1

0 Kilometers   1